W9-AGE-749

SEEING RED

SEEING RED

Roger
Ormerod

Charles Scriber's Sons
New York

First published in the United States by
Charles Scribner's Sons 1985
Copyright © Roger Ormerod 1984

Library of Congress Cataloging in Publication Data

Ormerod, Roger.
  Seeing red.

  I. Title.
PR6065.R688S4   1985   823'.914   85-2345
ISBN 0-684-18366-8

  1 3 5 7 9 11 13 15 17 19 F/C 20 18 16 14 12 10 8 6 4 2

Printed in the United States of America.

I

It turned out to be a small market town on the border of Wales, only fifteen miles from the motorway, but still operating in the traditional meaning of the word market. There was a cattle and sheep auction every Wednesday, during which it was almost impossible to move along its main street unless you had four legs. And I had to choose a Wednesday to drive there, with a gusty drizzle sweeping in from the dark mountains of Wales. The cobbled streets would be a slimy trap for cars, and utter misery for towed caravans, which happened to be what I had.

I came down towards the town from the hills to the south, passing my objective, the house called Viewlands, though I was not aware of this, and hit the first trouble a mile from the town. The County Council was driving a new road as a link to the motorway, and a mile of it was intended to ease off the swings and plunges of the old road. It meant I was suddenly trapped at a section of single-lane highway controlled by traffic lights, at red. I stopped. I was nose-down on a fair slope, to the right the part-formed new roadway, which just there was five feet below my level. The work had thrown clay onto the road surface and the rain had slicked it. I felt the back of my Rover 2300 move sideways as the caravan tried to jack-knife.

It was an uncomfortable situation to be in. When the lights changed I'd have difficulty easing the caravan away from the drop.

I cursed, and got out to have a look at it. The one-lane section was a two hundred yard steady curve, and I couldn't see its end. The annoying point was that there was nobody coming the other way, so I'd stopped for nothing. The lights were only two-colour, red and green, and while I stood there they changed to green. At once, a horn blasted from behind me.

If there was anything I wasn't going to do, it was hurry over it. Five hours of towing experience hadn't taught me much, but I knew that a downhill slippy slope meant I had to keep the car

5

ahead of the over-run brake, or the caravan could lock a wheel and slew over the drop. Backing out, with the over-run brake disengaged, would perhaps be better. If I could do it.

But it needed thought. I walked back.

In this district, the police would no doubt need different transport from the usual sleek town cars. This was a police Land Rover, behind its wheel a very large, dark and angry sergeant. I couldn't see why he was angry, unless he was rushing to an accident.

'You'll have to bear with me,' I said mildly, trying to smile. 'I think I'll need to try backing out.'

He climbed down. I realised from the smell of his uniform that he was very wet. The Land Rover was muddied to the top of its wings, and he to his knees. His impatience was reasonable. He'd been rushing towards a dry pair of trousers.

'I do apologise,' I said.

He looked me up and down. Perhaps he saw something that calmed him. He rubbed his hand down his red face, and sighed.

'Anybody who brings a caravan down here, and on market day . . . Oh Lor', mate, we do get 'em.'

'I wasn't to know, was I?'

'Another mile and you'd have been in real trouble. Just try to get that lot through!' He took off his peaked cap and scratched his bald patch. 'And where did you think you were heading? There's nothing but mountains the other side.'

'I was looking for a place called Viewlands.'

He looked beyond me and breathed heavily. 'You don't want to go there.'

'Don't I?'

He glanced at me, then away. 'Tell you what – I'll tow you out. There's a lay-by back there. Room to turn round.'

'You think I should?'

'You passed Viewlands a mile back.'

'Ah.' I took my pipe out of my pocket and stared at it. 'But you'd advise me not to go there?'

'Depends why you want to.'

'Just visiting.'

'Hmm! I've got a rope. We'll hitch it to the caravan. I can tow the lot in four-wheel drive.'

'You're very obliging.'

'It's just that I don't want to see another.'

6

I waited. He spoke in a series of leading questions, luring me on, like a game. I didn't want to play it. He went to get his rope, and when he came back I got the continuation.

'Since they started this section we've had three go over that drop. All at night, mind you, but in spite of all the winkers and cones. Madmen.'

He left the crawling bit to me, the part where you try to find somewhere to hitch the tow-rope. From under the caravan I asked:

'Not fatal, I hope.'

'One of 'em was. Turned over and went up in flames. Nasty.'

As I'd come to the district because of just such an incident, it occurred to me that it would be strange if he was not referring to the death of Angela Rollason's father. But if that was so, it had happened three months before, so the roadworks weren't progressing very rapidly.

'When was this?' I asked, sticking my head out into the rain. He said it had been three months before.

I scrambled to my feet. 'You mean it's been like this for three months?'

'They ran out of money,' he said in disgust. 'And just left it.'

He told me to release the handbrake when he took up the slack. He'd blast his horn. I was beginning to look as bedraggled as him, so I got back into the Rover and waited for the signal. I felt a complete faith in his ability.

He drew me out sweetly, though it was strange travelling a hundred yards backwards, with very little view of where I was going. We made it to the lay-by. We unhitched his rope. I thanked him.

'And to whom am I indebted, Sergeant?' I asked.

'The name's Timmis, sir.'

I'd got the 'sir' because of my careful grammar, no doubt. 'And if you'd just direct me to Viewlands . . .'

'If you still want to go there.'

I did. It was a mile back, turn right up the lane by the three dead elms, and I couldn't miss it. Follow his muddy tyre tracks, he said.

'You've come from there?'

'That dratted woman! And I warned her. The lower dale's treacherous in the wet. I did say.'

'I'm sure you did,' I comforted him. 'But they never listen.'

'Got her gelding bogged down. I had to pull him out . . .
Gawd, what a mess. She'd run two miles to a phone . . . I'll give
her that.'

'Headstrong?'

'You're not a relative, are you?'

'I've never met her.'

'Ah. Pity. Somebody ought to tell her.'

'Tell her what, Sergeant?'

He puffed out his cheeks and suddenly smiled, like the sun
breaking through.

'I knew her father, Gledwyn Griffiths. Went to school with
him, till we were eleven, anyway. I remember Angela Griffiths
as a kid. A right tomboy, she was. But tomboys are out of
fashion, and she's too old for it. You tell her from me, though,
that she's not too old to be spanked, and I reckon I could still do
it. Her dad not being around, you might say.'

He turned to climb into his Land Rover.

'He was the one in the car that went up in flames?' I asked.

He looked over his shoulder at me, no humour in his eyes
now. 'Yes sir. You tell her it'd be an honour to stand in for him.'

Then he tipped his hat with one finger, his Welsh version of a
salute, and drove away.

I worked the car and caravan round, and drove back towards
Viewlands, not with any enthusiasm, because I wasn't sure
what lay ahead.

I was doing Phil Rollason a favour. Now . . . that's fine for a
friend, but I had reason to hate Rollason's guts. So what the hell
was I doing there? Partly because I had to be somewhere that
wasn't where I'd been, and the Welsh border had seemed far
enough away, and partly because I'd had the vague idea that a
favour for Rollason might help to extract a little truth from him.

But basically, I'd been disturbed by the way he spoke about
his wife, Angela. I'd not have expected such an extroverted lout
as Rollason to be so moved.

Angela's father had died in a car crash, three months before
. . . or so. He'd left her his house and its contents, so she'd gone
along there to settle it all up. Probate, and that sort of thing, and
put up the furniture for auction. Nothing to it. Rollason had
driven her there himself, to Viewlands, and left her to it.

'I reckoned she'd need a week or so,' he'd told me. 'But it
went on and on. Drifted along, and damn it, the last time I went

to see her she'd done nothing, absolutely nothing. Two months now . . .'

'Not so long, two months.'

'But she's said she's not going to budge till she gets the truth of it,' he protested, waving his podgy hands. 'Says it wasn't a normal accident, but the local CID won't do a thing.'

'CID?'

'She's got this idea.'

'Oh yes?'

'That her father was murdered.'

As I said, I was disturbed, more so when he went on to talk about Angela. I listened, not interrupting, and he couldn't have been aware of the impression he was making. She had left for her father's home, not a happy woman, because she was heading for his funeral, but at least a woman with an apparent background of happiness to return to. He called her Angie. 'I drove Angie there, and when you see it . . . so damn lonely!' But time had progressed. He'd dashed there on weekends – eighty miles each way – and she'd gradually changed. He didn't tell me he was visiting a stranger, but now he was visiting Angela, not Angie. She became vague about her intentions. 'Angela's never been vague, you see, always definite, and sometimes blasted forceful.' She had seemed as quiet and remote as the house. Viewlands, her father had called it. Great vistas of valley and the lowering, black hills of Wales in the distance, I'd gathered.

Well, I'd now had a glimpse of those gloomy vistas, and they hadn't encouraged me. I headed back into the rain, which had become a tangible thing, enclosing me and limiting visibility, until it was the only living thing outside the car. I put on the headlights, but they drove into it and became lost, and I had to lean forward, close to the windscreen, searching for the dead elms. When I found them, they were like grey, beckoning fingers. The lane beside them closed in on me, with dry-stone walls each side, and I was committed. I certainly wouldn't have been able to back down. The rainwater streamed down the rutted old tarmac, so that it was like driving in a river. So much for Timmis' muddy tyre tracks!

'There, you fool,' I said to myself, just as I drove past a break in the left-hand wall.

I braked hard, feeling the caravan's over-ride brake thump

on. There was an open gate. Dimly, I could just detect that the name on it was: Viewlands.

Fortunately I was nose-up on the slope and could back down. Ten feet did it. I took as large an arc as I could and scraped through. There was no sign of a house, just ghostly trees, dripping dismally, and not much more than a hint of driveway.

My first impression of the house was of a low, wide shadow. There were no lights visible at the windows, but after all, it was still only afternoon. A grey, shifting gloom played with the façade. I thought the drive turned left across its front. I stopped the car, and sat, watching the wipers arc across the screen, trying to decide whether that was a light I could see to the right.

On that side of the house there seemed to be a wall with an archway, beyond it a shadowy line of low buildings. If the house had at one time been a farm, I could've been looking into a farmyard, with stables or barns facing the side of the main building. And there was certainly a light, but yellowish and uncertain.

I reached back for my anorak and climbed out into the rain, shrugging into it. I was standing on uneven gravel littered with puddles. Treading round them, I made my way beneath the arch.

The house was a heavy weight to my left, with a side door open into the cobbled yard, and with a light now visible behind a window. The line of buildings that faced it had clearly been stables at one time, but now only one was still maintained for that purpose, the far one. There was an enclosing fence linking it to the house. The rest of the line seemed to have been converted to garages, with at least one up-and-over door. There was a whole row of windows linking the stable to the end garage.

The light I'd first seen came from the stable in the far corner. The top of its split door was open, inside it a naked electric bulb, which seemed to be swinging. As I approached, I could hear someone singing, or crooning, a comforting mother-to-baby sound. I reached the door and leaned against it, peering over. She was currying the brown gelding, taking long, sweeping strokes along his flanks, telling him what a beauty he was and assuring him it was all over and he was safe. He was dry now and gleaming, but shudders were still tracing their way down his leg muscles, his eyes were wild, and his nostrils flared. He was clean and dry, but frightened; she was wet and muddied, bedraggled, completely and contentedly absorbed.

The gelding snorted at my scent and tossed his head. She turned. Her eyes, big and dark and heavily shadowed by the overhead light, were instantly suspicious. She, too, tossed her head, mainly to clear the dark and tangled hair from her eyes. She couldn't have been more than five-four, slim, her legs long and straight in the jodhpurs, her face drawn and tired, for all the contentment that flowed from her task. Then her chin came up and she was in control. A square chin, I saw, with determination moulding it.

'Yes?' she demanded. 'What is it?'

The jodhpurs were muddied to her waist and clung to her. The anorak might have been waterproof at one time but looked as though it had had enough.

'You'll catch your death of cold,' I said severely.

'Do you know about horses?' she demanded.

I shook my head.

'Then mind your own business. If you've come about the house, it's not for sale.'

'Phil asked me to look you up,' I told her. 'If I was passing.'

Then she laughed, put the back of one hand to her face and laughed, and at first there was amusement in it, before it cracked on a note close to hysteria. She was bordering on exhaustion.

'You were passing?' she gasped.

'With the help of a friendly police sergeant.'

She ran a hand down the gelding's nose, and allowed his velvet lips to play with her palm. Her eyes were huge. 'Phil sent you?'

'He thought I might help. But of course, he didn't know about this.' I waved my hand, embracing horse and rider, and her obvious physical distress. 'Perhaps I *can* help, though. The door opposite – I assume that's your kitchen. If you're reluctant to leave your horse, I could at least get you a cup of tea. I'd bring it across. Then you could run a hot bath. Really, you know, you ought to look after yourself.'

Then she buried her face in the chestnut, shining neck, and for a moment she was close to tears. I waited, patting my pockets, but it wasn't there. At last she whispered: 'Thank you.'

'I'll be back.'

I returned to the car for my pipe, then ran through the puddles to the side door and into her kitchen.

I'd guess the house to have been built around the turn of the century, and the kitchen had probably changed very little since then. It was wide, though the single window was small, with down its middle a solid pine table, scrubbed until the grain stood up, with six pine chairs scattered around it. The sink was the original glazed earthenware, though it now boasted a stainless steel draining board. The gas cooker was ancient, but there was a fridge, and the freezer against one wall was a recent acquisition. The other end wall was entirely cupboard. It had come with the house. The doors still hung precisely and were not in the least warped. The red tiled floor had a rush mat nearly covering it.

The general impression was that the kitchen had seen a lot of living, a vast number of happy meals at that table, and was stubbornly, placidly waiting for more. The smell was of cured bacon and cheese, as though smoked sides still hung from the hooks I saw in the ceiling, and somewhere curds might be separating from whey.

I flung open a few cupboard doors, exploring, and lit my pipe and the burner beneath the kettle with one of her matches, wondering whether a can of soup wouldn't be more suitable.

'Tea first,' I told myself selfishly, putting out two mugs.

Angela, I decided, was well stocked up for an extended stay.

I poured two mugs of tea, took a mouthful from mine, then hurried across with hers with a saucer on top to keep out the rain. This time she allowed me inside. She had a rug over the gelding, who'd stopped shuddering.

'Oh . . .' she said into the mug. 'That's good.'

'I sugared it.'

'Just how I like it.'

'Then I guessed right.'

She lifted her nose. 'And Phil sent you?' She still didn't seem certain about me.

'He asked me to look you up. He said you were in some sort of difficulty.'

She gave a short laugh of scorn, I supposed at my way of putting it. 'He just refuses to do anything himself. Does he think you can?'

It was not the place to discuss it. 'Will there be hot water?'

'We're not that old-fashioned.'

'Then, if you're coming in now, I'll heat you some soup. And then a hot bath for you, young lady.'

'Oh?' she said, raising an eyebrow at my tone, and considering my seniority of perhaps eight years.

'Yes. I'm sure the horse is fine. You can leave him now.'

So she came back with me, and sat at the table with a bowl of soup while I went to find the bathroom and put my hand to the cylinder. Then I sat at one end of the table with my own mug of tea, Angela at the other, and we said not a word.

A strange young woman, I thought, prepared to live here on her own, and not really querying my presence. Perhaps she was secretly glad to have someone with her, though she seemed self-sufficient. A tomboy, Timmis had called her. I suppose the modern equivalent would be a junior feminist, though sitting there she looked small and lost against the length of the table. She had thrown off the anorak and sat in a roll-neck sweater, her face dirty and her hair untidy, and she could not have looked more feminine. Once she glanced up, a startled look. I thought she was suddenly afraid, but perhaps she was only measuring me, wondering whether she could trust me.

When she'd finished her soup, she got to her feet, flicked me a small smile, and went off for her bath.

I'd had time to do no more than gain a general impression of the house. Solid and lived-in, with woodwork everywhere. Four bedrooms, I guessed, and I'd peeped into one that ran across the rear. On a clear day you could've seen for miles. Windows up to the ceiling, and panelling . . . a man's room, probably her father's.

When Angela came down the day had really finished, and all traces of the tomboy had died with the light. She was wearing a tweed skirt and a blouse, and her hair was now drawn back tidily, making her face look much thinner. And she had a genuine smile for me, now very much the mistress of the household.

'We haven't been introduced,' she said. 'You know I'm Phil's wife. They call me Angie.'

'And I'm Harry Kyle.'

'Friend of Phil?' she asked, getting it straight.

I had to be careful how I put it. 'I've had dealings with him –

as a detective sergeant. But I'm . . . kind of on leave just now. That's why I've got the time to stick my nose into other people's affairs.'

She laughed. 'You beat me to it.'

'I thought we'd start off on a basic understanding.'

She considered that, frowning, then she changed the subject abruptly. 'Is that your caravan out there?'

'Yes. Theoretically, I'm touring.'

'Well . . . it'll be fine there. I'll make you up a bed . . .'

'You will not, you know. How'd it look – just you and me alone in the house?'

'There's nobody to see.'

'When the weather clears . . . No – if I can put the caravan in the corner of the yard, that'll be fine.'

'If you're intending to stay.'

'That was the general idea.'

'If you're really going to stick your nose in, you can stay until you've found out who killed my father. There's a tap in the corner of the yard, if you really want to be independent, and an old outside lavatory . . .'

'Not *that* independent,' I protested, remembering that hot cylinder.

'But I'll cook for you. Had you realised we're halfway through September?'

I tried to capture the sudden change of thought. 'Not really.'

She threw back her head. 'And you said you're touring! Didn't you know that all the tourist caravan sites shut at the end of the month? You'll just *have* to stay on here. Now . . . you won't have eaten. I think we deserve a slap-up meal, don't you?'

There wasn't any disagreement about that. I allowed myself to be shown into what she called the study, which was a cosy, dark room, all flickering shadows from the log fire she had in there, with brasses over the fireplace and a grand old oil lamp, still in operation if I'd put a match to it, and beautifully counterbalanced so that you could reach it down for lighting and raise it smoothly to any desired height into the high, carved ceiling. Until I was called to join Angie in the kitchen, I sat placidly smoking. I'm good at that sort of thing.

She was a splendid cook, and I enjoyed the meal. I hadn't been eating well of late, but watching her – listening to her – I forgot my lack of appetite.

It was as though a fresh spark of light had ignited her. She came alive before my eyes, glowing and eager and chattering away a stream of nonsense. I began to worry that she might be seeing too much hope in me, and that I wouldn't be able to justify it.

'Tell me about yourself, Harry,' she said at one point, but I managed to steer round that, and she didn't really notice, switching to another subject with her habitual ease. The atmosphere was friendly. I could have sunk happily into relaxation, if the word murder hadn't been hanging in the air.

2

We ate. Then we retired to the tight, warm study, and there at last we got to the reason Angie thought her father had been murdered. Quite clearly, from what I'd already heard, he'd died in an ordinary motoring accident.

She lit a cigarette and stared at it in her fingers. 'Phil just will not listen to what I've got to say,' she said tensely.

'I'm here to listen.'

'They said my father drove off the road, going very fast, at the traffic lights where they're going to put a new road.'

'That's what it seems like.'

'What if I told you he hadn't driven a car for ten years?'

'I'd say he was driving one that day.'

'It was night. Particularly, he would never have driven at night.'

'But he *could* drive a car?'

'Oh yes. He could drive. But he hadn't driven since he killed a man on a pedestrian crossing, ten years ago.'

What she was saying signified nothing. I considered how to put it. 'I may be wrong . . . but you were not here, on the night he died.'

'No. Of course not.'

'And how long since you'd been to see your father?'

Her eyes snapped. She reached out with a poker and jabbed at a log. It collapsed in a shower of sparks and flame, catching light in her eyes.

'Too long.' It was a whisper.

'How long . . . please?'

'Nearly a year. But I kept in touch.' She raised her chin in defence.

'But you couldn't be certain he hadn't bought a car, or hired one or something, and started to drive again.'

'He wouldn't do that.'

'Do you *know* he hadn't?'

She drew in her lower lip and bit it, threw her cigarette angrily into the fire. 'You're saying just the same as Phil!' She had expected better. I should be showing more understanding than Phil.

'I'm sorry. But we've got to get it straight. Did he have a car?'

'I know now, from what I've found out since I've been here. My cousin – Neville – lent him one. An old Escort.'

'Well then.'

'To experiment with, not to drive.'

'Experiment?'

A flicker of a smile, but she kept something back behind it. 'I'll tell you about it, I promise . . . but now, I'll just say it didn't involve driving. Any driving, Neville did for him, or more often Lynne Fairfax, that's daddy's secretary and lab assistant. Was, I mean. No, my father didn't drive. They both say he didn't. In any event, it was night-time. My father could not have driven at night, and he would certainly not have driven in the direction of the town, because of the traffic signal, and certainly not . . . absolutely not . . . as fast as they said he must've been going.'

It's possible to get a fixation about this sort of thing. Someone close to you dies in tragic circumstances, and it's something very difficult to accept in any event. Sometimes the very details of the death are distressing, and make the acceptance even more difficult. But most usually the rejection occurs when suicide is involved. Nobody wants to believe their beloved relative has committed suicide, if only because there's a suggestion that in some way they've failed him. But that, as I say, is in respect of suicide. In her case there was no suggestion of suicide – was there? Yet the fixation was just as strong. Angie was not prepared to accept something as ordinary as an accident. It had to be murder.

I eased my way into it cautiously. 'You were here for the inquest?'

'Yes.' There was a dismissive toss of her head. 'Such nonsense.'

'He was driving it – that was the evidence, I suppose?'

'That was what they said.'

'But . . . with the law as it is . . . he'd have been belted in. That is – in the driver's seat.'

'That was what they said he was.'

'But you can't surely be saying he was strapped in, against his will, perhaps unconscious at the time, and the car was sent down that slope, all just on the chance it'd neatly turn over and . . .'

She waved me silent, not wanting to hear about the burning.

'I don't know. If you say you want to help, surely that's one of the things to find out.'

I sighed. 'If,' I said, 'someone wished to kill your father and cover it as an accident, and he had not driven for ten years, wouldn't it be strange if a driving accident was used to fake it with?'

'I don't think so,' she said stubbornly. 'Not with those road works there, so convenient, and that traffic signal there. *That* traffic signal! Have you seen it?'

I nodded, puffing out smoke.

'It's only got two colours. Green and red.'

'Yes. They don't need the amber because it isn't a crossing.'

'Well then. *If* it could be assumed that my father was driving – and it *has* been assumed he was – then that would be just the place to fake an accident. Particularly at night. Particularly him.'

'If you say so. But why?'

'Because my father was colour blind on green and red.'

I realised, then, that she'd led me into it, gradually building up the background until I fell into the trap. The normal traffic signal sequence is red, red and amber, green, amber, red. This is a help to the colour blind, as they get a clue from the sequence. With a traffic signal using only red and green, that clue is missing. It was, as she'd said, just the place to fake his accident. But equally . . .

'You've just said it yourself. You're implying it'd be just the place where the traffic lights would confuse him. So why shouldn't it have been a genuine accident?'

'Because,' she said, her voice loaded with the deep suffering of a person plugging desperately at stupidity, 'he'd know about the signal, and if he *had* to drive for some reason – some emergency nobody knows about – he'd drive with care. They said he must have been driving fast. Very fast! It's completely ridiculous.'

I sat back and gave it some thought. She was, fortunately, the sort of person who is not afraid of silences. She watched me, though, ready to pounce on any rejection.

There was something in what Angie said. Given a person with the background of her father, there was at the very least a considerable amount to be discovered before I could confidently say he'd driven himself to his death. But to suggest the facts fitted murder . . . that was a different proposition altogether. Murder would have been too awkward and difficult in that way, too uncertain.

'This colour blindness,' I said, stalling. 'Tell me about it. I know so very little . . .'

Then she smiled, and her face became radiant. She knew she'd got through.

'It's not really a good phrase. Colour blindness. Only a very tiny percentage of people are fully blind to colour. Those are the ones who see things only as black and white and grey. Like cats. That's all *they* see. But what's usually meant by colour blindness is the fact that they don't use all three of the primary colours in their vision.'

'Red, yellow and blue,' I put in, to show I wasn't completely ignorant.

'No,' she declared, denting my ego. 'That's pigments. We're talking about *light*, and pigments take away light, not add to it. Light. Red, green and a purply blue, roughly. And the most usual difficulty is between red and green.'

'What's happened to yellow?'

'You'll see, because it's light we're talking about. Put an electric torch in each hand, one red and one green, and shine them on a white wall, and where they overlap you'd see yellow. *You* would see yellow. A person who's colour blind on red and green can usually see something they call yellow, but to match that up with the two torches they'd have to dim one of them, in some cases switch it off altogether. That's how my father was. Traffic signals he could handle, but it took a bit of concentration on the sequence. One wet and rainy night his concentration lapsed for a moment, and he ran down a man on a pedestrian crossing that happened to be controlled by a traffic signal.'

'Was he prosecuted?'

'That's the ridiculous thing about it. Witnesses said daddy was in the right, and drove through a green. But he blamed himself. He said he wasn't sure – and he didn't ever drive again.'

'That would be difficult for him, surely. This place isn't exactly a short walk from the nearest supermarket. A car would be absolutely essential to him.'

Angie drew up her left knee and linked both hands around it. She began to rock gently back and forward in the easy chair, her eyes going distant and dreamy, her voice falling to a soft tone, with husky hints beneath it. I pretended to be casual, but I was concentrating on her, waiting for another little trap, hoping to avoid falling into it. She was clever, and subtle with it, and what she had in mind was based on intuition, her knowledge of her father, her love for him and her understanding. She'd work very hard to put that across to a stranger, now that she knew I was all she had to depend on.

'I was living at home then,' she told me, 'and we were very close. We both assumed I'd always be around to look after him, so I could drive him where he wanted to go. As it happened, it was the same for both of us. We were commuting to Aberystwyth – don't you hate that word . . . commuting? He was a professor at the University there, and I was in my second year. Daddy had it all planned. A PhD for me, in his footsteps. Even the same subject. You see, he'd always specialised in vision and light and colour. He lectured on the physiology and psychology of sight.'

'You're a doctor of philosophy?'

She laughed. There was just a hint of regret behind it, but she trapped it before it became obvious.

'I never finished the course. Daddy killed that man on the crossing, and though I could drive him in every day, if he wanted, he became obsessed. In the end he resigned, and came back here to set up his own laboratory – I'll show you in the morning. Then he devoted himself to research on colour blindness.'

'Oh dear,' I said. 'How sad.'

She leaned forward, frowning at what she thought was my sarcasm. 'Sad? But he's been very happy.'

'Sad for you, I meant. If you had to give up . . .'

'Oh no! You mustn't believe that. There were other reasons I didn't go on for my degree.'

I nodded solemnly. It mattered. 'Sorry.'

'There was my mother, you see, and later I met Phil. And that was the end of everything.'

It was an unfortunate way of putting it. I waited. She looked suddenly shy.

'Or the beginning,' she amended thoughtfully. Phil Rollason had never struck me as the romantic type. Mind you, he's good with engines . . .

'So he researched,' I reminded her, keeping my mind on the subject. 'In his own laboratory.'

Angie smiled vaguely. 'At first, I worked with him. But he really needed someone who could type, and things like that. So he took on Lynne, who's been just marvellous. You must give her that. Marvellous. And there was Phil . . .'

She paused. A year or perhaps more unfolded itself in her memory, but remained unexpressed. The struggle there must have been over leaving her father was indicated only in a ruffle that crossed her brow. She tapped her teeth with her thumb-nail. I stared at my pipe.

'The house,' said Angie gently, 'was very big for the two of us. When mother died and Paul went away . . . my brother, Paul – you'll perhaps meet him . . . after that the house seemed empty. Even more when my father spent twelve – fourteen – hours a day in the lab. There's so much unexplored in the field of colour blindness, you know. He wanted to help people afflicted in the same way he was. He treated it as an affliction, though with most people it's no more than a slight disability . . . I'm wandering off the point. I'm sorry. What was I saying?'

'The house was empty all day,' I said. 'And there was no place for you in the lab.'

'Did I say that?' Large, startled eyes, suddenly challenging me.

'That's what I thought you meant.'

'No. I had plenty to do. Riding. The orchard . . . I used to play in it as a child, but it became a responsibility. They don't just grow, you know.'

'What was your father trying to do?' I prompted. 'To help.'

'Towards the end – and he wrote to me regularly – he was experimenting with vacuum-coating spectacle lenses, trying to produce a stronger contrast between red and green. You can see the point.'

I grunted, and nodded.

'And he'd had some success in that way. So he wanted to try it with an actual car windscreen. That was why he borrowed my cousin Neville's old Escort. Or bought it, I suppose. It wasn't worth much.'

'Vacuum-coated a whole windscreen?' He'd need very special equipment for that sort of job. 'Surely . . .'

'Only a very small area of it – or so he wrote to me.'

'Now hold on. A second. Surely you're not telling me he'd treated part of the driver's side of the windscreen, and that he'd taken the car out that night . . .'

Then again I saw she'd caught me. She was smiling. She had already bounced all this off Phil, and found him unresponsive. She had made an assessment of the official police attitude, and had prepared her assault on me with all the objections in mind. I was getting the revised version, the interpretation most likely to influence me.

'It's just what I'm *not* telling you,' she said. 'It was an area on the passenger's side he treated. Neville can explain all this, because it's Neville who's been taking him out in the Escort. At first, it was with daddy wearing his special spectacles, and then, because they were such a success, it was with daddy in the passenger's seat of the Escort, looking to see the effect of the small patch.'

I thought a lot before I took it on to the next point. Her father had been found in the driver's seat of that car. Argue how she might, to me that proved no more nor less than the fact that he'd been driving it. But if he'd had some success with his vacuum-spraying process, and he'd gone out driving that night, surely he'd have worn the spectacles. Take it further, and you could even imagine that he'd had enough of being driven by Neville, and thought it time he gave the spectacles a genuine driver's test. Surely that must be reasonable, even to the intense young woman who was at that moment poised for me to speak, like a chess master waiting for me to commit my bishop.

'And was he wearing his special glasses?' I asked gently.

'They were found lying on the roadway, broken. It seems like he was wearing them.'

'Then surely you can see . . .' I leaned forward, pointing the pipe stem at her. 'Surely it's obvious that he *was* driving, because he must have put them on with the *intention* of driving. As a passenger, he wouldn't have needed them. You've thought this out. It must be quite clear it has to be an ordinary driving accident.'

'Oh heavens,' she said, 'is this how they use logic in the police? If daddy was wearing his spectacles, then why should he have made a mistake about the traffic signal? It surely shows – if he really was driving – that he'd driven out just in order to test the effect of those specific traffic lights. How could he possibly have confused them, *and* been driving fast, into the bargain?'

I saw then that I wasn't going to win, whichever way I turned. There seemed very little to be discovered about the accident that wasn't already known, and anything new that turned up, Angie would simply reject. I felt let down, depressed. But I'd taken it too far simply to withdraw.

The truth was that she was on a nostalgia trip, back here at her old home. Perhaps life wasn't too marvellous with Phil. She was using the manner of her father's death as no more than an excuse for prolonging the stay. But only prolonging, surely, unless I was over-simplifying the difficulty, which I could well be doing if Phil's attitude was anything to go by. He'd been too morose for the problem to have been no more than an extended stay. He had trapped me, no getting round that, and, come to consider it, so had she. Even before the background had been laid out she had made me her guest – as good as – to be released only when I produced a happy solution. Offhand, I couldn't think of any correct etiquette for simply rejecting the invitation and driving away.

'Ideas,' I said morosely. 'Thoughts and feelings and intuitions. That's all we've got.' It was a mistake, the 'we' instead of 'you'. She was on it in a flash, her eyes glowing, but I hurried on before she could take me up on it. 'There's no way of extracting anything remotely resembling proof from what you say. No way of slipping a wedge in.'

'But you'll try, Harry?'

I shrugged, looking away. Damn it, she could easily have charmed some sort of promise from me. I glanced back. She was leaning forward, hands clasped around her knee, two spots of high colour on her cheeks and her lips moist. A lock of dark hair had strayed across one eye. She tossed her head. She had the damnedest way of tossing her head.

'We could give it a try,' I growled grudgingly, and thought

she was about to throw herself on me with kisses of thanks, and . . . oh, what the hell!

I could understand now why Phil Rollason was so mad to get her back. I'd never have guessed he possessed the sensibility, the Phil I knew being customarily arrayed in black stained overalls, with greasy hands and a sly, oily smile. There was money behind him – had to be, seeing he owned five or six garages – but its evidence never showed. They even lived in a poky flat over one of his repair shops. But he was sharp, and as thick-skinned as you'll ever meet. Well . . . I ask you – he'd been the cause of my suspension, yet he'd still meet me with a friendly slap on the shoulder. 'Heh there, Harry, what can I sell you?' That sort of thing. Phil Rollason I would have liked to strangle, if I hadn't had enough trouble already.

'I'd better back-in the caravan,' I said. 'Tuck it in neat.'

There'd been too much silence, and I was beginning to get uneasy.

'I'll help you.'

3

I'd had rudimentary advice on backing a caravan when I bought it. You steer the opposite way to the one you wish to go. As simple as that. They don't tell you that you can't see what the hell the back end's doing until it's too late. They don't warn you about excitable young women jumping around in front of the bonnet and shouting 'left hand down' and 'easy does it', and generally confusing the issue.

In the end, I got the Rover stuck at one angle and the twelve-foot caravan at another, and couldn't see any way in or out, so we unhooked it and ran up the little wheel at the front, and manhandled it into the back corner of the yard, with a little shove here and there from the gelding, who thought it was great fun.

That gelding though! Come to think of it, she'd bought him since she'd arrived there, so there was every indication that she wasn't even considering going back to the flat. So what the devil was I doing there?

We went inside for a relaxing cup of tea, over which I told her all about backing techniques, but Angie was only amused.

It was time I got myself somewhere I could think straight. I looked at my watch and said I'd take a run into town. She was at once on her feet.

'Alone,' I told her, and she pouted. 'A drink with the men,' I explained, but plainly she was disappointed. Bored with herself, I decided, but you have to be firm.

I drove down into the town. It wasn't quite in Wales, but close enough to the border to have a Welsh name – Llanmawr. I'd said I was going for a drink, but there was more to it than that, because the route naturally took me past the scene of the accident to Gledwyn Griffiths.

The rain had eased, or rather had settled into separate heavy drops, at least improving the visibility. The market would be over and most of the visitors retired to their far-flung farms.

The road was quiet. I wondered how quiet it had been on the night he'd driven to his death. Perhaps there had been witnesses. If so, I'd heard nothing about them.

It was now dark, with the dead, solid blackness of the countryside under heavy cloud. Coming down from the hills beyond Viewlands I could see Llanmawr spread in front of me, an insignificant handful of tossed lights on a black velvet background. Also, from quite a distance, the traffic signal at the roadworks was visible. As I approached, I watched the light change from red to green half a dozen times, and no car lights ran through in either direction.

I drew the Rover into the lay-by we'd used earlier for turning, left the parking lights on in case, and got out to have a look, taking a torch with me. The warning signs started early. Roadworks. Traffic Signals Ahead. Road Narrows. A sign indicated that the narrowing was from the right. This meant that from my direction, the downhill one, the single lane was on the natural driving side, and thus should not have presented a problem. Nevertheless, red and white plastic cones stood sentry at two feet spacing for a full fifty yards, leading to the dangerous drop on the right.

The old road had been tricky. There was a long, sweeping curve, suddenly reversing direction, and a whole quarter of a mile was in the form of a switchback, with several rises and falls in that distance, one of them to negotiate a hump-back bridge spanning a stream. All this was going to be smoothed out by the new roadworks. Straight and level, they were, so that a new tarmac surface would appear on your right for fifty yards, then on your left; for a few seconds six feet above your eye level, then six feet beneath your wheels. Where there was a drop the cones were reinforced by iron uprights driven into the road verge, with a chain linking them. They would not have withstood a car at any speed. Apparently they had not done so.

There was no obvious reason why a vehicle, even rushing a red light, should not have driven through safely, unless he'd met someone coming the other way. But there'd been no mention of another vehicle. I walked back to the Rover and drove into town, looking for somebody who might tell me more.

Llanmawr had never been more than a small market town, sitting there in medieval times with the same purpose, and probably undisturbed when black Welshmen poured down the hills on marauding expeditions. Celts and Saxons would meet here to trade and barter. Battles would flow past the town. Even now, market days would sing with the lilt of the Welsh tongue, and auctioneers would use a gabble that was neither one language nor the other.

But more recently there had been a half-hearted attempt to introduce small industry. As I drove into the outskirts I saw a sprawl of buildings enclosing a half-acre of regimentally aligned tractors, and following that a corrugated iron structure with a gateway sign indicating that preserving and canning were carried out. A large, now dark, garage seemed to specialise in agricultural machinery repair. Ahead of me was the first of the streetlamps.

It was large enough to boast orange streetlights along its main road, a Woolworth's and a Boots', two cafés and four public houses, and a bingo hall. The central square was large, cobbled, with a clock tower at one end of it. The stock pens were still there, but now hosed down, canvas flapping around the tubular steel supports, and leaving vast empty expanses of pungent parking space. Hardly a soul moved in the streets. It was either too early for the night life to have awakened, or the town already slept.

I got out of the car. Somewhere a motor cycle burst into life, but the sound disappeared away from me. One of the cafés was blasting out rock, but the glitter of the sound was sad in the wet and bedraggled streets. The clock in the tower began its run-up to the hourly warning of our diminishing lives, and I stepped out, looking for the nearest pub.

At least there was warmth and a hum of voices, deep eyes resting on me for a moment before passing on, no smile, but equally no scowl, and the beer was probably brewed locally from water that began life halfway up a Welsh mountain.

I located Sergeant Timmis in the third pub I visited, the Mitre. He was at a corner table, in civvies now, chatting to four youths and a very old man. I caught his eye and he nodded, then bent his head to the conversation again, so I turned back to the bar.

'Nice town you've got here,' I said, as my glass was pushed over.

The barman nodded. 'It suits.'

'A good brew. Local, is it?'

'Just out of town. You'll see it on the hillside, next door to the tweed mill. Some say they share the water. You can taste the tweed.'

I swallowed. Nodded. 'Nice pattern.'

Then Timmis was at my shoulder, ordering for his table. 'Care to join us?'

'I don't speak Welsh.'

'We're talking English.'

I grinned at him. 'I wouldn't have guessed. I'd rather hoped for a quiet word with you.'

He raised his eyebrows. 'So she's been telling you the tale.'

'I'll go and sit over there. Just a few minutes of your time, if you can afford it.'

He stared at me, working it out, wondering what trouble I might bring to his town. 'I'm off duty, so the time's free. I'll be with you.'

He managed it with circumspection, after a few minutes slipping over to my table, bringing with him his nearly-full pint glass.

'She's been talking to you about murder,' he declared affably. 'I can see it in your eyes.'

'I think I'd better give you the background. Her husband owns a few garages in Birmingham . . .'

'I know. Straight, is he?'

'You guess. I haven't been able to prove otherwise.'

'So you're in the police.'

'Detective Sergeant. Sort of.' I stared at him through my glass. 'The name's Harry Kyle.'

He smiled, daring me to avoid his eyes. 'Trouble?'

'I'm on suspension.'

'Naughty.'

'Bribery.'

'True?'

I shook my head.

He eased himself in his chair. Timmis was a big man, topping me by a good four inches, and generally unsmiling. But now he smiled, like a slat lifting in a venetian blind. 'So now you're filling in time. On my patch, too.'

'Helping out a friend.'

'Rollason? A friend?' One bushy eyebrow was raised. 'Or did I understand you wrong?'

Sometimes I can't hold back a laugh, which with me comes out like a dog barking. Heads turned. I leaned forward. 'You're too quick, Sergeant. Yes, it was Rollason who was involved, and no, I didn't take a thing from him.'

'But you're helping him?'

'Helping his wife, I'd rather say.'

'Ah.'

There was a short silence. I probed into it. 'You met him?'

'He came here – like you. We talked about things – same as now.'

'What did you make of him?'

'Rollason? Is that what we're talking about?'

'For now.'

'Then I'll tell you I didn't like your friend. Too smooth. We don't take kindly to subtlety round here, Mr Kyle. I think he was trying to bribe me into running Angela out of town.'

Lot of chance he'd have. I smiled. 'I just want to help her. Thought you'd point me in the right direction.'

He had a strong jaw and a wide, expressive mouth. He allowed it to indicate a slight satisfaction as his eyes scanned me. 'I think maybe you're already in the right direction.'

'Not that I can see.'

'Rollason wasn't interested in helping anybody but himself.'

I nodded, and said nothing. That described Phil.

'I was supposed to give her a good old talking-to,' he went on. 'Fatherly, you know, heavy, because I was a friend of her father. But I'm not much good at that, Mr Kyle. Besides, it might not have been a good idea. Tell her not to be a silly girl and pack her off home! D'you think that would fit the case? You're talking about helping her. Was that what you had in mind? Is that what you want from me, ammunition to use for shooting down her arguments? I've got plenty, if you need it.'

I've learned to use my pipe for all sorts of purposes other than smoking. You can watch your fingers filling it, and have a good old think. I was thinking that this Sergeant Timmis was not a man it was safe to upset. He spoke quietly, and his angers would be quiet. He'd lean on you gently until you backed as far as you could go, and smile silently while he squashed you.

I looked up. He was waiting patiently, huge hands clasped round his glass. 'Get you another?' I tried.

'Keep to the point.'

I skirted it gently. 'I've known her for an hour or two. Not long enough to form an opinion. She seems to me to be a determined young woman who's got herself an obsession. She thinks her father was murdered. She said she does. Now I'm not certain.'

'Not certain it was murder?'

'No. Not certain she's told me her real obsession. I'm not even certain she recognises it herself. She's been alone in that house for a long while now, letting the atmosphere soak into her bones. I once put away a classical pianist. Hit and run. He'd kept going because he'd been terrified he'd drawn blood. Anyway, he was inside, for manslaughter, for two years. No piano. No music except pop. I'd have done him a favour if I'd blown out his brains. I went to see him when he came out. His wife said he'd been shut away with his records for a solid week, soaking it up, in tears half the time, but letting it soak into his bones. He wouldn't touch his piano, afraid he'd lost it all.'

'And now?'

'He conducts. He composes. But something died in that two years, Sergeant.'

He nodded. 'Angie's been soaking it in, you say?'

'I don't think it's a good thing. I never met her at the time I was dealing with Rollason, so I don't know how she might have changed. But she'll go back to him when she's convinced she knows exactly what happened to her father. I think she will. I don't know. We don't want another performer finishing up with no more than a baton, now do we!'

'I know what happened to her father, Mr Kyle. I've told it to her in detail. Do you think you'll find anything I missed?'

There'd been challenge in his voice. I sighed. 'Tell me, if you will.'

He rubbed his face with his big, beefy hands, said: 'I'll get 'em,' and was up and away to the bar before I could say a word. When he came back he'd made up his mind, judging by the force with which he banged down the glasses.

'A Friday night,' he said. 'He'd come home earlier than expected, as he was due back on the Saturday. He'd been at a Convention in Blackpool the past week. Occulists, or whatever they call themselves. Lynne – his secretary – she'd driven there to pick him up in her Fiesta. She said he was quiet and depressed. He'd read a paper and it hadn't been well received.

Or so I found out. She drove him up to Viewlands and dropped him at the gate. They must've had words, judging by the fact that she didn't go in with him, look after him, put his kettle on. She always fussed over him. So she left him there. The Escort would've been locked away in the garage. It was around ten-thirty at the time. Dark. Raining, like tonight. The visibility wasn't bad, she told me, but that stretch with the traffic signal is always greasy with clay.'

'She'd have driven this way, into town, to get home?'

'No. She lives out the other side of town. No reason she'd have seen anything of it, if that's what you're thinking.'

He seemed protective whenever Lynne Fairfax was mentioned. I shook my head. 'Just a thought, hoping you'd got a witness.'

'Oh, we had one of those, all right. An anonymous one. We got a phone call at the station, timed at eleven-three. A car'd gone off the road and set on fire. That's all. The caller hung up. A man, the duty constable thought, though the voice was high and a bit hysterical. I wasn't on duty, but they called me out, but it was all over when I got there. They'd put out the fire, but really it'd burnt itself out when the fire tender got there.'

He took a draught of beer, and wiped his mouth with the back of his hand. 'The car was lying on its back,' he said unemotionally. 'It was down on the new road, a hundred yards past the lights. You could see where he'd gone through the cones – the chains weren't there then. The skid marks were obvious. He'd been doing fine. For some reason he braked hard, and went over the edge. The car hit on its side and turned over twice before it stopped moving. Oh, I checked every mark in the morning, measurements, the lot. I think he must've been dead when the fire started. That's what I tell myself. But the pathologist's report mentioned scorch marks in the throat and smoke in the lungs. That didn't come out at the inquest, Mr Kyle. Nobody thought that was necessary. You get my point? Maybe he'd run a red, and somebody was driving towards him. Our anonymous caller, perhaps. Does it matter? It was still a driving accident, and I can't imagine anybody being able to force him off the road from behind, because it's only single-lane. An accident, and I wish to Christ you'd persuade her so, then we can send her home.'

I mulled it over. 'Her father got home that Friday evening.

He was upset. He barely settled in before taking out a car he'd not driven before and driving it towards the town at a dangerous speed. It doesn't hang together. There's something we don't know. D'you think I ought to try to dig it out, Sergeant?' I asked. 'Does that sound like a good idea to you?'

'We closed it down.'

'That wasn't what I said. I'm wondering why you didn't dig deeper.'

'Are you, Mr Kyle?' he asked blandly. 'Perhaps I didn't want to see any deeper. D'you know what? It occurred to me that Angie doesn't want to, either.'

'It sounded to me as though she did.'

'Like that awful fascination some people get on the top of cliffs. They're terrified they might go over, but they can't keep away from the edge. Try to help 'em, and it could be just that extra touch that'll have 'em over.'

'She's afraid,' I agreed. 'Of something.'

We both brooded quietly for a few moments. I was pleased to have met another brooder. At last I said:

'It's her horse, you know, not borrowed. The gelding. She bought it.'

'Perhaps she'll take him home when she leaves.'

'They're in a flat.'

He laughed, thumped his knuckles on the table and laughed, and perhaps he saw it as amusing.

'You know what I think?' I asked. 'She believes her father did it on purpose, deliberately drove off that road. She doesn't know why, but she feels she ought to know. But she's terrified of finding out. Do you think I ought to satisfy her?'

For a moment he was angry. I could see it in the sudden whitening of his knuckles. 'I don't like your imagination,' he growled. 'I'm not sure I ought to encourage it.'

'Risk it. Go on.'

I didn't really need his co-operation. There's no law that says you can't go round asking questions, only that you can't demand answers. But it's as well to keep on the right side of the police, especially in a strange town. This town was as close to being Welsh as I'd wish to get, which could make it very strange indeed.

He grimaced. 'Don't expect me to hold your hand. What had you got in mind?'

'There've been names mentioned. A brother called Paul. I'd like to meet him. A cousin of Angie's – Neville something. This secretary woman – Lynne. I'd like to speak to them all. Addresses, perhaps, from you, that's what I'd ask. Maybe a hint of official backing. I'll keep it all low-key. That much I promise.'

How easy it is to make promises. You can tell the farmer it's only a little fire you want to light in the corner of his wheat field, but then the wind changes.

Sergeant Timmis straightened his shoulders, and half reached up with his right hand, as though forgetting he wasn't wearing his peaked cap. He thrust back his chair.

'Reckon I could show you one of them, right now. Neville Green's in for drunk and disorderly again. We're drying him out.'

'I'd prefer him when he's sober.'

'Then you'd have to get him early in the morning. Drink up. It's only round the corner.'

I could hardly refuse. I got to my feet. He lifted a vast, belted raincoat from the stand in the corner. I finished my drink while he said goodnight to his mates. They eyed me with quiet concern, convinced he was taking me in.

'Thought a lot of his uncle, did Neville,' he said, holding the door for me.

'There's not much point in talking to him if he's drunk,' I told him quietly, beginning to feel he was using this as a form of obstruction.

'It isn't him I want you to meet. But Lynne Fairfax should be around by now. She always comes for him and takes him home. She's his fiancée, or something. Not actually living together, but either address can find both of them.'

The rain had stopped altogether, but the cobbles were still glistening under the streetlamps. Across the square a single-decker red bus was waiting, and farther up the bingo hall was just coming out, timing it for the bus I suppose. A group of youths came bursting out from one of the discos, and ran yelling past us. Sergeant Timmis did not react. The square echoed to their feet.

'It's round the corner,' he said.

The station was about the size to be run by an inspector, with possibly three sergeants and a dozen constables, with back-up from HQ, who'd supply any CID support as required. They'd possibly boast a single cell, more likely a room with one small window and one thick door. It had a lamp over the steps up to the front door, with a blue and white illuminated sign over it, and a grey Ford Fiesta parked outside.

A squat, vigorous woman was trying to lever a tall, angular man into the passenger's seat.

'Try!' she howled at him. 'Bend your stupid head, you drunken swine.'

'Ah!' said the sergeant. 'You're in luck. Both of them. This is Lynne Fairfax and Neville Green.'

'Don't stand there,' she said to me. 'Help me, can't you!'

I thought she was talking to Timmis, but when I looked round he'd disappeared into his station.

So I helped her.

4

He would have been around thirty, I thought, though he was not, at that time, in full control of his features. He had a decent thatch of hair and a fluffy moustache that looked as though it was stuck on, and great, long and floppy limbs that took a good deal of folding into the car. Truth to tell, Lynne did more of the work than I did. Perhaps she had the practice.

'Do this often, do you?' I asked.

'Enough. Push that knee in and I'll shut the door.'

'What about the seat belt?'

She shouted in his left ear. 'Can you fasten your belt?'

He fumbled around with it. He was at that stage of drunkenness when all was placid agreement and a fond attempt towards self-help. He played with the belt and finally got it to click, then he looked up at me and asked:

'Didn' think I'd make it, did y'?'

She slammed the door on him, and he grimaced at me in apology through the glass. Then she turned to me, solid legs planted apart and her square, strangely attractive face cocked, a knitted hat on one side of her head with hair flopping around above the other ear.

'Well!' she declared. 'I swear I'll kill him, one of these days.'

'I was trusting the sergeant to introduce us,' I said. 'My name's Kyle. I wanted a few words with you.'

She grimaced. It was a wide, straight mouth. She flapped her hands against her firm hips in their tight jeans. 'Hardly the time, is it?'

'About your ex-employer, Mr Griffiths.'

She stared up at me. The light was bad out there. I thought something crossed behind her eyes, but she shook her head, then looked away.

'There's nothing I want to say.'

'I know it's not convenient.' I was about to say I'd see

her another time, but she became immediately practical, and yanked open the car door again.

'Where did you leave the car?' she asked Neville.

He'd been asleep. She shook him awake and repeated it. He mumbled something. She demanded the keys, and patiently, slowly, he searched his pockets until he found them.

She banged them into my palm. 'Make yourself useful. It's a Metro, outside the Gun. Drive it round here, and then follow me. Huh? Then he'll have it in the morning.'

' 'Sa dark blue one,' he mumbled.

I needed directions to the Gun, which was down a side street two up on the right. I set off. 'Don't go away,' I called, and she shouted after me: 'Oh . . . funny!'

The Metro wasn't exactly where she'd said. Not outside, but round the back, where the light was no more than a naked bulb over the outside gents'. There were three Metros, and the key opened two of them. It took all my detective abilities, as both were new enough to be bare of personality. As I was deciding that the one smelling of scent was probably not his, a woman said from behind me: 'What the hell d'you think you're doing?' I withdrew my head, dangled the keys, said sorry I'd got the wrong Metro, and drove away in the blue one. She shouted after me that I must be effinblind, and I had to agree. As the headlights ran across her car, I saw it was red. Some detective!

Lynne watched me coming, and was moving away before I'd started the necessary U-turn to get behind her. Timmis appeared in time to wave from the steps. I found that Neville had got the seat right back, so it just suited me, though I kept changing up too early until I got used to the high-revving engine.

She took me out of town in the generally west direction of wild Wales. We left the street lighting behind and traversed the side of a hill, then abruptly turned between two hefty beech trees, emerging beyond them onto a sweep of gravel in front of a two-storey arc of modern flats.

They were so modern that they were not really finished. I could just make out the run of foundations to one side, where the garages would eventually be. The balconies at one end of the sweep of flats were not yet fixed.

They'd landscaped it to hide it in the trees. From the road below there'd be nothing but a wooded hillside. She drew up, me neatly behind her. A bluish light over the entrance showed me that her hair was blonde and untidy, most of the rest of her matching. She was round at my window before I'd got the handbrake on, and opened the door for me.

'This is the difficult bit,' she said. 'He's up on the second floor.'

Quite frankly, I'd rather have done it all myself. But she insisted on taking most of him, leaving me with the odd arm and shoulder, and her encouragement to him alternated wildly from: 'careful there, lovey,' to: 'watch out, you great lump!' at a full scream. I couldn't make out whether she regarded him with fond affection or abject disgust. His door key was on the same ring, so I let us in.

The entrance lobby, the double marbled staircase and the absence of graffiti, had given me a clue what to expect. The flat was modern and clean and indicated an unexciting personality. He had the right choice of G-plan in the approved arrangement, scatter cushions neatly tossed around and carefully selected to clash with the scatter rugs, and all the necessities of life, as seen through the eyes of the young man about town who is no longer so very young, and whose town is somewhat small. *Playboys* were tossed onto low surfaces, record albums thrown on top of them. The hi-fi was higher than last year's, and the colour TV located as far as possible from the remote control, to prove how well it worked. All that, and a row of bottles on a pale and angled sideboard. Seemed a pity he troubled to go out to get drunk, but I supposed he'd have to be one of the boys, and be encouraged to it.

She noticed my wince at the colour scheme. 'I've been trying to brighten him up,' she explained.

'What's he think about it?'

She laughed. 'Said I was making his life a misery.'

We laid him out on a low divan. He groaned, then mumbled himself to sleep again. Lynne blew out her breath, fluttering her lips, then drew off the woolly hat and tossed her hair free with an angry shake of her head.

'Thanks,' she said. 'You've been a great help. I can handle him now.'

'I'm free to leave?'

She stared at me. Her eyes had gone vague, opaque with worry. Pleasant, warm hazel eyes they were. I waited for it to register. We were a good mile out of town. Her eyes cleared.

'Oh Lor',' she cried. 'Aren't I the biggest idiot!' Then she laughed, a little tinkle of cool amusement.

'My car's parked in the square, and I did want to talk to you, anyway. About Gledwyn Griffiths.'

She turned away from me quickly, but not before I caught the distress in her eyes. 'Not now.'

'But when?'

'I don't know who you are and what you want.' Then her eyes were large, and considering me innocently. 'Are you another policeman?'

'I'm just a friend of Angela. She's not happy with . . . things.'

'Oh . . . that!' she said in disgust. 'I'm simply fed up with hearing about it.'

Keep your eyes on them every second and they become uneasy. I took a tour of the living room. Perhaps he'd call it his lounge. He'd got a hairy bit of Welsh tweed hanging on the wall.

'Nice place,' I commented.

'He works for the council.' But she was speaking absently, impatient to hear my true business.

'It's a council flat?'

'Oh no. He's a land surveyor. Good money. Good flat.'

Did I detect a note of envy in her voice? She wouldn't have earned much with Gledwyn Griffiths, and would now be without a job. But from what Sergeant Timmis had told me, she could probably have moved into this flat at any time.

'What are you fed up with hearing about?' I asked.

'That Angie!'

'Yes?'

'He's dead,' she said fiercely, a catch in her voice. 'A fine man, and he's dead. And no amount of talking's going to bring him back.'

'Then you're happy about the way he died?' I examined a record sleeve.

'Happy?' she snapped.

'You find it acceptable, then?'

'He was upset, that night. Strange. I don't know why he took the Escort out. I can't understand it. But he did.'

'You wouldn't have expected him to?'

'Never. He didn't drive. Or why would I have had to fetch him from Blackpool?'

'Had to? Was it an order?'

She was becoming angry, with the anger of distress. 'No, damn it. He was due back on the Saturday. We'd arranged that – for me to fetch him then. I'd got something else on, that Friday.'

'A date?'

'If you like.' She threw it at me, and walked away.

'A date with sleeping beauty, here?'

'Yes. No. What's it matter? Gledwyn had given me a holiday. A week. I've got my own life. He phoned on the Friday morning. Just like that. I want to come home. Fetch me.'

'Phoned you at the lab, up at Viewlands?'

'At my place. I wasn't at the lab. I told you, I was on holiday.' She gestured angrily. 'I'd better get Neville to bed. I'm not going to talk about it any more.'

'He's quite happy there,' I said, considering Neville's lax and placid face. 'And I'm here until you decide to drive me back. You don't have to answer any of my questions . . .'

'Then don't ask them.'

'You were annoyed with this fine and wonderful employer. Won't you tell me why?'

'At his beck and call . . .'

'I'll bet you loved it. Tell the truth, now.'

She growled in her throat, moved restlessly, and clamped her square jaw so that her mouth was a thin, straight line. 'It wasn't part of the job, driving him around, but I didn't *mind*. Take him to Blackpool – we'd agreed to that – and fetch him back the next Saturday. Right enough. There on Sunday, back on Saturday.'

'But he decided to come back on the Friday,' I murmured. 'Not Saturday.'

'I'm telling you about the previous Sunday,' she said firmly, nodding fiercely. 'Part of my holiday, I reckoned it. Right?' I nodded, a little amused at her emphasis. 'So he'd no cause to snap at me, no cause to sulk all the way to Blackpool. If something had upset him, he could've told me. To me, he could've said it. He always did.'

I was filling my pipe. The carriage clock on the narrow mantel indicated it was nearly ten. 'Always sulked at you?' I asked with interest.

'No . . . silly!' She almost stamped, her sturdy body taut

with impatience. 'Otherwise I wouldn't have noticed it – would I? But on the trip to Blackpool he barely said a pleasant word. No word of thanks for the typing I'd re-done for him the night before. Stayed late for it, too. Not a thought for me! He never asked why I could hardly drive for the tears. Never even noticed I was upset myself. I shouldn't have driven at all, that day. I knew that. But it was a Sunday, so the roads weren't too bad. A good thing. But *he* never noticed.' Then her voice softened. 'Any other time . . . Oh – what's the use!'

I had her going. It wasn't a pleasant sight, but you have to seize the time and place because they never appear again together.

'And why were you in tears?' I asked softly.

'My friend had died the night before. You know that. You *know* it. You're just teasing me.'

'I know nothing about your friend.'

'My friend Carla.'

'Your friend Carla died on the Saturday night,' I almost whispered.

'She was killed. Everybody knows. Killed by a hit-and-run driver, who didn't stop, didn't phone, didn't do anything. Otherwise she'd be alive now.'

Everybody knew . . . except me. Everybody included Sergeant Timmis. If I'd had him there I'd have strangled him. Nobody had said a thing about two deaths. Her friend Carla had died on the Saturday, her friend and employer Gledwyn Griffiths on the following Friday.

'If you want to know,' she said from behind me, a weak, childish voice now, 'it wasn't a date. Not on the Friday that I fetched him back. That was the day of the inquest on Carla. It was why I couldn't go to fetch him until the afternoon.'

She spoke almost as though Neville Green was awake, and it was him she was reassuring. But he did not stir.

I said: 'He looks safe to leave.'

She shrugged. 'I'll drive you back. I'd better spend the night here with him.' That answered a question in my mind. She ruined the impression of a loving twosome by adding: 'I suppose.'

We left him sprawled amongst the garish evidence of his professional success. She had become silent. As we climbed into her Fiesta, I asked:

'I got the impression you live elsewhere.'

'The other side of town.'

'Towards Viewlands?' I wanted to get it straight.

'No.' She dismissed it with a grated gear-change. 'Out on the Whitchurch road. I can get there from here without touching the town. If I want to. North a bit, then east. The same from Viewlands, if I want to. Miss the town, I mean.'

She was giving me unnecessary information, empty words to mask her feelings. But her driving betrayed her. No one should drive a car under emotional stress. Fortunately the traffic was sparse, and my concern was for her.

'I found her,' she said into the night ahead. 'Me. Going home from Viewlands. It was late. After ten, and dark. This was the Saturday, the day before I was due to drive Gledwyn to Blackpool, and I'd stayed on to type up the paper he was going to read there. Stayed on in case he wanted to alter it again. But he was late. He'd been to see his son, and he was late back. So I waited. I knew Carla was going to my place, on a visit, but I didn't worry because she'd got her own key. But I was driving fast, and suddenly there was her little Fiat, parked at the side of the road. I came round a bend, and there it was, with the rear lights almost dead, and no more than a glow from the dipped headlights when I walked round. I'd shouted her name, you see, and didn't hear a sound. This was half a mile from my place, and she could've walked, but why would she walk away and leave her headlights on and run down the battery? She'd know better than that. You see what I mean?'

She wasn't really asking. I said nothing. The police station was ahead and she was slowing, determined to drop me exactly where she'd picked me up. She'd stayed very late at Viewlands, the evening her friend died. It indicated a great devotion to duty, or to Gledwyn Griffiths. I had to listen out this distress of hers, or maybe I'd never get to the one that interested me.

'And there she was,' she said, drawing to a halt. 'They said she'd been thrown over the bonnet, because there she was, lying at the front, and there was blood everywhere. She'd have lived if I'd got to her earlier. I could have done something. But I was so late.'

We were parked outside the station, and Sergeant Timmis was standing in the doorway, feet apart, smoking a cigarette. He was looking beyond us, as though we were not there. Lynne took her hands from the steering wheel and stared at her palms. Then she went on to explain why she'd been so late.

'And when,' she said dully, 'Gledwyn *did* get back from visiting his son, he said not a word to me, just walked across the yard from the house with his face like stone, walked through the lab to the office, and threw his keys at the wall. Not a word. I gave him the typing I'd done and he barely glanced at it. Just tore it across and across and tossed it on the floor in a temper, so of course I had to type it all again for him, otherwise he wouldn't have had it for the morning. And otherwise I wouldn't have been so late, and perhaps Carla would have been alive . . .'

She said it simply. There was no bitterness in her voice, no blame for Gledwyn Griffiths and his strange mood. But how could there be, when a week later he'd died himself? His death was the deeper grief, and she now used Carla's death only as a screen, to shield her from contemplating his.

'And the following morning you drove him to Blackpool?'

'Yes.'

'He knew nothing about your friend's death?'

'How could he?'

'I thought perhaps you'd have phoned him.'

'I didn't get a spare minute. The police were questioning me.' She nodded sideways. I hadn't realised she'd noticed the sergeant. 'That great lump. He was there. I got hardly any sleep.'

I'd been playing with my pipe, not wanting to light it in somebody else's car. I wondered whether to close down the discussion right there. Her voice had been too even, too restrained.

'It was Sunday morning,' I said gently. 'Neville wouldn't have to go to work. You could have phoned him, and he'd have driven your boss to Blackpool.'

'I tried.' She gave a nervous laugh. 'But he didn't answer. I suppose he deserved all the sleep he could get, that drive he'd done the night before.'

'Drive?' I murmured. 'What drive?'

'I said.' She was impatient. 'Oh, you just don't listen! I told you – that Saturday, Gledwyn'd been to visit his son. Who d'you think drove him? I couldn't, because of the typing. It had to be Neville. Of course.'

Any driving Neville had done, I decided, I'd discuss with

Neville himself. I contented myself with one remark. 'For once, then, he wasn't drunk.'

'He didn't get the chance. Oh . . . I don't know what's the matter with him,' she whispered. 'For months now . . . and he never used to drink.'

'You'd better get back to him,' I suggested, hunting for the door catch.

'I've half a mind to drive straight home, and let him rot.'

I got out. She didn't look at me again and she didn't drive home, but did a U-turn over the opposite pavement and headed back to Neville Green. I hoped he'd realise what he'd got there, and walked up the steps to say goodnight to the sergeant.

'You're a very unnerving man to know, Sergeant Timmis,' I told him.

'I thought you'd better hear it from her.' No hint of a smile.

I nodded. 'She'd got it all neatly laid out. Did you ever get anybody for the hit-and run?'

'I'll walk you to your car,' he offered, falling into his patrol stride, which he hadn't lost from his youth. 'Hit-and-runs are difficult. You know that. No connections with the victim, except the damage to their own vehicle. Oh, we put out calls, all garages and body repair shops, over a radius of fifty miles. But there was nothing came back.'

'You know there was damage, then?'

'Must have been. The forensic lot said he must've been going at a fair speed, from the damage he did to her, and traces of headlamp glass were found. No skid marks. That was strange. Her Fiat had broken down. The petrol pump. She was obviously standing beside her door, waiting to wave somebody down. This was a clear eighty yards from the bend. We decided the other driver came up from behind her car, and couldn't help but have seen her. You wouldn't drive around there at night without at least dipped heads. So she'd have been seen. But there were no skid marks. He must have driven straight at her. And left her. The battery was flat when Lynne Fairfax found her, which might or might not mean she was lying there a long while. Take your choice. Nobody would spot her, lying beneath headlights, though.'

He stopped beside my new Rover and slapped the roof. 'Like your car,' he said.

'I wanted something that'd tow a large caravan.'

'It's up at Viewlands, is it?'

'I'm staying there.'

'Ah well . . . any more help I can give you, Mr Kyle – I'll be around.'

I slid in behind the wheel. 'Your help's more in the line of diversions, isn't it! All the same, I might take you up on that.'

I drove back to Viewlands. The single lane stretch was more tricky in the uphill direction, but I met no other traffic.

There were no lights on in the house. Suited me. An early night, I thought, but the gelding peered at me suspiciously over his half door, and whinnied, and before I got safely inside the caravan Angie was at my shoulder.

'The water's hot, if you want a bath.'

'Not just now, thanks.'

'I heated it specially for you.'

'In the morning, huh?'

I had gas and mantles in the caravan. I got a match to my lamp, and turned. She was peering in from the door, her eyes hopeful, disappointed. Hell, she must've been lonely. There was nothing sexual in it. But you have to be firm.

'Please,' I said. 'I've had a big day.'

She pouted, nodded. 'The bathroom's to the left at the top of the stairs. I'll be out of there by seven-thirty. All right?'

'Thank you.'

She closed the door gently. I felt like a louse. Coffee, a bit of a chat, a smoke – what would've been the harm in that? I nearly went after her, but had my shoes off while I was thinking about it, and it was too much effort to put them back on.

As I said, I'd had a big day. I fell onto the bunk bed, and slept.

5

With the morning emerged the full beauty of the valley, and the reason for the location of the house on that exact spot.

At seven-thirty there'd been no sign of Angie in the house. I'd soaked a while and felt great. On the landing, there was still no sound, so I ventured on a little exploration. The second door opened into the bedroom I'd already taken a look at. It was not hers. The set-up was masculine. The spaciousness – three windows on one wall – suggested it was the master bedroom. Gledwyn's. I ventured to the windows, fumbled for my pipe, gripped it, and failed to light it.

Green, grey and purple ran out into the distance, and though the mountains were not clear the aerial mist hinted at their weight, and shadows chased behind it along the far horizon. To the right the hill continued to climb, clothed in the mauve of heather and cut across by grey outcrops of slate. Cream specks of sheep clung to the slope. To my left the valley leaned away into swaying patterns of multi-toned green, and the far golden shades of wheat stubble. The stream flashed silver and blue, narrow and restless, and russet Guernsey cows paddled in it. Closer, the orchard Angie had mentioned was red and green with apples waiting to be plucked, green and gold with pears, purple with plums, and between it and the acre of Angie's paddock someone, who could not have been Gledwyn Griffiths, had planted a row of maples, just for this moment in autumn when the leaves flared into red, and the morning sun set them alight.

In the paddock, she was gently cantering her chestnut gelding, working the fear from him on the firm turf.

I sucked the empty pipe.

Gledwyn Griffiths must have gazed through that window onto a thousand beautiful mornings, and suddenly my heart went out to him, that he could not have seen this blaze of colour. Yet he must have loved the house. He'd never lived away, always making the long journey to wherever he happened to be lecturing.

But how was I to know the intensity of his enjoyment of the scene? My musical ear is poor, but I can still thrill to Tosca. If I'd had perfect pitch, would my appreciation have increased ten-fold? A hundred-fold? Or not at all? No one can imagine the intensity of another's pleasure. Cries of delight might seem brash to someone caught dumb by ecstasy.

Reluctantly, I turned away. With Angie safely out of the way, it was a chance to look over the rest of the house. It would perhaps tell me something about Gledwyn.

Perhaps on a grey day the interior would have seemed dark, but I knew from the previous evening that it would be a cheerful darkness. There was a tendency towards heavy, black mahogany and high Welsh dressers, solid furniture with maroon velvet upholstery and tall velvet drapes. The pictures on the walls were of Welsh landscapes, and were originals. Perhaps not valuable – there'd been an artist in the family maybe. But any gloom was denied by the high and wide windows, and every-where there was oak parquet and soft, oatmeal carpeting.

I went out into the stableyard and leaned over the white rails at the rear. Angie saw me and waved, so I went back in and set bacon to frying, then went out and watched her. She rode over, and this morning it was a happy Angie, erect in the saddle and laughing down at me while the gelding reached his yellow teeth for my hair.

'I learned to ride in this paddock,' she told me. 'Daddy bought me my first pony when I was nine.'

'You'll need to get your fruit picked.'

'Morgan Rees buys my fruit. He sends his men over. No worry.'

Her words had all the contented practicality of a woman who'd settled in to stay. What had Phil Rollason to offer, I wondered, one half so attractive?

She swung down and led the gelding into the yard. The sun caught her hair, and there was auburn in there as the wind stirred it.

'Evan's driving over today,' she said. 'I phoned him this morning, to tell him I had a visitor. He said he'd like to meet you.'

'Evan? I asked. 'Over from where?'

'Evan Rees. Surely I mentioned him.'

'You did not.'

'Dr Evan Rees. He's Morgan's son, and he's doing research at Aberystwyth University. He was a research student when daddy lectured there, that's why he studied the same subject. I *knew* you'd want an expert on it, to understand what daddy was doing. Then you'll agree he couldn't possibly have killed himself.'

We'd been crossing the yard towards the kitchen. Suddenly she stopped dead, raising her head, and clutched my arm.

'No . . . wait. A moment, please,' she appealed. 'Do you know how many years it's been since I've had this pleasure? Walking across from the stables after an early morning ride, and my mother cooking bacon and eggs. It's not the same doing it yourself. You need to come to it with a head full of fresh air.'

I turned my face to blow smoke away from her. 'Many years?'

'Eight or so.' She moved ahead, her voice suddenly brisk and dismissive. 'My mother was ill for a long while. It was why daddy had to give up research at the University. He'd had to go every day, and he was always kept late. It's why he switched to lecturing. Just once a week, that became.'

'Until the pedestrian crossing incident?'

'Yes,' she said shortly.

Clearly he'd wanted her to take his place. She had wanted it, too, for herself and for her father. But Rollason had come along, flashing those teeth of his, and with that smooth charm that he uses when he's trying to sell you a car. Whatever had she seen in him?

'Eggs and bacon!' cried Angie, bursting into the kitchen.

'Bacon, anyway. If it's not done to a crisp.'

'I like it crisp.' She glanced at me. 'But I'll need to do some shopping, afterwards.' She whipped off the pan.

The implication was obvious. She had no car in that garage at the end of the yard. But Rollason could easily have brought her something, towed it in if necessary with his breakdown pick-up. The mean bastard. He'd been deliberately making her life awkward. I supposed that Morgan Rees had been helping her out with the shopping. I supposed I'd have to step in.

'No difficulty there,' I said, trying not to sound too obliging.

'If we go straight afterwards,' she said happily, 'it will be all right. Evan won't be here till after lunch.'

She said nothing when I stopped at the same lay-by, to examine the same scene of death by daylight. I wondered whether I should do it, with Angie at my side, but she nodded when I asked her, and sat grim-faced when I got out of the car and walked away.

It was not really safe to walk along the narrow single-lane in daytime, now with more traffic. I jumped down onto the new surface before it became too much of a drop, and walked until I found the crash marks, which were still clear enough. Scars ran along the surface, crossing and impacting until I reached an area still black from the heat of the fire. Cars drove past, eight feet above, beyond an almost solid rank of plastic cones. There was nothing to see except in the imagination, which I didn't want to encourage. The car had been found on its roof, with Gledwyn Griffiths still dangling from the remnants of his seat belt. Only his special spectacles had been thrown clear, unless the small, half-melted lump of plastic at my feet had belonged to him.

I bent and picked it up. The thumb wheel and valve were still identifiable as the remains of a plastic zip lighter.

As I returned to the Rover I wondered where they'd taken the wreck.

We drove on, Angie averting her face.

'Did your father smoke?' I asked her.

'No.' She said it on an indrawn breath.

We drove for half a mile before I asked: 'Is there another way into Llanmawr?'

'Yes,' she whispered. 'But it's longer.'

'We should have taken it.'

'I wanted you to see.'

To see how far the gouging had run, and estimate how fast he'd been moving? She wasn't going to miss a trick.

'I've seen now. We'll drive back the other way.' I was a little short with her.

The town was alive that morning. Parking was no longer simple, but they hadn't progressed to meters. I left the car nose-in to the kerb, with barely room to open the doors. Angie said she'd wait in the café she pointed out – if I had business I needed to do.

This was rather pointed, but in fact I had none. I'd have liked a chat with Neville Green, but he'd be at work, sorry for himself but persistent, no doubt. I wanted to speak to Lynne again, but

I hadn't got her address, and anyway she lived some miles distant. There'd been mention of a brother, Paul, but I had no idea where he might be.

Not wishing to remain inactive, I called into a tobacconist's and bought some tobacco, then went along to see whether Sergeant Timmis was on duty.

He was. He smiled sourly when he saw me and leaned in exaggerated weariness over the counter. 'Still here, then?'

'Barely started,' I admitted. 'I'd rather like to get a look at the car, if it's still available.'

'Gledwyn's Escort? That'll tell you nothing.'

'All the same . . .'

He turned, and called out: 'David, where did they take the burnt-out Escort?'

'Old Cadwell's yard, I think.' The voice came from the office at the rear.

Timmis returned his attention to me. 'It's convenient. At the top of this street, where it fades out. He's dug himself into the old quarry. But don't count on too much.'

'I won't.' I stared at a poster about Colorado beetle. 'There's mention of a local you'll know. Evan Rees. A brain from the University at Aberystwyth. Can you tell me anything? He's visiting this afternoon, and I'd like to start with an advantage.'

This seemed to delight him. He put his hands together as though praying, and blew into his palms. 'Well now! Young Evan coming to visit Angie, is he?'

'Coming to visit me.'

'Guess whose eyes he'll stare into.'

'If it was like that,' I said severely, 'she's had plenty of time to send for him.'

He grinned hideously. 'But she's been alone. How could he visit her, with his family in the farm next door? They're very funny round here, you know. Things can get sexy, but they've got to be discreet.'

'For a good laugh, I'll know where to come in future.'

'And as soon as she's got a chaperone, Evan's on his way. What a coincidence!'

'I'm sorry I troubled you, Sergeant.'

'No, no. Don't go.' He drew himself up to his full height. In uniform he looked huge. 'If you're going to be a chaperone, it's only fair you should know what you're up against.'

'Much obliged.'

'Evan'd be about the same age as Angie. That'd make him – what? – oh, twenty-six or so. The apple of his father's eye, Evan was. The farm was coming to him. But you'd never see 'em apart, when they were kids, Angie and Evan, and that brought Evan close to Gledwyn, and *that* was the end of farming for Evan. Those days, any trouble either of them got in, you just looked round for the other. Angie was the leader, and Evan caught the trouble. A big, shy fool he was. She got him into scrapes, and she'd laugh, and he'd smile quietly, and they'd run off together after a good ticking-off . . . but as I say, Evan got too close to Gledwyn, and there were great plans for Angie, so how could Evan do anything different? Where Angie went, Evan had to go, trailing along, looking dull and stupid. But Gledwyn said he'd got a fine brain. Well, you probably know what happened by now. Angie dropped out of the University, but Evan went on. It'd got hold of him. In here . . .' He thumped his chest. '. . . Evan was a farmer. In here . . .' He tapped his forehead. '. . . he was a scientist.'

'On research now, I hear.'

'And doing well. Morgan Rees says he's disowned the lad, but he's as proud as hell of him.'

So . . . Evan Rees had lost out, or won out, whichever way you looked at it. While he was qualifying at Aberystwyth, going on for his doctorate, taking on research, Angie was meeting Phil Rollason, and who'd have predicted a motor mechanic for her?

'A bit of a shock for Gledwyn Griffiths, wasn't it?' I asked. 'A crummy garage attendant for his darling girl!'

I put in a load of disparagement there, but I couldn't shake him. Everything bounced off that great chest and the low, broad forehead.

'True, true,' he agreed.

I thanked him for his assistance, went and dug out the Rover, and drove up to Cadwell's Quarry.

The hill soon disintegrated to a section of the town they'd probably have preferred to forget. A row of tatty shops was too far from the town centre to attract attention, and an old petrol station had ceased to trade years before. The last significant building was a chapel, and I couldn't tell whether or not it was still in business. From that point I climbed between high banks each side, until the one on the left fell away to rolling hillside, and on the right the rise was cut into as a quarry. Somebody had noticed a seam of gravel or sand, and dug their way in until it disappeared. They had left Cadwell with an ideal place for his junk.

There was a corrugated iron shed just round the corner as I drew up inside. From it tottered a greasy old man, who took one look at the Rover and decided he couldn't see a customer. I got out and surveyed the chances.

He, or somebody – I couldn't imagine him managing any physical toil – had got things organised. Old vehicles from which something might be salvaged on the left, junk wrecks on the right. Presumably you stripped out what you needed. Bring your own tools, wave your own wallet.

He tittered, rubbed his half-gloved hands together, and said: 'Help you, squire?'

'I was looking for the car that was burnt-out at the road-works.'

''Nescort, was it?'

'S'right,' I matched him.

'It's over there. Help yourself.' He cocked his head. 'You buyin'?'

'Just looking.'

'Engine could be okay. Transmission, too.'

'I wasn't really in the market for either.'

He cocked his head again. 'Cost yer a quid for lookin'.'

I'd met a shrewd old fraud. I glanced round. He had hefty and high metal barred gates and a huge padlock hanging free. Nobody was going to be doing any free looking out of hours. I searched out a pound note.

'I'll give you its mate, if I decide to buy you out.'

I used up a pound's worth of looking to no good purpose at all. It was on its side, leaning against a couple of other wrecks, and it took me a few moments to decide it had been an Escort at all. When I climbed over shifting metal, I saw that the interior was an unpleasant mess, where the upholstery had shrivelled itself into black lumps. The tyres had gone completely, and one of the wheels seemed to have been wrenched off with the impact. At the rear – and I had a good view of its underside – the tank had clearly exploded, leaving a large, jagged hole in the metalwork. There was barely a sign of paint anywhere, and red rust was replacing the blackened surface of the shell.

I uttered a silent prayer that Angie had not seen this, and turned away.

From that angle I could see behind the shed, where Cadwell had his own transport. It was a nearly-new Audi 100. A lot of people had had a pound's worth of looking.

I drove back, and found Angie looking very intense over a cup of tea in the café and I found out later she'd been wondering what brilliant detecting I'd been doing. I hefted her shopping bags and we went for the car. Isn't it wonderful what weights these slim women can carry about? They nearly killed me.

She directed me out of town past a small park with ducks and two swans on its pool, and told me we'd get to Whitchurch if we kept going long enough. A mile out of town we took a left, and began a wriggly climb into the hills.

'It's longer, but the view's better,' said Angie. 'We used to do miles round here on our pedal cycles. You can see the house from just along here . . . the break in the trees . . . there it is. Oh, do stop a minute, please.'

I pulled in because she sounded so childishly delighted. There was a low dry-stone wall, beyond it the ground falling away to reveal our own road winding down through the valley, and way over to the left I got a much better idea of what the new roadway would look like when it was finished. Far down, a tiny moving toy, I could see a grey hatchback weaving its way in the direction we were going. If the light hadn't deceived me the night before, it could well have been Lynne Fairfax's Fiesta.

If so, there didn't seem to be any sign of it when we reached Viewlands – and where else could she have been heading? But when I drove into the yard there was evidence that she was there. One of the big doors next to the garage was open.

'Lynne's here,' said Angie, without any enthusiasm.

Come to see me, I guessed. There had been an incompleteness about our previous encounter, when I had perhaps caught her at a disadvantage.

But there was no sign of welcome when I wandered into what was obviously Gledwyn's lab, and shouted: 'Anybody here?' There was Lynne, at the far end of the building, fiddling around with something, and all she did when I approached was give me a glance and say: 'Oh . . . it's you!'

Then Angie called out, friendly enough, 'You here for lunch, Lynne?' and Lynne called back, 'I brought sandwiches.'

'You've come to show me around,' I declared, giving her the benefit of the doubt. Lynne shrugged.

'Angela doesn't know much about it.' There was a certain amount of prim pride, and a frigidity in the way she used the name.

'You're the expert,' I said cheerfully, and it got me a conducted tour.

What I had taken, the night before, for a row of windows, turned out to belong to the four large doors that had replaced the half-doors of the original four stables in the middle. These had been knocked together, which had given Gledwyn a wide but not very deep laboratory. The remaining stable at one end matched the garage at the other. Along the back wall he'd run his main bench, a solid pine surface on which was his heavy equipment. The centre of the floor space was taken up by two smaller benches, displaying the more delicate-looking instruments. The back, far corner was walled off to form a small square space, which Lynne quite proudly called her office. A door in the side wall, next to her office, opened into the garage at the end. I put my head in there briefly. There was no car, just a patch of oil where the Escort had stood, and an up-and-over door to the yard.

'Strictly speaking,' said Lynne, 'I'm not a technical person. I never had any laboratory training and science was my worst subject at school. I came here when Gledwyn advertised for a secretary, but really, you know, there was hardly any work in that line. So I got to following him round with a notebook, and he told me what it was all about and what he was doing, and I picked it up on the way. Towards the end, most of what I did was lab work. We worked together. He told me everything. We were friends – more than that. You know how it is, when you can work with someone without having to say a word. He trusted me, you see, in so many ways. Took me for granted, if you like. I was supposed to be there always, at his beck and call, to drive for him, type for him . . . cook for him sometimes, otherwise he'd have starved, I think.'

This was somewhat different from her previous attitude towards him, but I had to make allowances for the fact that her resentment, then, had arisen from the fact that his demands had impinged on the death of her friend. Any other time, and she'd have accepted them. There is a sort of person who takes pride in being taken for granted. They equate it with being trusted; something certainly to be proud about. But it can go too far. It sounded to me as though he'd walked all over her. But she did not see it like that, and her voice was soft with affection as she spoke about him.

'He was a very great man, I hope you realise that. If he'd kept on with his research at Aberystwyth, he'd have done wonderful things, I'm sure. He told me all about his plans and dreams, when he was there, and how it all fell apart when his wife became ill. Of course, it was impossible for him to stay away from her for long. Multiple sclerosis, it was, poor woman. Oh, don't get me wrong, he didn't feel that he'd been robbed. Gledwyn wasn't like that. Sometimes he was just a little sad when he spoke about it. That's all. What he could do here was so . . . restricted, really.' There was a sudden, oblique sharpness in her voice. 'But make no mistake, he martyred himself to his wife.' And abruptly she sounded ridiculously mature and bitter.

'Shall we make some coffee?' she asked.

She took me into her little office, which I'd been waiting to see. The ancient Royal rested on an old kneehole desk, and she had a plain, upright chair. There was a wooden filing cabinet and a small table, on which she had her gas ring. 'I get water from the lab,' she said, and, noticing my attention to the cabinet, 'His life's work is in there. Years of research.'

She adopted a fond possessiveness when speaking about the research. It had been hers, really, in her mind. Gledwyn Griffiths had done it, but she'd supervised, encouraged, probably bullied. It belonged to her.

While she was getting the kettle filled, I peeped out of her tiny window, and one mystery was solved. The rhododendrons that flanked the drive continued along past the lab building, but were set back a matter of eight feet. Here, tucked away, she had parked the Fiesta. There was a pathetic independence in the gesture, distancing herself from the house. This was her province, hers and Gledwyn's. She'd really have preferred it to be isolated on a mountain top.

When she returned with a full kettle, I said: 'I can see how you came to meet Neville. Did he visit his uncle often?'

'He was the only one Gledwyn could depend on.' She nodded. That set Neville high in her estimation. It was strange how she fluctuated between youth and age, perhaps not so strange when you considered the years of association with her older employer.

'After Paul left,' she said, her voice disturbed by possessive anger, 'Paul, that's his son . . . after the final row, and Paul gone, and Angela taking off like she did . . . you'd have expected something better, wouldn't you, the way he doted on her! But no, along came that Rollason – have you ever met him? A bit smarmy, I thought, the way he got round Gledwyn. Along he came, and nothing else existed any more for Angela. It hurt him, you know. I had to work with him, and I felt it. Suddenly he was an old, old man.' She seemed to flop loosely as she said it, following him into old age. She was wearing what I'd thought to be a smart outfit – certainly not what she'd have worn for working there – but for a moment it fell about her raggedly, and all her joints were stiff, her posture undisciplined.

'But I take it he recovered?' I suggested.

'Why do you say that?'

'Last night, you gave me the impression of a vigorous person, whose behaviour upset you, not a broken old man.'

'Yes. Yes, he was full of energy. I don't understand what you're saying.'

I wanted to bring her more up-to-date. I wasn't yet certain in my mind on the sequence: Carla's death and Gledwyn's death.

'You told me that on the Saturday evening, late, Gledwyn returned here from visiting his son Paul.'

'That's quite correct.'

'I don't really know about this son, Paul. Visiting him where?'

'Aberystwyth, of course.'

I might have guessed. But I was now having to extract the information sentence by sentence.

'Is he another researcher there, or a professor . . .'

'I'm sure he'd like to be.'

'He's *staying* there, then?'

'At some hotel or other. He's recently come back from America. You'd think he'd have come here – but oh no. That fine Yankee wife of his, I suppose. Not good enough for her.'

Now I had to restrain her. Once she got going . . . 'Paul Griffiths was staying at Aberystwyth with his American wife. Gledwyn went to visit, presumably because his son was reluctant to bring his wife here. And it was from this visit he returned in a terrible temper and threw his keys at the wall?'

'Over there,' she said, pointing. 'They landed down beside the cabinet.' Serious, nodding, marginally distressed at the memory.

'But you said Neville had driven him there.'

'Neville's been so good to him. You wouldn't believe . . .'

'I gather that. This was in Neville's new Metro, the one I drove last night?'

'Oh no. It was in the Escort.'

We'd have been sixty or more miles from Aberystwyth. 'I thought this Escort was an old wreck.'

'Oh it was. It was Neville's in the first place, and Gledwyn wanted a car he could experiment with. The Escort suited, and Neville was looking round for another car. So Gledwyn bought the Escort from him. Or rather, he helped him buy the Metro.'

'All right. But . . . this Saturday . . . Gledwyn had come back, and you were waiting for him. In here?'

'Yes. Waiting here in my office. He'd re-written this speech . . . oh, a dozen times. I had it ready, but there was always the chance it'd be changed again. So I waited.'

'And still it didn't satisfy him?'

'He hardly glanced at it.'

'Just threw his keys at the wall, and tore his speech to pieces?'

'He was so upset! What they must have said to him . . .'

'Then, I suppose, he marched back into the house. And where was Neville, while this was going on?'

'Picked up his Metro and gone home, I suppose.'

'He didn't come in and have a word with you?'

'He wouldn't know I was here. It was late.'

'Late, yes. And you – waiting here for Gledwyn and knowing that your friend Carla was driving over to your place on a visit – all the same you sat right down and typed it out again?'

'He'd need it the next day. He was going to Blackpool, to his Convention. I was driving him.'

'In your Fiesta?'

She was becoming a little impatient. 'Yes.'

'So eventually you took the re-typed speech in to him . . .'

'He came in here. He was flustered. He apologised.'

'It took you . . . how long to do it again?'

'A good hour.'

'He timed it right, then, appearing just before you could take it across to the house.'

She frowned, shaking her head. I was being abrupt with her, trying to shake her simplistic faith in him. 'How can you know that?'

'You'd be anxious to get away, knowing Carla would be waiting.' But Carla wouldn't have been waiting; most likely, at that time, she'd have been dead. It did not occur to Lynne.

'Oh, I see.' She nodded, and smiled weakly, acknowledging the logic. 'Yes, I suppose he timed it well. Another minute, and I'd have been across to the house.'

'He must have known how long it would take you.'

'I suppose he would.' A shade of annoyance framed her mouth for a moment. 'If it matters.'

'I don't know what matters,' I said casually. 'I'm just getting the background. He knew you'd type it again for him?'

'You keep getting at him,' she said tersely.

I sighed. 'Here's a man, in such a temper that he tore up your evening's work in front of you, and stormed . . .'

'Not stormed! Not that!'

I raised my eyebrows at her. 'Went then. Quietly but angrily he went into the house, but all the same he was sufficiently in control of his temper to realise you'd stay here and do it all again – and he timed it!'

'You're just making him sound . . .' She had raised her voice, but caught it with severe control.

'Sound what?'

'He was not his usual self.'

'That's quite plain.' Then I changed the mood. 'So eventually you were able to leave. You drove home, but came across your friend, dead in front of her car.'

She banged across the carriage of her Royal. 'Yes.'

'Then – in the morning – the Sunday morning,' I pressed on, steering her away from her friend's death, 'he was still moody. He didn't notice you were upset. Would a quarrel with his son still be affecting him?'

'I'm not sure it was that, not entirely.'

'What, then?'

'This was a paper he was presenting. A bit more than a speech, you see. His reputation was going to be resting on it. Or so he told me. And he knew it wasn't ready, and you can't blame him for being worried.'

Only for having been so short with her. 'He told you he was?'

'I knew. He'd rushed his results. The special spectacles he'd made – they weren't fully tested. And the work on the Escort's windscreen . . .'

'Passenger's side?'

'Yes. That wasn't proved, either. It was the reason he got Neville to use the Escort the previous evening, it gave him one more chance to check the results, before he went to Blackpool.'

'So obviously he was disappointed with them.'

She turned away. There was a kettle boiling its head off that neither of us had noticed. She gave her attention to the coffee mugs. Presumably I was using Gledwyn's. Suddenly I'd lost her. She'd felt I was reaching for something she believed should not be pursued.

'I really don't see what this has got to do with anything. I don't see why I should answer your questions.'

'I'm interested in his work.'

She made a sound of disgust. 'You're only trying to belittle what he was doing.'

'I did get the impression,' I suggested, 'that you were upset because of the way he ignored your distress on the Sunday morning, and because he didn't tell you what was upsetting him.' Her eyes were gravely on me. 'But perhaps he had a very good reason – if he was convinced his work wasn't much of a success.'

'I don't see what you mean.'

'He wouldn't want to tell you, would he! After all, if it was as much your work as his . . .' I left the thought hanging.

She was silent for a few minutes, stirring her coffee round and round, not realising she was doing it. Then she looked up at me with a small smile.

'He'd have shared it with me, if it'd been a success.'

'Of course he would.'

Her coffee was too hot and too strong. I put the mug down to cool off. 'One thing . . . you said Neville didn't come in to speak to you, because he wouldn't know you were here.'

She nodded, managing a real smile for me now, trusting me.

'But you didn't hear *him*, it seems, putting the Escort away, and the garage is right next door – the other side of this wall.'

'Oh, I was typing, wasn't I! Clattering away like mad.' She paused. 'How d'you know he put it away?'

'It was raining. Wasn't it raining? I seem to remember –'

She laughed. 'He wouldn't worry about that. A bit of rain on the Green Dragon.'

'The what?' Then I caught myself. Keep to the point, Harry. 'He might not worry about the Escort, but he'd have had to get out the Metro. *That* was new, so he wouldn't have left it out in the open. He'd have put it away in the garage.'

'Oh, you're clever!' She didn't say it as a compliment. 'Very cute, I must say.'

I grinned at her. 'And what's this Green Dragon business?'

'It's what Neville called the Escort. What it was called when he bought it. Oh, it must've had a dozen owners before he got it, and one of them had put that at the top of the windscreen. You know, a strip of green plastic with words in white on it. Green Dragon, it said. Neville seemed to think that was very funny. I'll swear he bought it because of that. Men can be so childish! His name, you see – Neville Green. But it meant I was always sitting under the dragon bit, when we went out in the Escort. He thought that was a joke. Does it seem amusing to you?'

'Nobody would take you for a dragon, Lynne,' I told her solemnly.

It seemed to please her. 'You wouldn't?'

'Never in a million years.' I took her for a rather naive young woman, who hadn't known where she was with the men in her life.

'It was stupid, anyway,' she said. 'It wasn't green at all. It was red.'

The only red I'd seen on it had been from rust.

She walked out into the lab with me, moving round, touching things. 'His vacuum chamber,' she said. 'His colorimeters, his Munsell charts.' Now she'd gone vague again. She hadn't come, this day, specifically to see me. I'd been the excuse. She just couldn't keep away from his ghost, which still prowled.

'You fetched him home the following Friday,' I said. 'You told me he was still in a mood.'

'I guessed the reason. Sometimes I could read him like a book, sometimes I could get nothing. But obviously his paper hadn't been a success.'

'But surely, in all that journey, he'd said something.'

'Oh yes,' she said brightly. 'He said he'd finally decided to alter his will.' She frowned. 'But he never got the chance, did he?'

6

We were going to have mushroom omelette for lunch, followed by fresh fruit salad. The fruit was all from Angie's orchard. As it wasn't going to need much preparation, I persuaded Angie to take me into the room she called the office, which was at the far end of the hall. It had a rattly old roll-top desk in one corner and a much-used easy chair by the fireplace, and not much else.

I asked her whether she'd been through her father's papers, and she said she had, in detail.

'His will was here?'

'No.' She seemed surprised. 'I came down for the funeral and his solicitor approached me. It was the first I knew about what he'd left me.'

The window looked out on a corner of the yard. I peeped out at my caravan, wanting to make it all seem casual.

'Which turned out to be this house and its contents?'

'Yes. Why're you asking this?'

'Interest.' I turned my attention to the desk. 'Did you come across the registration document for the Escort?'

'I think I noticed it,' she said indifferently, her mind still on my mention of the will. 'Somewhere in there.'

Lynne had told me that she knew the contents of Gledwyn's proposed revised will. It had been on his mind for some time, and, as seemed to have been his habit, he'd discussed it with Lynne. She had even drafted a copy for him, but he'd apparently taken no action to get it made legal. The existing will Lynne knew nothing about, except that the sum of £1,000 was to come to her. Presumably it still would. The revised will, she had said, would have left the residue of his estate to Neville.

I found the registration document. 'Did you know Lynne gets £1,000?' I asked, reading the details at the same time.

'Yes. The solicitor told me that.'

'Did he tell you anything more?'

'Nothing I hadn't guessed. The remainder of the estate to my brother, Paul.'

'Ah.'

The registration was for a Ford Escort, 1972, described as green. Clearly, it had been green when an early owner christened it. Previous owners? Five, it recorded. Any one of them could have given it the name of Green Dragon, any subsequent one could have had it re-sprayed red, without regard to the legal requirement of changing the registration details.

It was all I'd wanted. We locked up the desk, and left.

'Why did you say ah?' she demanded, halting me in the hall.

'Just something I couldn't understand. Lynne told me that your father was talking about changing his will. This was on the trip back from his Convention. He mentioned it. It sounded as though it could mean he was going to disinherit you, and I couldn't understand that. I mean to say, it wasn't you who'd upset him, it was your brother, apparently. So now it's explained. It was your brother he intended to cut out of his will.'

We walked into the kitchen. Angie was quiet. I could almost hear the hum of her brain working. She was silent over the meal, and it was not until halfway through the fruit salad that she spoke.

'I don't think I like what you said about the will.'

'There's no reason to doubt the truth of it. On the Saturday evening, before he went away for a week's Convention, your father seems to have had a row with your brother, and . . .'

'How *could* he? Paul's in the USA.'

'No he's not. He was at Aberystwyth, the week before your father's death. Whether he's there now . . .'

'He's in England? And he's not even phoned.' She tossed her head, her eyes avoiding mine.

'He might not know you're here,' I said comfortingly.

But Angie was distressed, her eyes bright and moist. 'The solicitor would have told him. Paul! And he didn't get in touch!'

I allowed it to cool. We had coffee. Angie was smoking. At last she spoke in a controlled voice.

'Where is he . . . Paul?'

'Possibly still at the same hotel. Your cousin – Neville – he'll know. He drove your father there. If there was trouble, he'll know. In any event, your father was deeply upset, and after the Convention, when he'd had time to think it through, he told Lynne he was going to change his will.'

'Oh, he'd tell Lynne! Everything . . . he told her.'

'So it seems he intended to cut Paul out of his will.' I paused, then asked quietly: 'Would it involve much?'

She jerked the cigarette towards her ashtray and made an angry sound when the ash missed. 'I don't know. Probably. My grandmother, that's daddy's mother, she had money, and left it equally between daddy and his sister, Flora. Neville's mother, that'd be. But Martin Green was a gambler, and all my aunt's money just melted away. But daddy . . . money wasn't of much interest to him. I don't think he remembered he'd got it in the bank . . . look at the way he bought that Escort from Neville! He could've bought a new one.'

I didn't say so, but it seemed he had – the Metro for Neville.

'Much money?' I prompted.

She shrugged exaggeratedly. 'How can I know? I'd guess between twenty and forty thousand.'

'But he didn't have time to disinherit your brother,' I pointed out.

'What the hell does that mean?' she flared.

I made a great performance of staring at my pipe, filling it, lighting it, and staring at it again. Anything to avoid looking at her and revealing my anger. She was lying. Of course she knew Paul was in Britain. He'd surely have attended his father's funeral, and he'd have met Angie there. So she was lying, and her pretence had been so false as to be laughable. If I'd been in the mood for laughter.

She had welcomed my efforts to help her, though beneath it she'd feared what I might find. The mention of the will had pushed her fear beyond the borders into panic. Did that mean she believed that Paul had killed her father? Did she fear that knowledge, yet know she had to face it?

But she'd been furious at me for mentioning the will. That was fine; just what I needed! And if I ever reached the truth – which I now believed was going to be unpalatable – who the hell was going to tell her, and face those frantic eyes and the distraught face?

Harry Kyle was.

I pushed on with it, seeing how far it would go before she told me to go to hell and out of her life. I didn't answer her angry question: 'What the hell does that mean?'

'Guess who'd have got the money if he'd changed it,' I said.

'Then who?'

'My information is: Neville.'

'Neville?' She stamped out the cigarette. 'Neville would've got it?'

'So I'm told. But after all, Neville's apparently the only relative who's really done anything for your father for some time. If he was looking for a new beneficiary, maybe your father would look close to home. And Neville's been on the spot.'

She glared at me. 'How dare you!'

'I know,' I agreed. 'It's rough. But you've missed the main point. Not who might have got the money if he'd changed his will, but who would have lost out.'

Angie had her chair back. She was motionless, half crouched, her eyes smouldering. Suddenly she spun the chair away and marched over to the window, clasping her elbows in her crossed hands, and her voice was so quiet I barely heard it.

'That's a terrible thing to say.'

'Is it? But you're forgetting I'm supposed to be helping you. And what did you say you wanted – to prove your father had been murdered.'

'I don't want to hear any more.'

I sat at the table, hands on its surface, my pipe cold between my teeth. 'Oh, that's fine!' I said heavily. 'You don't want to hear any more. I've been hearing things I don't fancy ever since I got here – but I suppose that doesn't matter. My ears aren't all that delicate. But you can put an end to it at any time, Angie. You simply tell me to leave. The caravan takes five minutes to hitch up, then I can be off. If you want that, you only need to promise one thing. That's to phone Phil and say you want to be fetched home. Tell him I did what I could for you, but you don't want to listen to any truth.'

She turned. The light was behind her, her features dimmed. Her voice was equally shaded. 'Then say it.'

'Oh come on! For God's sake, you spoke of murder. The car was crashed, at speed. How the devil could *that* have been rigged?'

'I don't know.' There was a catch in her voice. 'I don't *know*.' Now almost in tears.

'And if it was . . . no, listen. Don't you dare walk away from me now. Take one more step towards that door, Angie, and I'll know I've got to treat you like a spoiled child, wanting without the effort of reaching out. Sit down. Please.'

She moved back slowly, rescued her chair, and sat down again. I reached out my lighter for the cigarette she fumbled out, but had difficulty trapping its shaking end.

'Angie, if it was murder, then it was deliberately disguised as a car accident. I can't see how, but that's what it must have been if we're to consider murder. But we discussed the difficulty there. Your father hadn't driven for years, so it was a strange accident to fake – a driving one. It would have to be faked by someone who wasn't aware that he didn't drive any more – or somebody who thought he'd started driving again. The sight of the Escort in the drive might give that impression. Now don't you get mad at me. How long has your brother been in the USA?'

'Six years,' she murmured.

'So you can see what I'm getting at.'

'Not Paul! Paul couldn't . . . oh God!' Then she clutched at a sudden thought as at a liferaft. 'But not for money,' she said in triumph. 'Paul wouldn't need money, his wife's rolling in it.'

'Is she, now. Is she.'

There seemed nothing to add. I didn't trouble to point out that a wife with money might create an even more desperate personal need. Silence built up, and across the yard the gelding whinnied shrilly.

'Did you know,' I asked eventually, 'that the Escort was red? It was called Green Dragon.'

'How interesting,' said Angie dully.

More silence. Then I said something about washing the crocks, but she made no move. Suddenly she got to her feet and marched out into the yard. I gave her five minutes, then I followed her. She was leaning over the white rails, gazing down into the orchard. I went and brooded beside her.

'There was an orchard like this,' I said, 'smaller perhaps, just along the road where I grew up. We used to scrump the apples, more than we could ever eat. It was the getting of them that was the thrill, because of the dogs. You were robbed of that, having your own orchard.'

She tossed her head. It was a gesture of freeing, but not just her hair – her mind too – of what had passed.

'It hasn't always been like this. Some of those trees I helped daddy to plant. Doesn't it show how time flies!'

'Makes you feel old,' I said lightly.

'Older, certainly.'

'Paul – is he older than you?'

She no longer reacted to his name. 'Two years. You'd think he'd have got in touch . . .' She was still trying.

'So he went through college that far ahead?'

She laughed lightly. No recriminations were attached. 'Not through. He went *to* college. But he was sent down at the end of his first year. It was just no good. Psychologically, Paul wasn't suited for it. In school, oh he was clever. Daddy was very proud of him. But then he could be watched over – at school and at home. At Keele University – that was where he went – doing Science . . . at Keele, he had to do his own pressuring, and poor Paul . . . there were so many distractions. Sports – he was mad on sports, but he never seemed to get down to any solid work.'

'Self-discipline, that's what it needs,' I said grandly. 'Did you have that, Angie?'

'Me?' She turned in surprise, taking a whisp of hair from her eyes with one finger. 'I didn't need it. Daddy wanted me to get a first, and I always felt he was at my elbow. It didn't take any self-discipline.'

But she hadn't got her degree after all. It had been necessary to look after daddy in his misfortune.

'So Paul was given the proverbial shilling and banished from the family home?'

'It wasn't like that. There was another try, this time at Loughborough, but it still didn't work out. *Then* there was an almighty row, and Paul marched out. The next we heard, he'd found his way to the States, and was working hard at UCLA.' She laughed. 'It was clever, when you think about it. Paul knew his own faults. He knew he couldn't keep up the pressure on himself if there was one single distraction. So he went to a University where there wasn't any cricket or his sort of foot-ball.'

'It worked?'

'Yes. Daddy was right . . . Paul's got a fine brain. He got his

PhD over there in social philosophy, and he's been lecturing at his old University.'

'Then why has he come home?' I wondered. 'Why has he brought his rich American wife to this country?'

I wasn't even aware that I'd said it out loud. It had been a thought, and Angie treated it as such, so that we were silent there, me puffing smoke with apparent content, when I was not contented at all. Even disturbed.

Angie had confirmed what I'd suspected. If she'd thought of murder, her mind must have embraced all possibilities, including the one that her brother must be a suspect. But that was not the limit of her fear. She wasn't necessarily trying to prove her father had been murdered, there was also the possibility that he'd committed suicide. Otherwise, why had she reacted strongly to no more than a hint that she'd neglected him? But – consider suicide, and there has to be a reason for it.

Already, with his death, she would have had to face her conscience. Her father had been deserted, first by Paul and then by herself, and of the two her own desertion was the more deserving of blame. At least, Paul's flight had followed an almighty row. Hers had been the purely personal satisfaction of an urge. It might even be said to have arisen from a growing, perhaps subconscious, desire to get away from what had become a responsibility. After all, she'd been the only one left with him. She would perhaps have felt trapped into a situation that could become permanent, she an old maid, with her first love, Evan Rees, gone from her completely into his academic flights.

I could imagine her, at that time, suddenly becoming aware of her predicament, with her father self-absorbed in his eccentricities and research, and in himself, and she caught in something he would not even realise existed. Had Phil Rollason been no more than a lifeline to be grabbed for, the Phil Rollason Lynne had said became everything to Angie? The death of her father – so suddenly and tragically – would appear to Angie to offer her a re-birth. Or would it more likely be a trap? The tragedy of it would be the trap. If there was now nothing left of what she had felt for Rollason, then her childhood home, without the entrapment of her father's presence, could well seem a release. Once it became too attractive, what chance had Rollason then?

But the prospect was soured by the tragedy. She could have no peace at Viewlands until I'd absolved her of any blame, however distant, for his death. By solving the problem, I might be denying Rollason what he'd asked me to do for him.

And was I going to worry about Phil Rollason? No sir, I was not.

Glancing sideways, trying to detect something of her dreams, I saw only an abrupt awareness, an excitement, a sudden tenseness in her.

I looked to see the cause. Climbing over the far rail of the paddock was a stocky, dark young man in working jeans and a roll-neck sweater, who advanced with the easy, space-consuming lope of the hill farmer, but with something else, a confident lift to his chunky face and a confident eagerness.

Timmis had described him as big. Evan Rees couldn't have been more than five feet eight, but he was broad and strong, resilient. That was what made him seem big.

When Angie flung open the gate and ran towards him there was no change in his pace, and not even a smile on his face that I could see, but his pleasure was apparent in every movement. His head came up. They reached out and clasped hands, looking at each other.

'Evan!' I heard her say.

'You're looking well, Angie.'

Then their hands fell apart and they walked back towards me, side by side, with, apparently, no more to say.

They had both come home, and I knew Phil Rollason had faded a little further into the background.

We were introduced. He had a small smile for me, though he was not one for expressing his feelings too openly. Perhaps Angie had trained him in that. Getting the blame loaded on him, and always responding with a shy smile, was no doubt good grounding for one whose emotions ran deep and stubborn. So a tentative smile for me, a firm handshake and a hard, steady stare from deep-set dark eyes. He was wondering whether he could trust me with Angie's tender constitution. I was the one who'd be needing his protection, I had no doubt, before all this was over.

Tactfully, I wandered into the lab. So many years for them to retrieve. But maybe he wasn't fully prepared; he followed me inside, Angie standing in the open doorway and watching from a distance. She quietly and unnervingly stared, as I'd done with the Rover when I'd picked it up at the showroom, deferring the pleasure of touching, using, savouring its solidity and power.

I moved quietly at his shoulder, observant of his silence. He was a man of strong silences. I wouldn't have wished to arouse his anger. So I walked round with him, allowing him to make observations in his own time.

'Still using the Munsell system,' he commented, opening a cupboard on what looked like a bundle of multi-coloured little trees. 'A bit out of date, now.'

'Oh yes?'

'It relates everything to hue, or colour, and what Munsell called value, which is luminosity, and chrome, which you'd call saturation.'

'Would I?'

'We all use the CIE System now. It's more mathematical. With the Munsell, it was a colour atlas, like the charts the paint people issue. In the CIE System it's all numbers. Poor Gledwyn could never have handled metallic colours, or the fluorescents.'

'He was behind the times?' I asked.

'Oh, certainly.' He moved along the back bench. 'Colorimeters, too. I see he's got a Burnham-Wright. Useful that. It's quite portable.'

'I suppose it would be.'

'And here's a Lovibond.' He touched it. Not at all portable, this one, a box with a single eyepiece protruding from the top. 'That's a bit better, but all the same, a colorimeter.' He turned, scanning the rest of the equipment. 'But no spectrophotometer anywhere. Dear me.'

'It's bad?'

'Really, you know, he was years behind the times.' But he was cheerful about this eccentricity. It had been an observation and not a criticism. He caught my eye, and his mouth assumed a shape close to a smile.

'But he did some fine work here,' he told me.

'You know that? But you haven't been here for years. So I understand.'

'I met him at Blackpool. That's really the basic idea behind these Conventions. Meeting old friends, chatting, searching each other's minds for ideas. We spent hours together that week. I've got a lot to thank Gledwyn Griffiths for.'

We were standing in front of a large steel globe. This seemed to interest him more than the instruments had.

'It's his vacuum chamber,' he explained. 'He'd need it for the spraying technique he was using.'

I felt he was trying to slide me away from personalities. 'A lot to thank him for, you said . . . so you had time to express it all?'

'I did.'

'And how did you find him, at that time?'

'Older. More tired. But still trying.'

I persisted. 'My information is that he was very upset, on the journey to Blackpool.'

'Gledwyn wasn't a person to load you with his troubles.'

Yet Lynne had felt Gledwyn's distress. He'd loaded it on her, all right, so much so that he'd had no time to notice hers.

'He didn't mention anything that was upsetting him?'

'Not to me.' His attention was still on the vacuum chamber. 'It was this idea he had – that by vacuum spraying spectacles, with some special formula he'd developed, he could make some sort of change in greens and reds. That'd be a great advance.'

'Would be?'

'If it'd worked.'

'But I thought it did.'

He shook his head and moved on, not speaking.

'He tried it on a windscreen,' I said. 'Or so I'm told.'

'He'd have to spray small pieces of plain glass, and stick 'em on the windscreen.'

'You're not optimistic?'

'He was.'

'Optimistic? But he would be, wouldn't he?' I asked. 'I mean, he'd been testing the spectacles he'd coated, and I've been getting the impression he'd had some success.'

'Have you? Perhaps you weren't listening.'

'I was. You're saying it failed?'

'I wouldn't say that.'

'But he *was* upset. Would it be because of the failure of his process? Or maybe something more personal?'

He did not shrug, but there was something in his voice that warned me he was impatient with the subject. 'He mentioned no personal problems to me. All his old enthusiasm came back.'

'Came back? It wasn't there on the first day?'

'I don't know what you're trying to get me to say. The first two days I thought he seemed exhausted. Working on your own can be a strain. He was pale and absent-minded. But we went for long walks together. The sea air seemed to do him good.'

'You both missed the lectures and the papers being read – and the rest?'

'As I told you, it's for meeting old friends. He was more than a friend.'

'Yes,' I agreed. So had Angie been.

'I had a paper I read on the Tuesday. He read his own on Thursday.'

'Successfully?'

'Everybody knows my work on genetics and vision. I'm trying to isolate the pigments that affect the cones. It was nothing spectacular.'

'But Gledwyn's was?'

He moved away. I hurried after him, aware that I was close to something. There were discs of semi-smoked glass on a bench in the centre. He picked one up and looked through it in all directions. I noticed that Angie was no longer standing in the doorway to the yard, but Lynne, whom I'd assumed to have left, was standing in the doorway to her office. Evan Rees seemed not to notice her through his bit of glass.

'But Gledwyn's paper was spectacular?' I insisted.

'You can't leave it alone, can you!'

'No.'

'If you must know, it was a spectacular failure.'

Then he noticed Lynne. He put down the glass disc. 'Hello,' he said.

She found him a small smile. 'We haven't met.' A hint to me.

I introduced them. He nodded, but did not shake hands with her.

'He mentioned you,' he said.

She blushed.

'With pride,' he told her, smiling now. 'You helped him a lot.'

She looked away. 'I was just leaving.'

'Don't go. Not for me,' he appealed.

'No. Really, I must.'

I noticed she kept a bench between us as she moved away. The blush was still in her neck.

'It was a failure,' I prompted him, when she'd gone. 'In what way?'

'It's complicated. I'd need to explain.'

'I wish you would,' I said patiently.

'Briefly, then.' Now there was more than a hint of impatience in his voice. He was anxious to get to Angie. I stared at him encouragingly. 'All light can be broken down into a mixture of three primary colours – call 'em red, green and blue . . . near enough. Using those three, you can create any colour there is by overlapping, sometimes using only two of them, sometimes using all three, in various proportions.'

'Angie said something . . .'

'You're with me?'

'With you,' I agreed, my brain reaching for it.

He was wandering into Lynne's office. On his own subject, now, he was becoming enthusiastic. 'I wish I'd got time to rig something for you.'

'I'd like to see that.'

He sat at her desk. 'And where all three rays of equal intensity overlap, you'd get white light.'

'Yes.'

'Now you've got to understand that colour blindness, or at least some colour deficiency, is most common in men. In effect, these sort of people can match every colour *they* see with only two of the rays, or they use just a touch of the third. I'm simplifying, you understand. And because they use only two we call them dichromats. The most common difficulty is with reds and greens. Trouble with blues and reds is pretty rare.'

'It seems I might have that.' I told him. 'In poor light, anyway. The other evening I mistook a red car for a blue car.'

He smiled. I'd nearly squeezed a laugh from him. 'I could test you, if you like. We'd call you a tritanomalous dichromat. But if it's only in poor light, I wouldn't worry.'

'It sounds like some fearsome disease. Go on, though. I interrupted.'

'Let's keep it to Gledwyn Griffiths. He was a dichromat, because he could match any colour he could see by using only two of the primaries, and because he was red-blind we'd class him as a pronatope. Red and green are the trick colours for these people. We test it by checking what mixture of red and green light they use to match a pure yellow light. Gledwyn would use a very high proportion of red light. You – for instance – would need equal quantities of red and green.'

'How does this relate . . .'

'Very importantly, I can assure you. He saw red and green differently, but as grades of grey, I suppose. Who can ever say what somebody else sees? It's all in the mind, after all. But what he'd done was fatal to scientific procedure. He'd found some method of spraying glass – his spectacles at first, then the windscreen bits – that changed the emphasis. But he'd related it to *himself*. With the glasses, *he* saw red as smaller but very much brighter, green as spread out larger, but darker. You can see his mistake.'

I couldn't. The scientific mind baffles me. I shook my head.

'It was completely unscientific,' he said, with the nearest approach to emotion I'd seen so far. 'I can't understand – he'd have known! As a researcher, he must have grown up with the basics, and one of them is that you don't claim anything on the results you've got from experimenting on yourself. I know . . . there've been hundreds of examples . . . mostly doctors. *They've* tried serums and vaccines after injecting themselves with diseases. But they didn't stop there. Dozens – hundreds – of other experiments had to be made, before they were sure. But Gledwyn rushed it. Damn it, he was only fifty. Lots more years . . .' He stopped. 'Oh, hell!'

'It doesn't affect your argument,' I assured him. 'He should have taken it further – I can see that. But where would he get all his colour blind subjects?'

'It's no excuse. No reason. But it was worse than that. All his experiments were aimed at one aspect of it, which was the help he could give to drivers. At night. It's too small, too tight, it embraces so little.' He made a small impact with his fist on Lynne's desk. 'If only he'd have come to me. I could have broadened the sphere of investigation.'

'But if he helped only a few, in just that way . . .'

'Lord, but it was even worse than *that*. He based it all on himself. He was a dichromat/pronatope. I said that. The glasses suited him, because he'd made them for his own colour deficiency. But what if a green-blind person used them? God knows what that would've done to his night vision. Gledwyn was red-blind. Hell, it would've made a green-blind person a killer on the road at night. Or take yourself: a trinatope. A pair of Gledwyn's magic spectacles could completely confuse you, when now you're probably quite okay, because the balance is only slightly out. You see what I mean? He hadn't done his research, and he'd concentrated it on himself. It was interesting, as a theory, but . . .'

'But his paper was not well received?'

'They barely let him finish it.'

'The spectacles worked for him, though. You said that.'

'He said they did.'

'Reds smaller but brighter, you said. Greens spread out but dimmer.'

He raised his eyebrows, cocking his head with interest. 'What are you getting at?'

'The night he died, he seems to have been wearing them. If they did that for him, he'd be less likely to make a mistake over a traffic signal. He'd tested them, and he knew the effect they had. So he wouldn't drive through a red – at that roadworks, I mean. Have you seen it?'

He nodded, his eyes deep and serious.

'So he'd hardly drive through a red and meet somebody coming the other way.'

'It's unlikely.'

'And yet that's what he seems to have done.'

He was silent, his fingers playing with one of Lynne's ballpoints. At last, without raising his eyes, he said: 'I'm not sure of your interest in this. I've been talking about my own subject, so I got carried away. But I'd like to know what you're trying to do.'

'Angie hasn't told you?'

'Only that she had a guest.'

'She believes her father was deliberately killed, and didn't simply die from an accident. I'm trying to find out the truth.'

He took a long time thinking about that, but there are time-wasting things you can do with a pipe. I took it into the yard and reamered it out, strolled back, and found him examining the smoked glass discs again.

'Look through,' he said, handing me one. 'Go outside and look at the maples.'

I did. He didn't come with me. I closed one eye and scanned the scene, and the effect was most strange, even to me. The red maple leaves seemed to lose their colour but grow brighter, and the green apples in the orchard were blurred into a dark mass on their trees. I turned it round. From the other way it was like clear glass.

I took it back to him. He was absently turning a hand viewer in his fingers.

'Have you tried to talk her out of it?' he asked.

'I haven't got all the facts together.'

'You know I didn't mean that.'

'I've tried my sort of reasoning.'

'It's not right,' he declared, his voice empty. 'She shouldn't think such thoughts.'

I placed the glass disc on the bench under his nose. 'Try telling her that.'

He brought down the brass viewer suddenly, smashing the disc. 'Oh hell!'

Then he would have marched out, but I hadn't finished, and caught his arm. The eyes he turned on me were hot with fury. Then suddenly he relaxed.

'One more point,' I said patiently.

He actually smiled. There was not much warmth in it, but it was a smile. 'You're taking a lot of my time.'

'I simply wondered – does this mean that Angie could have the same colour trouble?'

'Oh no. Certainly not.' He relaxed. 'Here – have you got a bit of paper?'

I found him an old envelope, and he swept away the shards of glass. 'The trouble's transmitted down the female line, but the actual colour deficiency's very rare in women. They simply pass it on to their male offspring. Most likely, Gledwyn's mother had the latent genetic deficiency. Like this.'

He drew me a little diagram.

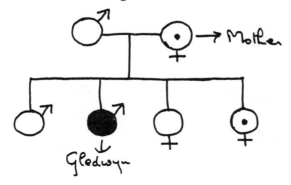

I'd come across the symbols before. ♂ for male, and ♀ for female.

'The blank circles,' he said, 'are normal people, the ones with the dots have got the latent tendency, but usually not the actual deficiency, and the blanked out ones are the colour defectives. You can see that out of the children of the family, a family like this, one boy's likely to be normal and the other have defective colour vision. Out of the girls, one could be normal, and one have the latent deficiency. A fifty/fifty chance for both. But now have a look at the next generation.' He drew another diagram.

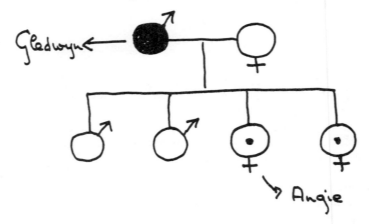

'You see, any sons – that's Paul in this case – would be normal, and the girls – Angie – wouldn't have it, but it'd be latent. They'd be carrying the gene deficiency. Waiting, kind of.'

'Which assumes, though, that Gledwyn's wife was colour normal,' I pointed out, having studied it for a minute.

'She was very normal,' he assured me. 'Those paintings in the house, they were all hers. Every one was done after she got that blasted sclerosis. They used to drive her out into the mountains on fine days and set her up, and just leave her. She insisted on being left, you know. Very determined, very independent, Margie Griffiths. I admired her tremendously. It went on until she couldn't hold the brush. No – she wasn't colour blind.'

'So Angie's got the latent gene deficiency? What does that mean to *her* children?'

'Then we go back to the first diagram. If the father of her

children is normal, she'd have a fifty/fifty chance of having a son with defective colour vision, and a fifty/fifty chance of having a daughter with the latent tendency.'

'Phil Rollason's quite normal,' I told him. 'Her husband, that is. With colour, that is.'

He stuck his pen back into his pocket, and tossed me the hint of a smile.

'That wasn't quite what I said.'

Then he walked out into the sunshine, leaving me wondering and disturbed.

7

The weather looked like holding fine all afternoon, so I decided to try to locate Neville Green. Angie, perhaps in an attempt to demonstrate to me a lack of interest in Evan's company, said she'd come with me. She wasn't fooling anybody. He was one of those dark, handsome and morose types, and I couldn't offer any of those but the morose bit. So clearly she wasn't going to enjoy the trip, and to tell the truth, I was beginning to feel uneasy in her presence.

But all the same, we took the Rover and I drove down through Llanmawr, pausing only to call at the local council office, which turned out to be not much more than a typist and a phone console. As Neville Green didn't work from there, but from the central County Council office, the telephonist phoned through to discover where he was that day. If it'd been his own office, then I'd have waited until he got home. I was simply hoping he would be within reach.

It happened that he was. The council was exploring the possibility of supplying Llanmawr and its outskirts with a different supply of water. A new reservoir and pumping station were involved, high in the mountains, and there'd be a considerable cost advantage. Only the brewery and the tweed mill might not be pleased.

The difficulty was in finding him. Drive out west, I'd been told, take the third left off the main road, and then, apparently, abandon all hope of a decent driving surface for a matter of nine miles. Which was understating what we encountered.

We were skirting a mass of mountain that never seemed to want to reach a peak, revealing around each shoulder a new valley and a further rise. The road surface was crushed slate, which gave the appearance of having slid down from above on one side or the other. They'd never have troubled to bring the stuff all up there, where only shepherds lurked, their sheep bleating plaintively from the far side of the valley. The grass was sparse, cut through with slate outcrops, and tiny streams trickled down, quite often cutting across the loose roadway. To the north, now, the air being quite clear, it was possible to see the far peak of Eglwyseg Mountain, or so Angie claimed.

She told me that very soon we would run out of road altogether. My instructions had been quite clear. 'Keep going and you can't miss him. The Land Rover will be parked at the side.' It was quite true that I wouldn't miss a Land Rover; I wouldn't have been able to get past it. When I did spot it, there was no sign across the expanse of valley on our right of anybody running around waving a theodolite.

I drew up behind. When I walked round he was up in the cab sharing a flask of coffee with his helper, a young person who could have been either sex.

'By God,' he said, 'it must've been urgent, if you'll chase out here after me.'

He jumped down. What I'd already seen of him had indicated he was taller than me, but his face then had been lax and formless. Now it was firm, the face of a man who frowned a lot, the eyes of a dreamer whose dreams have not materialised.

'Not urgent,' I assured him. 'It's a fine day, lovely country. But I was wondering why you found it necessary to come all this way to dodge me.'

He twisted up one corner of his mouth, and fell into step beside me. In wide open spaces I become restless and need to walk. We wanted privacy. The wind whipped away our words, and I found myself turning my head and raising my voice. He'd spoken in a mock plaintive tone. Perhaps meeting there amused him.

'Not trying to dodge anything,' he protested.

'I gathered from your office that this trip was unscheduled.'

'The headache wouldn't go. I couldn't even see the drawing board. Fresh air seemed indicated.'

It was too full an explanation. I suspected then – as I had not before – that he *had* been dodging me.

'I hope it's worked.'

'Just fine now, thanks.'

We had walked a hundred yards along the crisp turf beside the track. Now he halted, legs apart, looking out over what he clearly considered his territory.

'They're bringing a pipe-line right through the valley,' he

explained, 'down between those two peaks there. See. Over to the left. You can just see the line of red poles . . .'

He must have had eagle's eyes. Squinting, I just managed to see one red pole.

'Then we go over the brook,' he was saying with enthusiasm, 'and farther on it'll go over the old railway line. To your right . . . that run of yellow poles going away through the valley. This year . . . next year . . . I'm doing a preliminary – a practicality study, they call it. Don't they love their fine words! Feasibility! Next summer I'll spend weeks out here. Do you envy me, Mr Kyle?'

'Lynne told you my name?'

He nodded. He was cupping his palms round a cigarette, flicking his gold Dunhill. His anorak was an expensive model, his jeans tailored, and his boots were leather with a roll top, displaying the fur lining. The outfit set him off well, lord of all he surveyed.

'You're Harry Kyle,' he said. 'The one who's staying with Angie.' He worked a grain of tobacco onto his finger. 'Yes, I heard. I hope you're progressing.'

'Lynne told you what I'm doing?'

'Nosing around, she said.' The smoke was dragged across his face by the breeze. 'I've been trying out our new theodolite. It works with a laser beam. You wouldn't believe! The little light actually shines a spot on the measuring rods, and you can work accurately right across the valley.'

'Gledwyn would've liked to see that.'

'He was going to come out with me to watch it working.' He stamped out the cigarette, grinding it to total extinction.

'Was he interested in your work?'

'Was he just! Interested in everything, that man.'

'Funny, I got a different impression. So far, it's been the devoted and single-minded scientist.'

He lifted an eyebrow at me. 'The mad professor type? Just between you and me, mate, he wasn't all that dedicated, and not much of a bloody scientist, either.'

I walked away from him for a few yards, but he didn't seem inclined to follow, so I walked back.

'But you liked him, in spite of his faults?'

He shrugged. 'You get to like people. You know. And he helped me a lot. Shoved me through school and helped me get my qualifications. But it wasn't the same, you see. I hadn't got the brains he thought ran in the family. Academic stuff, that's what he was interested in, not the practical things I studied. It nearly finished him, I can tell you, when Angie flunked out of college.'

It wasn't how I'd heard it. Hadn't she had to come home because of her mother's illness? Or was it her father's driving accident?

'It's the first I've heard of that,' I said.

'Come to cousin Neville for the facts. That's what I'd advise.'

'Would you? Then tell me – while we're on facts – when you started drinking so heavily – and why.'

'Now . . . who's taking liberties!'

'As one who's helped carry you home . . .'

'Hell, why shouldn't I have the odd jar? It gets you down.'

'It?'

'How long d'you think we've been engaged? Go on. Guess.'

'*Are* you engaged? I didn't see a ring on Lynne's finger.' I laughed, but it got carried away in the wind. 'I thought you people didn't trouble with engagements, these days.'

'You people! Hah! That's going it a bit, and we've only just met. You people! I like that. Insults, now.'

'Modern young people.'

'Everybody's modern,' he declared. Had he argued this with teenage friends? 'It's the same *now* for all of us. I want to get married. Any harm in that?'

'No harm at all. I apologise. But . . . engaged?'

'There's an understanding.'

'Which, I gather, has been going on for some time?'

He was mollified, but so easily that I wondered how much of what he did and said was an act. Come to him for the truth, he'd said. For pretence, more likely.

'Three years,' he went on. 'Lynne and me. That was where I met her, up at Uncle Gledwyn's place. Did she tell you how he's been using her as a dishcloth? He always acted the part well – the absent-minded scientist with no practical ideas in his head. Had to be carried around . . . and Lynne loved it. What chance have I had to get her even to think about getting hitched? So I tried to give her a hand with him. Well, you would, wouldn't you? He wanted a chauffeur – well, Neville's at hand. You know the sort of thing. I was pretty well at his beck and call, as much as Lynne.'

'But he was so absent-minded that he didn't notice your kindness?'

'No kindness, mate,' he said. 'Don't get me wrong. It was all for me. We were going to be married, and I had to do something . . . Heh, you know, women are funny. D'you find that? The more I did . . . hell, the more time it left her to find things she could do for him. Well – I ask you! Wouldn't *you* get a bit desperate, and take in the odd pint here and there? Between 'em, they got me running round like a mad thing, getting nowhere.'

'Such as the trip to see his son, Paul?'

All I had to do was keep him going by dropping in a remark here and there. He didn't want me to think too highly of him. There was nothing disinterested about Neville Green, he'd have you believe.

'Well, how the devil would Lynne have managed it? His speech to type for the Convention . . .'

'Because, of course, he couldn't drive himself?'

'He *could* drive, but he hadn't got any intention of doing it. Far too comfortable being chauffeured, uncle Gledwyn was.' And yet, from the tilt of his head and the half smile, I could tell this was intended as a fond remark.

'Are you telling me he *had* been driving?'

'Oh no. Not on your life. He'd got this psychological block of his. His eyesight was rotten with traffic lights. Did you know that – have they told you?'

'The way I heard it, a pedestrian got killed.'

'His own fault!' he cried, waving his arms. 'Witnesses all said the same. Uncle Gledwyn didn't make any mistake. But he had to go into some sort of fugue – ain't that a marvellous word? – went into this thing he'd got, that told him he couldn't drive again. Like an invalid. No, no, I couldn't touch a steering wheel again!'

'You sound as though you hated him.'

He stopped waving and turned directly to face me, staring in surprise. 'Oh Lor', did I? No . . . no, nothing like that. It was the rest of 'em, pandering to him. They got up my wick. What he needed was to be shoved in a car and sent off on a long drive.'

'But all the same, he *was* colour blind. He was tested.'

'You really ought to get your facts right. Really you should. D'you know that one man in eight or ten is colour blind, some way or other? But d'you see one man in ten sitting at home because he daren't drive? Nah! They all made too much of it. They let *him* make too much of it.'

'But all the same, he didn't drive.'

'Crafty old bugger, no.'

'So you and Lynne did it all for him?'

'It got me a new Metro, didn't it?' He grinned tauntingly.

'You're telling me you didn't do it to help out Lynne, and you didn't do it to help out your uncle Gledwyn. You just did it for yourself.'

'He wanted my old Escort – the good old Green Dragon . . . heh, there's a laugh for you. Me Green, and Lynne . . .'

'I heard.'

'Yes. Well, he wanted it to play around with – mess about with the windscreen or something, and that suited me, 'cause I'd only have got scrap price for it, anyway. And he offered to help me replace it, so who'm I to grumble! I reckon he felt easier, buggering up an old Escort's screen, rather than a new car's.'

'He seemed to think highly of you,' I suggested.

'Why shouldn't he? I was the only relative still hanging around. A bit of plumbing at the house, Neville will do it. The lights've fused, send for Neville. You know how it is. He could've done it all himself, but he didn't want to slip out of his own bit of typecasting.'

I didn't know what to make of him. He said disparaging things about his uncle in a fond tone; he disparaged himself with a sardonic tongue.

'It could well have paid off,' I tried, venturing on a deliberate insult, to see whether he could be shaken.

'Did you hear about that?' he asked with enthusiasm. A fresh cigarette was jiggling between his lips. 'He told Lynne, on the way back from his Convention. He was going to change his will, and let me in for a bit.'

He lit the cigarette, and, catching my eyes on the lighter, tossed it in his palm. 'A birthday present from uncle Gledwyn.'

'But he didn't get round to his new will,' I said.

'Nah! That same night, he was dead.'

'Disappointing, hearing about it when it was too late.'

'Oh, don't worry. I'd heard before. Hints, you know.'

'From Lynne?'

'Not Lynne!' he said in fierce defence. 'She called herself his private secretary, and that meant private. No . . . he'd hinted at it to me. You know the sort of thing. "Help me out with this, Neville, and you won't find me ungrateful." And: "I appreciate what you're doing Neville, and you'll find I shan't forget." ' It was as though he'd carried the words in his memory. 'But he *did* forget, didn't he! Bloody hell, there's a laugh for you. There was me, working myself to the bone for him, running round in circles if that was what he wanted, and him knowing why I was crawling . . . and in the end he forgot to change his will.' Then he threw back his head and did genuinely laugh.

'You thought he'd already changed it?'

But he saw the trap in that. 'If I'd thought that, I'd have eased off a bit, wouldn't I? No – Lynne wasn't *that* private a secretary. If he'd actually gone to a solicitor and changed it, I'd have known soon enough.'

'So you drove him to Aberystwyth, to see his son, Paul, knowing that Paul was still going to inherit under Gledwyn's will?'

'Put it like that . . . yes. But I didn't –'

'Using the old Escort, and not your new Metro?'

'Yes. But I didn't drive all the way muttering to myself: "Paul's going to get his money, Paul's going to get his money." '

'Of course not. You'd have to pay attention to your driving.'

'He wasn't in a good mood. He left me to concentrate on the road.'

'This bad mood of his – it was because he was going to see his son?'

'That's what I guessed.'

'But my information is that he hadn't seen him for years.'

'Which is dead right. Can't fault you on that.'

'Why would he be in a bad mood, d'you think?'

'Wouldn't you? With Paul running off to the States and hardly ever getting in touch.'

'You know that?'

'Uncle Gledwyn told me.'

'On this trip to Aberystwyth?'

'Will you let me tell it, for God's sake! He mentioned it. On

84

the trip. He didn't sit there like a stone every minute. Paul just turned up in this country and phoned. Phoned, mind you, not even came to Viewlands to see his dear old dad. And then expected dear old dad to come to him.'

'Strange he didn't refuse.'

'Well . . . he'd want to *see* him.'

'And therefore, I gather, this wasn't just a social visit.'

'You can guess, Paul wanted something.'

'What?'

'How do I know? Uncle Gledwyn didn't say. All I know is, he didn't get it. There must've been a God-awful row, judging by his face when he came out.'

'Out of the hotel, you mean?'

'The Regent. I was waiting in the car park.'

'So you didn't go in to see your cousin?'

'Me? Lord no. Why'd I want to meet that snooty bastard? Why would he want to see me?'

'But you do know there was a row?'

'We'd better walk back,' he suggested.

'No hurry, is there? You knew there'd been a row, from his face?'

'And from something he said on the way back.'

'So he did speak?'

'One thing. After about ten miles, he said: "Neville lad, you can take it you'll be hearing something very soon to your advantage."'

I smiled into the distance. He'd been unable to leave it. It wouldn't have looked good if he left me with the impression he knew he already had the inheritance. I tried blunting his confidence.

'But that was a week before he died. There'd have been plenty of time to do something about it.'

'He was in Blackpool all the next week.' Neville shrugged. Easy come; easy go. But it hadn't come. It hadn't come within a mile of him.

'Though there was always the chance he'd have gone to a Blackpool solicitor,' I suggested.

'Lynne told me he hadn't. He was still only *talking* about it on the way back from there.'

'But she couldn't have told you that until *after* he was dead,' I pointed out.

He stared at me, flicking the cigarette end away negligently. Then he used the same hand to slap me on the shoulder. 'Hah – you're cute! I never thought of that. Makes it look bad, don't it!' And he grinned.

'You're right out of luck,' I agreed evenly.

Then he was suddenly cheerful. 'Still, could be worse, I suppose.'

I grinned at him. 'Yes. You've got the Metro – and got Lynne to yourself at last.'

'Yes . . . haven't I?' And he tossed his head, openly challenging me to make a motive out of that.

I said: 'You brought him home, that Saturday night, from Aberystwyth. You were late, I understand.'

'That bloody rain! It'd been on all day, and the Escort's wipers – he'd done his side of the windscreen with something – something stuck on, you see, only he'd done it on the outside. It meant the wipers kept sticking. Nearly drove me crazy. So we were home later than we expected. Poor old Lynne . . .'

'Waiting there. But she said you didn't go in and see her.'

'Well – I wouldn't know. The office is round the side . . . and where she leaves her car . . . have you seen? So I assumed she'd gone home. I was in a rotten mood myself by then, anyway, what with the rain and the wipers and him sitting there like a thunder cloud, and assuming I'd missed Lynne. So I took him into the drive –'

'Not into the yard?'

'The drive. He said: "The front." Like I was a soddin' servant or something, and he'd already got his keys in his hand. I pulled up in front of the porch and he got out – no good night or thank you or anything – and dived for the front door. I thought: bugger you, too, mate, and dug out the Metro, and went home. And d'you know what! It was my birthday. A right day it'd been for me.'

'And you didn't see Gledwyn again?'

'No. Should I have done?'

If Gledwyn had marched straight through the house and across the yard, yes, I'd have expected Neville to see him.

'Did you put away the Escort straightaway?' I asked, at last allowing him to walk me back towards the cars.

'What? That minute, d'you mean?'

'That minute.'

'I suppose . . . you want details . . . Gledwyn didn't smoke, and he didn't like me lighting up in the car. I was dying for a ciggy. I reckon – yes, I remember now. I lit up and sat there while I finished it, cussing him and the weather. Does it matter?'

'I don't suppose so.'

Yet somehow it did, though I couldn't quite work it out. I could imagine Neville, in a rotten mood, digging out his Metro from the garage, where he'd surely have left it. But I couldn't see him putting away the Escort. More likely he'd drive out the Metro, glance at the parked Escort and the rain, and think: bugger him, he can put it away himself. That would seem a joke to Neville, making Gledwyn accomplish that bit of driving, at least.

'And the following morning,' I said, 'Lynne drove him to his Convention at Blackpool, so that you didn't see him alive again?'

'That's about it. Would you like to see our new theodolite in action?'

'Thanks, but I think we'll get back.'

Angie had stayed in the Rover, I thought because she'd not wish to stand out there and distance herself too obviously. Neville had not noticed who was with me. He came up to the car, and said: 'Hello . . . it's you, Angie. How're things going?' She nodded and smiled, and I climbed into the driving seat. Their conversation seemed to be over, so I backed and edged the car round, with some difficulty, and we drove away. I glanced at her. Neville, apparently, was not one of her favourite people.

'Seems he's upset you,' she said. 'You look harassed.'

'It's through standing face on to the wind. It's quite keen.'

'Neville was his usual difficult self, I can see it in your eyes.'

Now how the devil could she do that? I'd thought there was a weakness in his features, one he recognised and played on. But he hadn't been difficult; rather too open, really.

I slowed to negotiate a particularly deep stream-bed. The car rocked. I was worried about Neville Green. He'd had time to prepare his attitude, and he'd known I'd be wanting to meet him. Had his openness really been secretive?

'What would you say,' I asked, 'about somebody who happily admits he's been fawning round your father for what he can get out of it, and grabbing up all he can get his hands on, and at the same time speaks about him with scorn? Come on. You know Neville better than I do.'

She glanced at me. 'The wind seems to have made you facetious.'

'I caught it from him.'

'I don't know him all that well. Perhaps he was being deliberately facetious.'

'He chose a strange time to display it, then.'

'Or maybe,' she suggested in a neutral voice, 'he's over-sensitive, and I never noticed it before.'

'Good Lord!'

'Too sensitive to risk showing an affection for my father, so he has to cover it, even if he's clumsy about it, by being too outspoken. And too sensitive about accepting presents, so he pours scorn on the giver. Does that make sense?'

I took time out to look at her suspiciously. 'Of a sort. But he came up with a very poor lack of motive, and I hadn't even mentioned murder.'

'What was that?'

'Your father was intending to leave Neville his money – as you know. Our friend back there knew about the intention a week before Gledwyn died. If he'd had reason to believe the will had been altered legally in his favour, that could well have been a good motive for killing his uncle.'

'It's strange,' she said acidly, 'how you calmly come out with these things, as though we're talking about objects instead of people.'

'It's why it's called objectivity. You mustn't consider it in an emotional way, Angie, or you get so upset you can't see past the personalities.'

She was distant. 'You were saying?'

'Only that he had no reason to think the will had been changed. Gledwyn was in Blackpool. It was a social event, and hardly a time he'd trouble to go into legal matters. Neville had been expecting something to happen about the will for a long while, and his fiancée, Lynne . . .'

'Fiancée? She hasn't said a word . . .'

'He wants to marry her. Let me finish. Lynne would have told him if and when there was any new will. So he'd surely wait to be certain, if he'd got anything drastic in mind.'

'But they're most unsuited!' she declared.

'I put to you a proposition . . .'

'You're right, of course.'

I tested her attention. 'About what?'

'There's no real motive there. Looking at it objectively, that is. But looking at those two as personalities . . . can you see them as man and wife? Really, now. Seriously.'

'It seems to have been his target for some while,' I ventured.

'Lynne'd make him a wonderful wife, I'll grant you that. Devoted to his needs, and organising his domestic existence . . .'

'Would he like to be organised?'

She nodded her emphasis. 'It'd take the embarrassment out of accepting, and make a formality out of what he had to offer. That would suit Neville splendidly.' She delivered this cool assessment with confidence.

I could see the town below me now, the street lights flicking on. We were on better surfaced roads. I relaxed.

'Do women think of marriage in such a way? You surprise me, really you do. Such a cold and dispassionate consideration of all the pros and cons.'

'Women take seriously matters of birth and marriage. We leave the men to be dispassionate about death.'

I grunted. 'You're too clever for me. I wish I hadn't brought it up.'

I drove steadily into and through the town. Again I took the route past the roadworks, and she made no protest.

'If,' I said at last, 'you say that marriage would make a formality out of what Neville has to offer, then there can't be much happiness in store for Lynne.'

'I told you – they're quite unsuited.' She was determined to get the last word. She added to it. 'Unless, of course, it's quite untrue that he's over-sensitive. In that case, it'd mean he's completely cold and calculating – as I've always thought – and marriage for Lynne to Neville would be disastrous.'

There seemed no point in trying to cap that. I drove into the yard beside Viewlands, and found she'd left the side door unlocked. On the kitchen table there was a note:

Angie. Can you pop over for an hour? My parents would be pleased. Evan.

Evan would, too, I had no doubt. Angie looked at me, frowning.

'I ought to go.'

'Of course.'

'Can you cook . . .'

'I'll manage.'

'Make yourself at home,' she said, the eagerness to be off already nudging the words. 'The big room at the back of the house . . . you'll find it. There're records and books . . .'

'You run along. I'll be fine.'

When she'd gone – after a dash upstairs for a quick change and to check that her face was still there – I phoned Phil Rollason, and arranged to meet him the next day.

8

It was not so much that I had any positive progress to report, as that I now believed the matter was drifting into deeper and deeper shades of domestic crisis, and I was best out of there. I couldn't say too much about it over the phone, but told him there were things I needed to know that would best come from him. This was true enough.

'There's a café in Shrewsbury,' I suggested, and told him how to find it. It was just about the one place I knew in Shrewsbury, and it spread the journey between us.

He agreed. 'Is she there?'

'She's visiting.' I decided to be diplomatic. 'The next door neighbour, a farmer called Morgan Rees.'

'Oh yes,' he said. 'I've met him.'

I'd tried to be off-hand with him, but you could hear the worry in his voice. I returned to the kitchen, feeling disturbed, and hammered three eggs into submission.

Afterwards I went out and raided the lab for one of those glass discs from the bench, and, being alone, had a closer look at the arrangements. Lynne had left her desk tidy. Well, it would be, as there'd been nothing for her to do since Gledwyn's death. Nevertheless, she'd found odd tasks that drew her there from time to time.

In the filing cabinet was the work Gledwyn had accumulated on vision, colour, and colour blindness. I fetched out one or two folders and looked at them, but they were very technical indeed, far beyond my understanding. And there were perhaps two hundred of these folders, all neatly annotated and carefully kept. Lynne's work, that. There'd been some disparagement of his scientific success and authority, but this seemed to me to be a considerable body of work, and quite an accomplishment for a man working alone and without a trained assistant, however enthusiastic Lynne might have been.

I saw – what I had not noticed before – that Lynne had

her own private door to the office. It opened onto the space where she always left her car. Here was more evidence of the way she distanced herself from the house. She had to prove she was devoted only to his scientific work. But prove it to whom?

The door was locked. She protected her own province, yet Angie had left the lab doors open at the front.

Then I went indoors and prowled around the house. Gledwyn had owned no television set, but his radio and record-playing equipment, which I found in the long rear room, were of the highest quality. And, judging by his record collection, his blindness did not extend to colour in musical composition. Richard Strauss, Mahler, Bruckner, Stravinsky, Bartok, as well as the more usual classics. His choice in books – and he had a large collection of fiction – extended from Chandler to Priestley, and indicated that he was not so unworldly as people seemed to consider.

The room was long, taking up nearly the whole of the rear of the house, and clearly matched the large bedroom above. But for all its length, I found the proportions elegant, and it had been furnished with period pieces showing excellent taste. Three french windows matched the bedroom's set, and were hung from floor to ceiling with sweeping velvet. I felt happy there, accepted.

Therefore, with a Mozart symphony on the turntable, and a bound collection of *Punch* for 1972 on my lap, I sat contentedly on a settee that would have taken three more, and waited for Angie.

She returned at eleven. I heard his voice at the side door, but Evan didn't stay, and she came in on me all bright-eyed, and walking with the stiff-legged gait people use when they're trying not to dance.

'I do apologise,' she burst out. 'Whatever must you think of me! I hope you got yourself something to eat.'

'I made myself at home.'

But Angie, restless, had turned away. 'Mozart? Is that number forty?'

'It is,' I agreed. 'I see you own a good collection of records. All the Beethoven symphonies and concertos . . . And wonderful equipment.'

She whirled round, flaring her skirt, partly to show it off, I guessed. 'But where will it all go?' she cried, abruptly aware that she did indeed own it all. 'If you saw the size of the flat . . .' She laughed, bit her lip, and looked out at the night from the tall, dark windows. I had not drawn the curtains.

The speakers, I'd already observed, were matched to the dimensions of the room. They talk of eigentones at hi-fi shops, the longest wavelength of sound you dare aim for being calculated from your wall dimensions. These speakers, with that amplifier, would shake down the ceiling of a flat and blow out the gas fire. Angie had realised something like that in a flash of despair.

'The equipment could be sold,' I suggested, 'and more appropriate stuff bought. The records you'd keep.' And play them with the din of the garage filtering from below?

'Yes,' she said dully, turning slowly, fingering the curtains that swept up so sumptuously in magnificent folds, her head averted. 'Yes, I could keep the records.' And yet her eyes dwelt on the solid, old furniture that her mother had polished, and her mother's paintings on the walls.

Then she seemed to tear her mind free, and was at once relaxed, swinging herself into the far corner of the settee.

'Tell me about yourself, Harry,' she said brightly. 'I know nothing . . .'

When they say things like that, with another man claiming their thoughts, it's no more than subtle flattery, and even more subtle denigration. She wanted to line up Evan's qualities against any meagre ones I might produce; she wanted to use me to calm the disturbing feelings that haunted her.

'There's nothing to know,' I said shortly.

'A friend of Phil's, and I don't know you! Oh . . . come on.'

'Hardly a friend.' I decided to discourage her. 'I met him as a detective sergeant, when I was investigating a series of car thefts.'

All thoughts of Evan Rees evaporated. I can be efficient when I try. 'You can't mean . . . you suspected Phil?'

'The facilities were there. But you don't want to hear about it.'

'You can't say a thing like that, and just drop it. Tell me, Harry, please.'

I shrugged. 'He offered me inducements. Bribes to you. Not actual cash. He wouldn't be so crude, and besides, we were friends. Remember? The slap on the shoulder and the: "Come off it, Harry, you know me." But the bribe was dangled. Now . . . can't we drop it?'

I moved to get to my feet. She spoke sharply. 'No!' Bit her lip. 'What bribe?'

'The way it works . . . it's the offer of a car, something second-hand, on rock-bottom terms. "I can give you a good price for your old one, Harry." And he happened to know my wife'd been worrying me to get her a car.'

'Wife?'

'Name of Cynthia. Two cars – on a sergeant's pay! I ask you.'

'But you refused?'

'Ever tried refusing Phil anything?'

'And what does *that* mean? I'm going to hear the truth of this, Harry, so I want a reply.'

'Oh hell!' I got to my feet anyway, but only to prowl about the room, gesturing with the pipe, looking anywhere but at Angie. 'I got home one evening, and there it was, a nearly-new Renault 5 in my drive, and Cynthia dancing round it and waiting to throw her arms round me. I knew what I'd got to do – drive it straight back and tell Phil what he could do with it. But how could I . . . it would've been like a slap in the face to her. So I stood there like a fool, grinning, and watched her take it out for a trial run, knowing I'd have to tell her when she got back.'

I'd stopped at the window. Nothing but reflections against the black night, my face distorted by a fault in the glass. Or maybe it wasn't the glass. I heard her speak quietly from behind me.

'And did you?'

'She didn't get back. There's a hill, a bridge over a canal. She went through the parapet.'

Then I turned to look at her, aware that I'd thrown it at her as a challenge. But . . . what *could* she say?

'Oh . . . Harry!'

I went on savagely, turning my distress to the purely professional. 'So how could I ever prove I'd have taken it back – or hide any of it? With Cynthia dead . . . I'm on suspension. And that's it.'

'And . . . and Phil?'

'It'd all been done with the best intentions, of course.' I

flapped my arms. 'You know Phil. It'd just been a sales trick – see how the little woman liked it. That sort of thing. "If there's anything I can do, Harry." When I could've killed him.'

She was shaking her head, hair flying. 'Not Phil. Not dishonest. And you're *still* friends.'

'Sure. He took pity on me. There I was, with nothing to do. I'd put the house up for a quick sale – you know how it is. I couldn't get away fast enough. Then I bought the Rover and the caravan, and Phil came round and said I could do him a favour . . . if I happened to be round this way . . . look you up.'

'So you're doing him a favour?'

'It started like that. But Phil can look after himself. It's you I'm trying to help, Angie.'

'Are you? Asking questions and making rotten suggestions . . .'

I tried to smile, but my jaw was stiff. 'I've been sitting and thinking. I'd like you to do something.'

'What?' she asked suspiciously.

'I'd like you to come out in the car,' I said gently.

Startled eyes. 'Now?'

'It's not far.'

'But . . . whatever for?'

'You'll see.'

I waited for her to get to her feet – my masterful act. She could not refuse. I had to get the talk away from myself. She shrugged, suddenly scared. I reached out a hand for her arm.

'It's rather late, and I'm tired,' she protested feebly.

'It needs to be late.' It wasn't a pleasure trip I had in mind. As we coasted out of the drive, I explained.

'I've now got a lot of information about the last week before your father died,' I said. 'Not all of it, perhaps. I'd still like to see your brother – he's at the Regent, by the way. But a number of unpleasant things happened in those last few days, and you ought to know about them.'

'Must I?' she asked bleakly.

'If we're going to get anywhere.'

She gave a little shrug, and a click of her tongue from annoyance.

'Your cousin, Neville, drove him to see your brother at the Regent,' I told her. 'That was the Saturday before he died. Your father was upset before they even started, Paul not having been to see him, perhaps. But something happened there that upset him even more, and he was in a very bad humour when they returned.'

'That was a whole week before he died,' she protested.

'And things didn't improve very much. The morning after his visit to Paul, he went to his Convention, met all his highly acclaimed friends and ex-colleagues, and later read a paper that fell flat on its face. He was very nearly accused of non-scientific investigation.'

'I thought we weren't going to use this road again,' she complained pettishly.

'You'll see. Your father . . . by the time he got home – and this was half an hour before he died – by that time he was as low as he could get. His life's work rejected!'

'But his spectacles worked!'

'Not in the way he wanted. Not in the minds of his peers – and it was *their* approval he'd want. No, he would've been in a really desperate mood by then.'

We were coming up to the traffic signal at the roadworks. The lights had been flashing out at us for the past minute or two. I drew into the lay-by. She sat stiffly beside me, unresponsive and remote.

'I'd like you to get out,' I said quietly.

'You're going to tell me he committed suicide.' Her voice was small and dangerous.

'No . . . not that. Get out please, Angie. There's something you must see.'

Reluctantly, she got out. I went round and took her arm, but she shook herself free angrily. In that second I'd felt her shaking, but I had to admit that the dress, even with the little jacket she had over it, was hardly thick enough for the thin night air.

'Get it over with,' she said.

The night was clear, but very dark. There was no moon. I had seen no traffic since we'd left the house, and it seemed safe to experiment. Ahead of us the traffic signal dutifully flashed red to green, green to red, almost blindingly bright.

'I want you to look at those lights through this.'

I thrust the disc into her cold hand. She nearly dropped it.

'If you get no effect,' I said, 'turn it round.'

She made a movement as though to throw it away, but I caught her wrist. 'Please.' Her face was almost invisible, only my sidelights throwing back palely at us.

She raised it to her eye. I told her to close the other. She was very still for a full minute. Then she lowered her arm.

'Well?' she demanded. Then, as I tried to speak, she went on wildly. 'You're going to say he confused the lights. But this works – even for me, it works. His spectacles worked, and he had them with him. You think I'm a fool, don't you! He didn't . . . he couldn't . . .'

'It's not what I wanted to show you,' I told her soothingly. I turned, reaching inside the car for my motoring jacket. It was ridiculously too large for her, but she was beyond any consideration for her appearance. She huddled into it, hiding from me, but I wouldn't allow her to escape, and walked her down the road to the signal, on until it stood at her shoulder.

'I want you to stand here. Tucked in, see, where you'll be safe, and you won't be blinded by the signal. I'm going back to the car, and I'm going to drive you. I want you to watch me through that piece of glass . . . and use a bit of imagination, Angie!'

I paused. There was no response. She drew in on herself, motionless.

'You're all right?'

'Oh, get on with it!' she snapped.

I turned away and walked back, and slid into the seat.

There was no point in taking it at any speed, and I wanted her firmly in my lights before I drove past her – the clearance was only two feet. But there she was, the piece of glass to her eye, as I'd asked her. I went on a further fifty yards and touched the brake, drew to a halt, then started up again and repeated the process. Then, as I was only a hundred yards past the light, and there being no sign of traffic in either direction, I backed out, stopping beside her.

I reached over and pushed open the door. 'Jump in.'

She did, awkwardly, taking two goes at slamming the door. I reversed up to the lay-by, used it to swing round, and drove back to Viewlands.

'Well?' I said, as soon as I'd completed the U-turn.

'I don't know.' She sounded choked.

'What did you see?'

There was a pause. 'Your . . . your tail lights were almost . . . almost white,' she whispered.

'And your colour sight's normal. How d'you think they'd seem to your father, wearing his glasses?'

There was no response. When I looked at her, she was quietly and desperately weeping.

I drove fast, and swept into the yard. The kitchen light from the window picked out her bent head as she stumbled from the car. She'd thrown off my motoring coat, and ran with head down ahead of me, to wait in the kitchen indecisively, looking round as though not recognising it. I pushed past her. Hot tea, I thought. Bang went the kettle onto the gas ring, clatter came the cups and saucers from the cupboard. Angie sat at the head of the table, her face in her hands.

Tea, I suppose, is the quickest hot drink to prepare, but to me the time dragged. I knew what I was doing, and the realisation that I'd acted instinctively and thoughtlessly was chastening. I'd not been able to continue thinking about Cynthia, remembering, so I'd crushed the memory with a display of more present brutal reality. I couldn't remember that any consideration for Angie had entered into it at all. Good old Harry, I thought. True to form.

Her hands round a cup, she sipped, and raised her eyes. They were red and swollen, but there was no defeat in them. 'I know,' she claimed, 'what you're going to say.'

'You keep telling me that, but you haven't been right once. What I wanted to *show* you . . . well, you've seen now . . . just use your imagination, Angie. Your father, driving along to that traffic signal. He's going fairly fast . . . no , just let me say it, please. He comes up to the signal, and he's quite confident about his sighting. He goes through a green. But suppose there was a car ahead of him, going slower, but in the same direction. Do you see it? He comes up behind it rapidly – and it brakes for some reason. By that time they're both well past the traffic signal. Now – what would those braking lights look like to him? Remember that modern cars have large and bright braking lights, designed for motorway driving. Do you see the point I'm trying to make, Angie? They would look like white lights to him, through his glasses. Dipped headlights. Suddenly – and he'd have a split second to think about it – he'd see a vehicle that was apparently driving *towards* him. Logic might dispute that, but there'd be no time for logic. He'd think, in that split second, that he'd made a mistake with the signal. He'd think he was driving head on towards another car. He'd brake frantically, and skid on that slippy surface. He might even have a brief thought that from his own error he was endangering somebody else. He'd remember the pedestrian he killed – and he always believed *that* was his fault. So he'd deliberately turn off the road to save the other car.'

I stopped. I'd managed to get it all out in one go. Those big, luminous eyes had not seemed to blink once during the whole of my explanation. They'd bored into me, rejecting the pain I was causing, and I'd had difficulty finishing.

'Isn't that reasonable?' I asked. 'There *was* another car – there was a telephone call.'

She looked away, and began slapping the pockets of her jacket for cigarettes.

'He had no reason to be driving fast,' she croaked. Cleared her throat. 'No reason.'

'I think he had a very good one,' I told her, sliding my lighter along the table top. 'He'd just got home from a perfectly disastrous Convention. For him. In fact, he'd cut it short and come home a day early. He'd want to prove to himself the small success he'd made with the spectacles. It was all he'd got left. He'd take out the Escort, and he'd drive it fast, deliberately pushing his vision on a lousy night with sticking windscreen wipers. The more difficult the test, the more the triumph. So he'd drive fast. He *would*, Angie. Where's the test if he'd drifted slowly up to that damned traffic signal?'

She drew on her cigarette as though desperate for the smoke, and banged my lighter down on the table. Then she got up abruptly and I thought she was going to walk away from it. But she seemed to have herself in hand, and was only getting another cup of tea. The pouring of it steadied her, and when she turned back to me she'd made up her mind about something. She remained standing.

'I know you're trying to help,' she said in a reasonable tone. 'And I'm grateful for what you're doing. But I should have told you more about daddy. He wasn't like that, you see. He wasn't a *strong* man, who could carry on in the face of setbacks and come up fighting. Poor daddy! I loved him so dearly, but he was easily discouraged. I didn't mislead you deliberately. You'll have to believe that. He was a wonderful man, but not . . . not resolute.' She smiled thinly, pain compressing her lips. 'I'll bet – if you went through all his records at the lab – you'd find he'd started a dozen projects and abandoned them. One little setback, and that'd be it. Impatient with himself . . . oh, you wouldn't believe. I'll tell you what daddy would've done, if he'd really been in despair that Friday night. He'd have gone into his lab and smashed every scrap that related to his experiments, got drunk, played his Mahler, and gone to sleep on the settee. That's what daddy would have done, with me not here to tell him he was the best and silliest . . .'

She stopped abruptly, put down her cup, and said: 'That's what daddy would have done.'

Then she walked steadily out of the kitchen, and the 'good night' that floated back must have taken all her courage.

It's always like that. Slap 'em in the face and they bounce right back; be kind, and they weep on your shoulder. Maybe I'd tackled it correctly. I didn't think I could handle Angie with her head on my shoulder. There, you see, another lie. Handle myself, I meant.

It was just another good idea down the drain, when a bit of luck would have meant it was the finish. Angie back with Phil – if that was what I wanted. Ah well, maybe – if it made her happy. But she'd loved her father, faults and all, and she had come back to Viewlands remembering only the happiest times. Gledwyn at his finest and most noble. Wreck that, Harry, and she'd never return to Phil with happiness.

I didn't know what I could do for her, and couldn't bear the thought of facing her and telling her that.

I put off the light, shut the back door after me, and let myself into the caravan. Home. That was how it was beginning to feel. I broke the blasted mantle, trying to light it.

9

In the morning I made a quick call from the phone in the hall, not caring whether Angie heard. I told her I'd be away most of the day, and she must have realised I was intending to see her brother. But I was not asked to convey any loving messages.

She stood at the side door watching me back out of the yard. The gelding snorted and tossed his head, I thought in contempt.

There were two routes I could take to Aberystwyth, either north to pick up the A5, and through the Horseshoe Pass, or pick up the A483, south to Welshpool, and west through Powys and Machynlleth. Each looked to be around sixty miles, so I chose the northerly one, mainly because I fancied the run through the Cambrians and past Lake Bala. Given two choices, I always make the wrong one, and up in the mountains the mist closed down. I saw nothing of the lake, nothing really but the wet, black tarmac ahead and dry-stone walls each side with sheep every now and then wandering beneath my wheels. It was only when I got down to Machynlleth, with eighteen miles to go, that I came out into sunlight again. When I reached Aberystwyth I didn't even get a sight of the sea, the hotel being well short of the town, where the road is still three miles from the coast. I'd seriously miscalculated the distance, as I registered eighty-three miles. I wondered how the run – either route – would have seemed to Neville in the clapped-out Escort with sticking wipers, in the dark and in the rain. No wonder he'd been dying for a smoke.

Paul Griffiths had sounded distant and suspicious, but had agreed to a meeting. I couldn't remember what I had to ask him.

The Regent had more the air of a country club than a holiday hotel. It stood placidly in its own grounds, had its own tennis courts and nine-hole golf course, and the dignity of ivy crawling over its red walls. It was the end of the season. I'd been a little chary of the suggested meeting in the lounge, our business not being exactly public, but I found it was empty when I got there. They rang up from the desk to say I was there. I took one of the easy chairs that made an arc round a coal fire that was there for atmosphere rather than warmth, and waited.

He was tall and slim, with the clean-cut, close-shaven appearance of the American male, tanned and confident, his gold-rimmed spectacles tailored to enhance his facial planes, his hair styled, his clothes draped in the loose, casual style that shouted out: West Coast. I almost expected an American accent, but he'd hung on to his English, and there was even a trace of Welsh when he introduced me to his wife.

She was a different proposition, the hard, diamond-cut elegance of the West Coast American born to money. Her tan was more a natural shade of her skin, and probably went in half an inch. I felt that there'd be no light bikini patches if you stripped her down; no warm passion either, if you got that far, more likely a polished expertise. She was dressed simply in a light two-piece that'd probably cost more than my Rover, was clutching her purse – as I believe they call them – in her right hand, and offered her left when he introduced us, holding it out palm down, probably just to put me out.

'My wife,' he said, then, to my surprise, he added: 'Rena McGaffey.'

They're peculiar about their maiden names, American women, an indication, I believe, of their determination to hang on to their independence. The smile she gave me was thin and hard. Nothing personal, I thought. It was just because I was a man.

'I'm not sure of your business,' Paul added, ignoring his wife as she made a great performance out of taking her seat, smoothing her skirt beneath that pert little bottom, wriggling her shoulders, then sitting on the extreme edge.

He sat to one side of me. Answering him meant speaking directly to Rena McGaffey, who set her eyes on me behind a pall of cigarette smoke and tried either to hypnotise or seduce me, neither to good effect.

I explained that I was a friend of his sister, who was concerned about the circumstances of his father's death.

'I've ordered coffee,' he said. 'I hope that's all right.'

I nodded, wondering whether he'd heard me. It was his wife who answered.

'We see nothing to question, there.'

Texas, I thought, but I was going only on what I'd heard on television. The flatness of her tone did not necessarily indicate any lack of interest.

'She's staying at Viewlands,' I told him, 'and I thought she seemed upset that you haven't been to see her.'

Fortunately, the arrival of the coffee rescued him. He paid attention to that. His wife told me:

'She never came to visit us, in LA.'

'Los Angeles is some way away.'

'We offered to pay her expenses. The complete package. She could've taken time out.'

'She wouldn't want to leave her husband,' I offered, accepting a cup.

'You reckon?' she asked. 'But – now you correct me if I'm wrong – but she has, hasn't she?'

Before I could ask how she knew that, Paul cut in quickly. I felt he was annoyed to have the conversation taken out of his hands, but nervous of retrieving it.

'You came to talk about my father, not about Angie.' He glanced at his wife. 'Correct me if I'm wrong.' The last words took on a Texan twang. I felt he'd heard them too often. She pouted at him, and sat back.

'He visited you here . . .'

'He did just that,' she put in.

'And my information is that he drove away in a distressed condition.'

I was choosing my words carefully, hoping he'd lead me in. He was quite calm and unshaken.

'That was a week before he died. I can't see the connection.'

'He didn't mean that, honey,' Rena said, wagging one finger at him.

'Then what did he mean?'

I got no chance to say, because they were man and wife, then, engaged in what must have been an eternal verbal warfare, and I might not have been there.

'You're such a trusting fool, Paul,' she told him dispassionately. 'Can't you see he's a private eye, or something?'

'I see that, I see it. So what?

'He's not goin' to lay it on the line, lover, he's gonna trap you into it.'

'Into what, for God's sake?'

'The will, honey, the will.'

'There's no possible reason . . .'

'You poor idiot,' she said, smiling her affection, 'he's heard the old fool was going to change his will. He's come to ask if you knew about it.' Cause if you did, then you'd got a whole week to do something about it. Think about that. He came to ask if you knew.'

'As you clearly did,' I said firmly. 'But I'm not a private eye or a dick or whatever's the current jargon. I'm just a friend. No doubt you've got a beautiful alibi for the night he died, but I'm not even going to ask you what it is. All I'm interested in is his state of mind when you saw him.'

She laughed shrilly and emptily. Paul blinked at me in apology.

'When he came to see you,' I repeated, not sure it'd got through. 'His state of mind.'

She waved her hand, dismissing herself from the conversation, and sat back as though exhausted by battling with two ridiculous men.

'For instance,' I said, making it easy for him. 'Why did he come here?'

'Because Rena wouldn't go there.'

'There was some . . .' I thought.'. . . disparity of intellectual interests?'

'I didn't wish to, either. We were never close, father and me. You've heard how we parted – I'm sure you'll have heard that. So all right, I didn't do too well at Keele . . .'

'Or Loughborough.'

'There too. Hell, father expected everybody to be like him.'

'Heaven forbid,' she put in, staring at the ceiling.

'I didn't wish to visit my father at my old home,' said Paul forcefully, each word spaced like heavy feet tramping on her interruptions.

'Aw, come on!' she cut in with disgust. 'Tell the man. He didn't want us. That's the truth of it. You phoned. Tell the man how you phoned and he didn't want you there. That's a nice thing. A father who didn't want his own son as a house guest. Will you believe that, Mr . . .'

I said I would believe it. 'So he came here instead. You persuaded him?' I asked this directly to Paul.

'And did I have to crawl!' he said moodily. 'But in the end he said he'd come and talk with me.'

'So,' she said, 'we're stuck in this God-awful dump. How far d'you have to go for a Hilton in your damned country, Mr . . .'

'Kyle, Mrs Griffiths.' I thought I'd save her the embarrassment of having to slide off it every time. 'It must have been something important, that you'd crawl to get him here.'

Paul gave me a bleak grimace. 'I've been lecturing at UCLA. I don't know how to put this . . .' He glanced at his wife, who snorted and tossed her head. 'But I've had my fill of American push and scramble, and between you and me a lecturer out there's as important as the guy who slaps a hamburger under your nose.'

'Christ, don't start again,' she pleaded. In England, she pleaded; in the States she'd have pled.

'There's the prestige, lover,' he told her. 'Mr Kyle, I'd heard there's a chair of Philosophy coming vacant at Aberystwyth University. I'd be a professor at my father's old University, Professor of Philosophy.'

'Get him!' she cried. 'Now that's what I call a hypocrite. Left home after a flaming row with his father, hates his father's guts, has nothing but contempt for him – but he'll fly six thousand miles for an effing chair of Philosophy in a dump that doesn't even remember his father's name.'

'Now Rena, honey.'

'Don't give me that crap,' she said flatly, lacing her language now with obscenities with the easy grace of a navvy. 'What've you heard about this shit of a father of his, Mr . . . er?' She compressed her lips, chiding herself for having nearly recalled my name. 'The great man, huh? The University professor whose brilliant career was cut short? Don't you worry your sweet ass about any of that, my friend. The guy was a wash-out. You ask me, he was a pain in the butt to the whole bunch of them, and they were glad to see the back of the old fart.'

There was a brief, contemplative silence. She'd stopped merely to draw a breath, which she did through the length of one of her long, brown cigarettes.

'But all the same, sweetness,' cut in Paul, his voice like gravel, 'it's still a professorship.'

It mollified her. It seemed she was a career woman, her career being the thrusting forward of her man. Perhaps when he ceased to move forward she might have to dispense with him for a more durable product.

'And your father,' I murmured, 'how did he enter into this?'

'It's his old University,' he said brightly. 'He always claimed he'd been a friend of the Dean, and the Warden wasn't exactly unknown to him. A word in the right ear . . . you know the way it works.'

I knew. Paul's use of his father was a sick reflection of Neville's. But Neville's had been blatantly claimed, and so was probably less serious than stated. Paul's was complacent. He'd been childishly hurt at the outcome.

'And I suppose he refused?'

'We gave him dinner!' Rena claimed. 'A good dinner. Wine.'

I wondered why she claimed that. Would even a vintage Sauternes smooth away six years of separation? I wondered, too, about Neville. What had he done as he waited in the car? Where would *he* have gone for food and drink?

'He refused to lift a bloody finger,' said Paul, not so versatile as his wife with his language.

'Do you know why? Did he say?'

'He didn't have to say,' put in Rena. 'I saw through him. I wasn't going to let him get away with that. You know – all his big words and his prestige. He didn't even *know* them, not to expect a favour. That's the truth of it. The Dean said this, the Warden congratulated me on that! All breeze. He was nothing at that place. Absolutely nothing.'

I looked at Paul, who was completely miserable.

'If it's any consolation,' I said, 'I wouldn't think the appointments are made like that.' I looked at Rena. 'Whatever the system in the States.'

'You gotta have leverage.' She pronounced it levverage.

'My father,' Paul declared, facing the fact philosophically, 'was a complete fraud. I knew, of course. But you don't face these things. He was a professional, all right – a professional martyr.'

I had to allow for the fact that he was naturally annoyed. But perhaps his father's refusal to help had been based not on his lack of friendship with the Dean and the Warden, but on the depth of it. He'd not wish to strain it by implying that their influence could be so lightly bought.

'It wasn't the impression I've received from your sister,' I told him.

'She always did go round with her head in the air,' he said distantly. 'But she'd know – she was up at Aberystwyth at the time. He said he was in charge of the science projects – all he ever had was a section. And *that* he buggered up, tell the truth. He came down because of mother's illness, but he'd have found some other excuse if that hadn't been there. And from then on he never let up on claims of all the great things he'd have accomplished if it hadn't been for mother. Believe me, he really revelled in it. Everybody spent all their time sympathising. And when Angie dropped out, oh the sighs and the sad shakes of his head! You had to know how much that had upset him, Angie's failure. But what'd he expect? How'd Angie stand a chance, with mother ill, and all the time getting letters from him complaining he couldn't manage on his own! All he needed was a housekeeper, so that he could disappear into his blasted lab and play with his instruments, and kid himself he was a great scientist, robbed by fate of his full potential.'

Rena made a move, leaned forward, was about to speak, but he said: 'For God's sake!' and she desisted.

'He even managed to bugger up Angie and Evan Rees,' he went on. 'Evan didn't see through him, thought he was the greatest. So Evan studied father's subjects, and when Evan visited Angie at home too much, father put a stopper on it. Dedication, he'd say, dedication, my boy! The bloody fraud. And then we all had to suffer when it broke up, 'cause I don't think Angie ever knew why Evan called less and less and grew colder and colder. You ought to meet Evan. Now *there's* your dedicated scientist. That's what father made of him – single-minded, and nothing exists that can't be fed into a computer. But daddy claimed Angie had robbed him of what he'd expected from her. Oh, he didn't complain to her, just to everybody else. What in God's name had he expected, when he'd loused it up himself – Pierre and Marie Curie?'

He'd really worked himself into a stew. And yet this man had asked his father for help, and been surprised not to get it.

'And you?' I murmured.

'D'you think I wanted his crappy science?' he demanded. 'But he got me down for it at Keele. So of course I didn't do a tap. Oh dear, the lamentations! He'd bred a moron. Another try at Loughborough. "If you knew," he said to me, "what I've had to do to get you accepted!" I did a year, and dropped out. What'd he got to moan about? Wasn't that what suited him? Everybody letting him down, but look how *he* carried on, against all odds, making world-shattering discoveries in his little lab! Christ, the hypocrite! And he couldn't put out a hand to help me.'

I was making a grand performance of filling my pipe, not caring to look too long at his hot, frantic face. It had stewed for too long in his mind, bubbling away. He was silent. I looked up. Rena was staring coolly into the fire, nearly putting it out. Her face was thin, the cheekbones prominent, her eyes slightly protruding. In a few years she'd be a harridan, and he hag-ridden, and both bitter, intent on destroying each other.

'And of course,' I observed, 'you told him what you thought?'

'It needed telling,' he said defensively.

'Do you think I'd let him leave, and think we didn't know!' Rena McGaffey Griffiths flared her nostrils at me. 'I told him. He'd gotta know what a contemptible piece of garbage he was. I gave him the lot, and he knew right well what we thought of him. Correct me if I'm wrong.'

I didn't correct her. There remained nothing useful to ask, so I said I hoped Paul would get the appointment – hypocrisy is infectious – and that they'd continue to enjoy their stay, and drove away before they asked me to join them for lunch, which I didn't think I could stomach.

I had another sixty miles to drive in order to meet Phil, which gave me time to attempt to reconcile the opposed views of Gledwyn Griffiths, and eventually I came on a compromise that could fit the facts. Devotion from Lynne and Angie, hatred from Paul, esteem from Evan Rees.

The way I saw it, he'd simply been a weak man, reaching for the stars and not even touching the branches of the trees around him. His family had been his trees. He'd expected so much from Angie and Paul, and been disappointed because he could see them only as an extension of himself. Perhaps Angie, too, had not been a born scientist, but had not dared to say so. She'd maybe inherited from him only the desire not to inflict pain. Paul certainly had not inherited the scientific mind, but he'd fought back, though not with compassion. Angie would have been pleased to drop out of college. It would be a relief, perhaps, one she could disguise in her concern for her mother. And Evan would have to take the place of both of them in Gledwyn's claim to posterity. Yes, he'd feel martyred, but he'd wield it gently. Gledwyn, I felt, could not bear to witness suffering. He'd claim a martyrdom to cover his distress over his wife's illness. He'd use the lab as a retreat from it.

Perhaps Angie realised this, and adored him for it. Perhaps Paul was too blinded by self-interest, and therefore hated him. Evan Rees, the only natural scientist of the lot, quite simply revered him for what Gladwyn had given him, and in repayment worked so hard that he lost sight of Angie.

This speculation used up the whole of the journey, and even then I was not pleased with it. I'd stopped for lunch, wasting time because Phil had said he wouldn't be able to reach Shrewsbury before six.

It was nearer seven when he arrived. I was standing outside the café by that time, calmly smoking but with my brain tossing it all backwards and forwards. He made a bit of a botch of the parking, and seemed to me to be exhausted when he climbed out of the Sierra he was using. Then he saw me and his shoulders straightened, his old grin appeared, and his step became firm.

'Hungry?' I asked.

'You bet.'

There was a restaurant I'd located that seemed solid and plain, and therefore would suit Phil. We ordered steak and chips and peas, and he demanded: 'What've you got?' almost as though I was offering him a part exchange. I stared at the table and collected my thoughts.

'What – d'you think – would persuade Angie to come home?' I asked.

'You know what. She wants to hear her father was killed.' He'd baulked at the word 'murdered'.

'Then I'd better tell you straight out that I can't see any chance of that. There're motives, but damn it, Phil, the very circumstances . . . And accident? Last night I put together a reasonable and solid theory of how he might have killed himself in that car. It was good enough, though I say it myself. But she rejected it.'

'That's Angie for you,' he said with gloomy pride.

'I can put together that final week of his, which was a complete disaster for him, and produce evidence that could lean towards suicide. Now tell me . . . what effect would that have on her?'

He treated that as a rhetorical question, too obvious to require discussion. I'd never seen him looking so smart, in a businessman's fine grey worsted and a blue tie. Usually you got him in soiled overalls, with hypoid all over his hands and a smudge on his forehead. It fools you, you know. Meant to. You get to thinking of him as a greasy, ignorant mechanic, so that when you settle on the shiny banger he's flogging you, you think you've pulled a fast one on him. Technique. He was intelligent behind the show. Now he was twisting an ashtray in his fingers, tapping his cigarette against it every two seconds, while we waited for our order. I thought at first he wasn't going to say anything, but he'd only been arranging his thoughts, considering no doubt how much he dared to offer me. When he did speak, he seemed to have flown off at a tangent.

'I knew him well, you know, Harry. For a while I seemed to live at that house. Angie's mother was still alive, but terribly ill, and I knew it'd be . . . ridiculous to mention marriage at that time. But Gledwyn saw what I had in mind. I got the impression he was pleased – it was difficult to tell. A strange man. Has anybody told you how small he was? One of those men with bright eyes and a very quick brain. Chirpy, the way he walked, but if you came on him suddenly . . . how shall I put it . . . you got an impression of defeat, which he didn't want anybody to see.'

'He felt the world hadn't been kind to him?' I suggested. 'Ah, here it is now. Let's have a bottle of their plonk.'

We did. He picked up on my question. 'There're people,' he said, with a kind of contemptuous awe, 'who're basically kind. I've met 'em. They don't like to upset anybody, just can't face anybody else's pain. I suppose it's something to do with imagination. And there was his wife. I think her condition broke him up, and he didn't want her to see it. It got to be an act with him, a cheerful kind of martyrdom, if you can have such a thing, only it was so obviously faked that you knew he'd have given his right arm . . . hell, I'm no good at this sort of thing.'

Embarrassed, he attacked his steak vigorously. I chewed. I said:

'You're doing fine. Carry on.'

But he'd ventured into fields too wet and chilly for him. Shaking his head, he went on: 'I met her in Aberdovey, you know. We were plodding over the dunes. I was there on a weekend break, testing out an Austin Healey I'd been tuning up. I walked her to where I'd parked it, and . . . phew, she couldn't wait to climb in. For three days I met her – that's all it took – and then she took me home. Strange . . . I've just thought . . . it's never occurred to me that she must've driven sixty miles each way, and what for but to meet me? Harry, I . . .' He stopped, his fork still, then he shook himself free of the thought. 'She took me home. Her father seemed more amused with me than anything else. And somehow pleased. There'd been this Evan chap, you see. I never got to the bottom of that. Gledwyn seemed to blame himself for something. He was a great one for blaming himself – even . . . and you wouldn't believe this . . . even for the fact that Angie didn't get her degree, when it was obvious she didn't come down from the University for him. She'd never have been able to stay away from her mother at that time. But he blamed himself. It amused him that I was a complete loon in their academic atmosphere. When we made up our minds, he said, "By heaven, a daughter of mine working a petrol pump – what have we come to?" Then a laugh, and some Latin tag or other.'

'*Mea culpa?*' I suggested.

'You too!' he said in disgust.

'My motto. You were saying?'

'I've forgotten now. I can see him now, though, walking into that big, long room of theirs, where Angie's mother used to sit in her wheel-chair, and him crying out, "What results I'm getting, my dear! My thesis is almost complete," and in a kind of mocking whisper to me, "and what heights I might have reached, my boy. Ah . . . responsibilities!" And we'd all laugh, because Angie's mother had been intended to hear, and I think we all knew the heights he was reaching. Am I making any sense at all?'

He knew he was. I could tell from his smile.

'And he'd never accept that I felt easy with him,' he went on. 'He was suspicious of it, as though I was putting it on. He played a lot of chess. He'd challenge me, to see if I'd let him beat me. Did you know I play chess, Harry?' It didn't surprise me at all. 'Not well,' he said modestly, 'but I tried as hard as I could. If he won – and he usually did – it was because he was the better player, and he realised that, I think. Appreciated it, that I'd done my best. Angie used to beat him time after time. It seemed easy for her. She said he liked her to beat him. He admired a better brain than his, she told me. But he liked to beat me, and I don't remember any contempt for *my* brain. And I could always beat Angie. Can, even now. I think he didn't really try, against Angie. It gave him a kind of satisfaction, allowing him to admire her.'

He was showing himself to be even more subtle than I'd imagined. Subtle and dangerous. I wondered why he was letting me see it, and tried not to let him realise I'd noticed.

'But he'd be upset when you married her and took her away?'

'I offered to try and sell up, and move to the area, but she wouldn't hear of it. Neither would he. And it turned out that you really had to be Welsh-speaking, even though they weren't officially in Wales. And anyway, Gledwyn knew my operation was getting too big for the country. He almost insisted on us leaving. I wonder if I did right, taking her away. Do you think I did, Harry?'

'I'm sure Gledwyn knew what he was doing. Every move.'

We were onto the coffee. Phil brightened, having unburdened himself. 'Now . . . what did you want to see me about?'

'You've said it all.'

'Have I? Has it helped?'

I smiled at him. Good old crooked, double-dealing Phil, who'd probably cost me my job and had tried so hard to show me how clever he was. I smiled, wondering why the hell I should save *his* marriage, when he'd destroyed mine. What was he up to? Keeping me out of circulation, was that it, when my presence in the Midlands might have done something to indicate my innocence?

'Sold any good cars lately?'

'You know how it is. You decide to slack off, but the business grows . . .'

'Nice flat you've got, though.'

'Did she tell you that?' He seemed surprised. 'She's not really a flat person, is she?' The play on words amused him. He emphasised the lack of good taste by slapping the table with his palm.

'It'd help,' I said, 'if you'd come and stay at Viewlands for a while.'

'Hell, I couldn't leave things.'

'Try.'

'They're pushing me, you know.'

'They?'

'Your lot. The police. Harry, I told them you're a *friend*. Damn it all, would I trust my wife to anybody but a friend? The little Renault . . . Harry, you know that was just a sales trick, pushing it. You'd have brought it back. I told them that.'

'That's very good of you, Phil.'

'Any time.'

'But all the same, I could well need you at the house. We might have to carry her away, kicking and screaming.'

That wiped the smile from his face. 'It's as bad as that?'

'I'm beginning to see something – a pattern. If I'm right, screaming could come into it.'

'Bloody hell,' he said.

It was later than I'd intended when I pointed the Rover's bonnet towards Viewlands. From what Phil had told me, a clearer picture of Gledwyn Griffiths was emerging, but there was still a lot of detail missing. I didn't know whether I dared to leave it unprobed.

By the time I was within two miles of Llanmawr I'd made up my mind. Late as it was, a diversion was clearly necessary. I spotted a phone box and tried to call Angie. There was no reply, but there was no reason she'd be sitting by the phone waiting for me to call.

I skirted the town, hunting for the Whitchurch road, and went to visit Lynne, on her own ground.

The address itself was intriguing, Wilmington Court, and the location a village four miles out of Llanmawr. When I found the place, it was as though somebody – probably a councillor called Wilmington – had had a spare six-storey council block doing nothing, and they'd hunted round for somewhere to drop it. Incongruously, they had chosen this village, and where they got enough council tenants to fill it I don't know. They had recognised an environment problem, and hidden the first storey in a belt of trees, but there it stood in the dark countryside, looming away with its banks of lights, a tiny portion of a large town miraculously in the country.

In town, the walls would have been covered with graffiti and the lifts out of order. They had their graffiti, but there were no lifts. Six storeys, and no lifts, and Lynne way up the top. Perhaps one to five were reserved for the elderly.

I had parked in front of the row of twelve lock-up garages, hidden away at the side. I'd walked cautiously into the darkened courtyard, and paused, getting my bearings. This bare expanse of tarmac was intended as a playground. A see-saw and a set of swings with no ropes loomed ahead. I stepped carefully around a pit of sand, from which a dog ran suspiciously.

It was very quiet. About half of the windows of the flats that overlooked me were showing lights, but all, as they faced inwards, were curtained.

It was built in the form of a U, each floor delineated by a continuous balcony running around the full length of the three sides. There'd be a central entrance, with stairs, I decided, and headed that way. I was right. The lobby was gloomy and cold, the concrete stairs running upwards in both directions. I climbed slowly, the way lit on each landing by a tiny bulb trapped in a wire cage. Somewhere, echoing, a group of children were playing tag in the dark corners, but I caught no sight of them. I emerged on the fifth balcony. It ran past each front door. Communal living. Shadows moved at the far end, and there was a suppressed giggle.

I strolled the balcony looking for 69. Television sound rose and fell as I progressed. A light was on, somewhere in the back of 69, but with no sound from behind its door. I pressed the bell-push.

She peered out suspiciously, then clicked a light switch. The other way round would have been more sensible. She did not seem surprised to see me.

'If you wanted to see Neville,' she said, lacklustre and with indifference, 'he's gone. Half an hour ago.'

'Oh,' I said, 'what a pity.' I hadn't given him a thought. 'But perhaps you can help me, Lynne.'

'How can I?'

'Can we try?'

She backed off. The door faced five feet of balcony walkway and a three foot iron rail to the drop. It opened directly into a kitchen, to one side of it, and straight through into her living room. A tiny flat, a single person's unit they'd call it. The rear, uncurtained window stared out over a few miles of fields. The door in one wall no doubt led to her bedroom, but the bathroom door I hadn't seen.

She had it furnished sparsely but neatly, with conventional prints on the walls, and a row of paperbacks along the top of her low sideboard. Several plants graced surfaces where there was space. She had a two-seater settee and an easy chair, not matching, and a small, very old television set, probably mono. I couldn't see what I'd interrupted. No book lay face down; no knitting was tossed aside. I looked sideways at her, not making it obvious. Her hair was untidy and her eyes red. I saw what she'd been doing – she'd been crying.

She was flustered, gesturing in all directions. 'I'm sure I don't know . . . will you sit down?'

I tried the easy chair, which was not built for my width. She had not mentioned taking my motoring coat.

There was silence. I could hear the wind blustering against the window.

'I wasn't sure I'd see you again,' I told her. 'You're not really working at Viewlands now.'

'I call in . . . nothing else to do.'

'You haven't found another job?' Pretty well hopeless, I'd have thought.

She had taken a seat on the settee, her knees spread, her voluminous skirt in a hammock between them, her hands balled together in it.

'I haven't really looked,' she said. 'Carla was talking about putting in a word for me at the council offices, but it'd be a long drive.'

'You'd have to move.'

'She said she could fix that up.'

But the necessity for employment hadn't arisen until after Carla's death.

'You had a job, though, at that time.' Her eyes were empty. 'At Viewlands,' I prompted.

'I didn't think Gledwyn needed me any more.'

Now her eyes were wide, the eyebrows high, that square forehead puckered. I smiled, trying to lighten the mood.

'But if he needed anybody, it was surely you, Lynne.'

'You'd think he'd have told me, then,' she said sharply.

This was a reflection of what Neville had said, Gledwyn using her as a dishcloth, showing no appreciation. Yet now I knew more about Gledwyn, who'd been all prickly sensitivity. She couldn't mean it in the same way as Neville. If Gledwyn could've seen her now, he'd have winced. She looked dumpy and unattractive, sitting there like that, and lost.

'I'm sure he realised how much you did for him,' I said, as gently as I could.

'No!' she said defiantly. 'He'd send me away. "Lynne," he'd say, "what're you doing here at this time?" As though time mattered.'

It'd mattered on the evening Carla had died.

'You were too good to him.'

'He was a great man,' she burst out. 'A wonderful man.'

'But all the same, you were thinking of leaving him? Carla was helping you with that.'

'But he'd have been lost!' she cried. 'How could I walk out on him?'

'He'd have got somebody else.'

She bared her teeth, then suddenly flounced to her feet. 'I'll put the kettle on.' Women have a tendency to resort to the kettle.

'It's all right.'

'No.' And she marched into the kitchen.

I didn't follow her, simply raised my voice.

'Then it's Carla who'd have been disappointed.'

Silence. Then she appeared in the doorway, a teapot in her hand. 'It was only a suggestion – I was a bit low, and Gledwyn had been so difficult that day. I said to Carla I'd got half a mind to chuck it in. But she pounced on it. She was always so very forceful.' She pouted. 'Oh . . . once she got going, she walked right over you. Took charge. You know.'

And she disappeared again, and it was no good shouting over the rattling of cups. I waited. Carla kept coming into it; I couldn't reject her. Then Lynne came back carrying a tray.

She was now more animated, and the lines of her face were smooth. A woman always looks well, carrying in a tray. She was at once completely feminine, though if the slant of her eyes and the toss of her hair were anything like a recognition of my masculinity, I was sure it was subconscious.

'It was what Carla wanted to discuss,' she said, 'on the evening she was killed. To tell you the truth . . .' She gave a little pout and a pucker of her nose. '. . . that was one of the reasons I wasn't in too much of a hurry to get away from Viewlands. That and the fact that I was worried about him – it was such a terrible night. And by that time the new job was all Carla's idea, and I couldn't – just couldn't – tell her it'd only been a silly mood.' She looked at me innocently. 'Do you take sugar?'

Well . . . the minx! She'd told me so much in that casually thrown-out speech, and I couldn't decide whether it was cold-bloodedly intended. I'd noticed she'd been worried about

Gledwyn, that night, and hadn't referred to Neville. And while we were on the subject of that night . . .

'You were worried about Gledwyn, but you didn't see the Escort arrive?'

'I was in my office,' she reminded me, pouring tea.

'Not in the lab? Anxious because they were late, and peering out of one of the windows?' I took the cup from her, and she sat with hers, immediately asking: 'Would you care for a biscuit?'

'You didn't actually *see* it arrive?' I said it shaking my head.

'No. No, it stands to reason. Otherwise I'd have seen Neville in the car and I'd have shouted to him.' She nodded, satisfied with that. 'The first I knew they were back was when Gledwyn came into the office and threw the keys at the wall.'

'But then you'd know that Neville was outside,' I pointed out.

'I didn't know how long Gledwyn had been in the house, did I?'

'Well clearly, with his house keys still in his hand, he must have walked straight through.'

'Oh, you do go on about things,' she said in exasperation. 'He was angry. Upset and angry. I wasn't thinking about Neville.'

'No. Of course not.' Poor Neville outside, hungry and tired and dying for a smoke. 'So you didn't actually see the Escort, out there in the drive?'

'Haven't we talked about this? He'd have put it away, and I didn't hear him because I got on with the typing right away.'

'But now I've got the idea it wasn't put away at all.'

The tea remained untasted in her hands. 'Why should you say that?' She was suspicious.

'No need to get worried. It was just something Neville told me, about the mood *he* was in. He might well have got out his Metro without you hearing, but I don't think he put the Escort away.'

'If that's how you want it.'

'And it took you an hour to do the typing, you said. The re-typing of Gledwyn's speech.'

'Yes.'

'It was a long speech?'

'I was a bit upset. He'd been so . . . abrupt.'

'Yes. So the Escort stood out there for an hour.'

'I just don't understand what you're trying to say,' she appealed.

'And Neville would have left the ignition key in.'

'What *is* this?'

She put the cup and saucer down on the cushion beside her. It had begun to vibrate alarmingly, tea in the saucer. I held up a palm.

'It's just that I like to get a clear picture. The car key wasn't with Gledwyn's house keys, you see. I'm guessing that, because of the way Neville described him walking away from the Escort with his keys in his hand.'

'All right. So it wasn't.'

'And Gledwyn wouldn't have put it away in the garage if you were there to do it. He didn't even *try* to drive, you said.'

I'd been pushing on, trying to get to my point before she broke down into tears or fury. It's not a situation I enjoy.

But she was sitting up straight and prim, being very dignified and feminine, and she'd got a reserve I hadn't guessed at.

'I'm sure you're trying to make a point,' she told me. 'So please will you make it.'

'The Escort was sitting in the drive, with the ignition key in, for an hour. That's all.'

'It seems a lot of effort to decide that.'

'But you didn't see it when you drove out?'

'I wouldn't would I! I backed straight out and down the drive, looking over my shoulder.'

'Then who,' I asked, 'put it away later?'

'Oh, you are exasperating.'

'I mean, it wasn't still in the drive when you drove up, the next morning – Sunday – all upset because of Carla's death the previous evening, to take him to Blackpool.'

'It wasn't there. Why did you have to mention Carla's . . .'

'To make sure we know what evening we're talking about. You didn't answer my question.'

'It wasn't there,' she said impatiently. 'Gledwyn wasn't *helpless*, you know. He could do that much.'

'Thank you.'

She stared at me, expecting me to go on, but there was no more.

'And that's what you wanted to know?' she demanded.

'And to cadge a cup of tea. I was ready for it.'

'There's more in the pot.'

'Thank you, but I really ought to be moving. Perhaps I'll see you again? Can I phone you if I need your help? Are you on the phone?'

She got to her feet. The cup and saucer rattled. She gave me a number. 'Gledwyn had it put in. He'd phone any damned hour, and I'd go running like a ninny.' Her voice broke. Then she went on calmly. 'Phone if you like, but I don't seem to be much help.'

'Oh, you are, you are,' I said.

As I walked across the courtyard I looked up. She was a dark shadow leaning over the balcony railing, most dangerously I thought. I waved, but there was no response.

The route took me over the alternative road Angie had shown me, and past the scene of Carla's death, if I'd known just which bend she'd been parked around. It was late, getting on for ten, and I felt exhausted. As I approached the point where Angie had shown me the view I slowed, intending to stop a moment and try to spot the lights in the house, always a cheering sight after a long day. But there was a car parked there already, a head on a shoulder in the front seats as my headlights swept over it, so I drove on.

The house was dark and empty. I let myself into the caravan and lit up inside, then went to try the side door. Angie always left it open. Careless of her. I snapped on the kitchen light.

She'd left me a note. 'This came! What next? I can't sit waiting for you, Harry. Cook yourself something. Angie.'

'This' was an envelope lying beside her note. It had been torn open raggedly. I stared at it, hardly daring to look inside, regretting bitterly that I'd left, that morning, before the post delivery.

It had been posted in Whitchurch the previous evening. The address and Angie's name – but as Griffiths – was printed in ballpoint. Inside was a plain sheet of cheap paper, printed in the same hand.

WHY DONT You GET OUT, You BITCH.

YOUR FATHER /DIED AND SO CAN You.

What struck me at once was that the suggestion of a deliberate death for Angie was coupled with the death of her father. The inference was his death had also been deliberate. I was struck, too, by the insertion of the word DIED. A mistake is easily corrected in a thing like this by doing the whole note again. Perhaps this was a person unused to printing – or somebody very clever pretending to an uncertainty with capitals, when in fact he, or she, was very sure with them.

I waited. I brewed myself tea and smoked, and thought about the information Lynne had given me, whether consciously or unconsciously.

There was a car engine buzzing gently in the yard, a slammed door, voices. I was careful not to get up and look out of the window. Then she came in. No more the relaxed head I thought I'd seen on a shoulder, but blazing eyes and a purposeful stride.

'God, but he can be exasperating!' she said. She stared at me angrily, as though I was just as bad.

'The letter,' I reminded her tersely.

. She snatched at it. I caught her hand. Instinct, that was, thinking of fingerprints and handwriting analysis, though it was doubtful we'd ever get to that.

'Temper,' I said. 'Have you been discussing it with Evan?'

'I had to discuss it with somebody. You weren't around. Why is it that you're always missing . . .'

'There's tea in the pot. Might be stewed by now, though.'

She flopped herself down on a chair, fumbling for a cigarette, and I went to pour her a cup of tea. It was close to black. She didn't seem to notice.

'And what did Evan say?'

One shoulder moved. 'Something ridiculous – that I ought to leave.' She tried the tea and grimaced. 'At first.'

'And later?'

'He said he reckoned he could hang around and keep an eye open for me.'

'Protective.'

'I can look after myself.'

'Of course you can.'

She was silent. After a few moments she gave a wry twist of her lips, and glanced at me sideways with mischief.

'Well . . . I can.'

'Tell me,' I asked, 'who'd gain if you packed your bags and left?'

'Gain? How can there be gain? The person who'd buy this house, I suppose.'

'And Phil. Let's not forget Phil.'

'Are you seriously suggesting –'

'Of course not. I just thought I'd remind you that Phil's involved.'

'If they think they're going to chase me away . . .'

'Or perhaps it's simply hatred. Somebody who feels they'll be happier if you're dead.'

Her eyes were bleak. 'You're a great help!' she snapped. Then she flapped her palm on the table, but the little laugh she gave was in itself a slap. 'Sorry. I'm being stupid. Of *course* you're being a help. Don't you see what this really means? It means that daddy *was* killed. You can't get round it. Whatever it is you're doing, they don't like it.'

I nodded. 'I don't like it either.' I cleared my throat. 'When Evan told you you'd have to leave – you were angry?'

'He knows me better than to suggest such a thing.'

'But you were angry.'

'I was furious.'

'But of course, he wasn't serious. As you said, he knows you better than that. Probably nobody knows you better than Evan.' I cocked an eye at her, then blew down my pipe.

'You're getting at something,' she said dangerously.

'I asked who gains if you leave. Perhaps it's the other way round – who gains if you stay. And who, knowing you so well, would realise that a message like that would make you even more determined to stay . . .'

'You're crazy.'

'And take it one stage further back, and ask yourself: who gained by your father's death? It brought you back home here, and it's brought Evan running – to lend a hefty shoulder.'

'How dare you!'

'And just when I might be heading for something that'd send you back to good old Phil . . .'

She was on her feet, pointing at the door. 'You can just get out of my house . . . off my property . . .'

I stood and considered her calmly. My, but she had a temper.

'It's your own fault. You want me to prove your father was

killed, but it hasn't got to be by anybody you like. Your trouble is that you like everybody.'

You can't stand for ever with your arm outstretched. She lowered it. 'You can go off people.'

'And vice versa. I was leaving, anyway, so don't fret. Things to do, something to look into.'

'You're determined, aren't you!'

'It's not finished, is it! And . . . I was going to ask you, Angie. Could you find me a key to the garage door? It's a new car, and I'd like to lock it away.'

'Well . . .' On an outward breath of exasperation, that was. She stared at me a moment, and I'll swear that humour crept into her eyes. 'What is there to look into?'

'I've found out, from Lynne, that the Escort was out on the drive for a full hour, with the keys in, on the Saturday that Neville brought your father back from seeing Paul at Aberystwyth.'

She frowned, perhaps at the mention of her brother's name. 'What of it?'

'That was the evening that Lynne's friend, Carla, was killed by a hit-and-run driver.'

She turned away abruptly, I'll swear so that she wouldn't have to consider the idea. Then she began searching in the back of the cupboard, and came up with a jingling bunch. There must have been a dozen keys on it. She was grimacing.

'He kept them all together. Most of these are for drawers in the lab. Here, I think this is it. Better try it on the way out.' She detached it, and handed it over.

I suddenly realised how exhausted she appeared. 'I'll be about an hour.'

'Does it have to be now?'

I gestured to the letter on the table. 'That makes it a bit urgent.'

'Give me a minute to get a jacket or something.'

'I'm going alone.'

Big eyes watched me. 'Because it's dangerous?'

'Shouldn't be.'

'I couldn't rest. Give me a minute.'

Then she was gone, clattering up the stairs, exhaustion shaken off with the same ease as her anger.

I went out into the yard and tried the key in the garage door lock. There was a T-handle four feet from the ground, with the cylinder lock in its centre. The key slipped in easily enough, but when I tried it the cylinder went round and round, and nothing happened. No click as the latch slipped back. I tried the handle. It turned, and when I heaved it the door went up and over as smooth as you like.

The lock had been broken. Put a bit of tube over one end of the handle, and you can snap that kind of lock easily. So much for the key! I slipped it into my pocket as she came running into the yard, leaving the side door wide open.

There was no point in telling her about the garage door lock. She'd ask me what it signified, and I didn't know.

After a minute, she said: 'This way again, Harry? It's beginning to give me the creeps.'

'The quickest way into town.'

A dark, nearly-deserted town again, but this time with dry cobbles. I went straight on through, turned up past the police station, and on towards Cadwell's quarry. I wasn't sure of my ability at climbing gates, but I needed to see the wreckage of that Escort again.

'The torch is in your side,' I said.

As I'd previously observed, there was very little activity towards the upper end of the street. The small row of terraced houses seemed to have been abandoned, and only scraps of paper chased around the concrete of the deserted petrol station. The chapel lay silent, apart from the flap of a sheet of corrugated iron in the wind.

We approached the quarry. I switched to sidelights, feeling ridiculously theatrical, but after all I was about to commit an offence. I was still close enough to being a copper to be concerned about that.

The crashing sound was so rhythmic that at first I thought I'd lost a main bearing or something. But then, twenty yards short of Cadwell's gate, I realised it was external. I cut lights and engine with one movement, and slid on the handbrake, holding off the ratchet.

The noise was coming from inside the scrapyard. I whispered, 'Torch!' She slid it into my hand. I clasped her arm, restraining her. 'No sound,' I sighed into her ear. I eased open the door and slid out into the night.

The gate consisted of vertical iron rods set at four inch gaps, with a diagonal strainer to each half. A chain and the massive padlock secured them, and both were intact. To climb it was easy; you simply worked up diagonally on one of the strainers, then jumped clear of the spikes. It meant an eight foot drop, but that was a minor consideration.

I peered through the bars. Over by where I'd examined the Escort there was a faint light, breaking the shadowy mass into accents of jagged metal. A shape was swinging an object – which had to be a sledgehammer – high into the air, catching a gleam, then pounding down onto the Escort. Somebody was trying to destroy the wreck.

I got to within two feet of the top before I dropped the torch. It clattered down the other side, unfortunately timed for an upstroke, and thus in a period of silence. The silence extended into a pause. I'd stand out against the sky. There was a clang when the sledgehammer was dropped, and a flicker of dancing light as the lamp was swooped up. I plunged my feet into the painful angles between strainer and rods, almost ran up the last few, and hurled myself over. I felt and heard the lining of my jacket tear as it caught on the spikes. It flung me off balance, and I fell on hands and knees painfully. I groped for the torch, found it, but it failed to respond to the switch. I turned, and began to run towards the Escort.

Already the light was dancing towards the rear of the banked wrecks, the clatter of pounding feet dying away. He was heading around to the left. I stopped, and remained still. He had no way out but the gate. I had him trapped. Now all I had to do was trace him by sound, and wait for him. Slowly, my ears doing a radar act as my head swung, I backed towards the gate. A yard, stop, listen. No sound now. Was he prepared to wait me out? A yard, stop, listen. The silence became oppressive. Yet he could do nothing, unless there was a graded ascent to the vertical sides, which I hadn't seen in daylight. I backed and stood still, and heard nothing until Angie's scream brought my head up.

'Harry!'

It was the last thing I heard until I struggled up from the darkness to hear myself whimpering with pain. I got myself to my knees, making myself stop, but the whimpering appeals continued, and something was tugging at my jacket.

Angie was lying full-length on the ground, her arms stretched between the bars, reaching for my jacket and trying to drag my dead weight towards her. I blinked at her. Blinding lights shattered the image. She took my hand through the bars, steadying me as I hauled myself upright. My left hand went to the back of my head. There was no stickiness.

'I'm all right,' I heard myself say.

She was almost sobbing. 'You didn't move.'

'You saw it?'

'I heard you cry out.'

Had I? I'd been knocked out before. Had I always cried out, and not known it?

'Did you see him?' My brain felt sluggish. There was something I should have been realising. Yes – he must have climbed over the gate. 'Did you see who it was?' I repeated, more hopefully.

'Harry,' she whispered, 'I was down on my knees, trying to reach you. I didn't look.'

I groaned, not at her failure to watch my assailant climbing over and running away, but that she'd been there, on her knees, only feet from him. And I'd thought there'd be no danger!

'Can you get back?' she asked anxiously.

'Not yet.'

She thought I meant I couldn't make it – which wasn't far wrong. 'You're hurt!' she moaned.

But I'd climbed that gate for a purpose, and it wasn't accomplished. I reassured her quickly. 'There might be another torch in the car. Will you look for it, Angie?'

'You *are* infuriating.'

'Please.'

While she was looking, I felt my foot knock against something. I reached down. It was the sledgehammer. My assailant had been so considerate as to belt me with the wooden handle! The head of it would have cracked my skull like an egg.

'Will this do?'

It was her own little pocket torch from her handbag. It would have to do. I thanked her, and stumbled over to the Escort.

One flash of the torch confirmed my complete theory. The attack with the sledgehammer had been on the nearside front wing. Bright, lacerated metal was reflected in the weak little light. I crouched in front of it, my pain repressed by the excitement.

The headlight had been destroyed completely in the crash, and the wing buckled. But the recent attack on it had broken free a mass of black, crumbly material, which came away now in chunks in my fingers. The do-it-yourself fanatics use a resin-bonded paste to repair bodywork damage. When this is subjected to heat it bubbles and flames into a nasty tarry mess.

Satisfied, I pursued the idea. Colours were difficult to detect in such conditions, and as I've explained, my colour sight isn't too good. But that's on blues and reds. Here and there I could see that traces of the body finish still remained in crevices and indentations. I reached out my penknife and detached two flakes of red paint, and put them in an envelope. There should also be some green. I laid them on my white envelope – three bits of green. And then I looked again. I shone the torch closer. There were, to my eyes, two different greens, not much in it, but just discernible. To make sure, I hunted out two more tiny bits of green, so fragile I had to balance them on the blade of my knife to tip them into the envelope. I put it inside my pocket, and straightened.

Greatly heartened, with no thought for my throbbing head, I made for the gate, retrieved my damaged torch, and climbed over with rather less agility than before, though now with a hand to help me down. I wondered at the strength of Angie's arm, turned, and found myself face to face with Sergeant Timmis.

'Breaking and entering, Mr Kyle?' he asked stolidly.

'I haven't broken anything,' I claimed. 'Entered, yes. But I paid a pound for looking at that car, and I only had a few pence worth.'

I didn't mention that I was taking away a few flakes of paint, which could be worth a great deal. That, I supposed, made it burglary. Even grand larceny.

There was some jocular discussion about charging me, but his heart wasn't in it. If he'd witnessed the attack on me, surely he'd have arrested my assailant, so I didn't mention it. There might or might not be fingerprints on that handle, but police intervention I didn't want at that stage.

We said good night. Angie insisted on driving us back. She then insisted on settling me onto a chair in the kitchen and applying a cold compress to my head.

'But it's only a lump!' I protested.

She decided I should spend the night in her father's room, which was the big one at the back I'd already strayed into, but there I asserted myself. She was talking about keeping an eye on me. Oh no. That I wouldn't be able to stand.

I groped out to the caravan, trying not to betray my double-vision.

11

My eyes were still troublesome over breakfast, but the head was feeling better. No skin had been broken, and the bump was going down. I was aware that I ought to hunt out a hospital and have checks made for concussion, but I said nothing about it. I had an idea I wouldn't be able to spare the time.

Carefully calculated to help finish the coffee, Neville Green decided to pay a courtesy call. Had I commented critically on the fact that he hadn't visited Angie? I couldn't remember. He'd met the postman at the gate, and brought in three letters. One of them had Angie's name and address on it, and printed in a style I recognised. It had been posted again in Whitchurch.

'Bet you're surprised to see me,' he said, smiling in a set way that indicated strain. 'Just popped in on my way to Whitchurch.'

My head gave a thump. Angie was clattering away at the sink, carefully ignoring the letter that lay on the table. I'd seen her flinch at it. She had not welcomed Neville with any eagerness.

He was dressed with the same casual expensiveness as I'd noticed before, and moved around the kitchen with an air of belonging that I found irritating. Angie remembered her manners.

'You should have called before, Neville.' Not chiding him, but lightly, as though she'd have been glad to see him.

'You know how it is . . .' He shrugged, accepted a cup of coffee, and sat with the letters under his nose. 'But I've come now.'

'You wouldn't have a specific reason?' I asked.

'Wanted to see how you were getting along.'

'We manage,' said Angie.

'And frankly,' he admitted, with one of his challenging grins, 'I was wondering if anybody's mentioned the records.'

We stared at him. He raised his eyebrows. 'Uncle Gledwyn's

jazz collection,' he amplified. 'He did say I could have them, me being the only one who appreciated them, sort of.'

'I haven't even heard of them!' Angie burst out.

I glanced at her. It was not a subject that required that tone of near-hysteria, but the incongruity of it probably shocked her.

'Old seventy-eights,' he explained. 'Priceless now. Some Coleman Hawkins, and a lot of the Duke's that're unique. Some others, too.'

'Well,' said Angie, recovering. 'You're quite welcome to come along and look them out. When you like. But not now.'

He nodded. 'Thanks. No time now, anyway.' He glanced at his watch, but made no move to leave.

I waited a minute. He stirred his coffee. Then I asked: 'There was something else?'

His eyes glinted at me, then down. 'It's Lynne. Tell you the truth.'

'What about her?'

'She's not well.'

'What d'you mean by not well?'

'Last night – damn it, she's usually full of life. But she didn't want to go out, didn't want to talk, or go to my place and play a few tracks. You know. In the end . . . well, we had a bit of a row, if you want to know, and I walked out. This was round at her place.' His eyes met mine. 'Have you seen the dump?'

'I've seen it.'

It was what he'd been angling to hear. The spoon clattered, and suddenly he looked tensely violent. 'I guessed it! She wouldn't say. You've been talking to her. What've you been telling her about me?'

You have to maintain a placid tone for this sort of thing. I smiled to help it along. 'Nothing, I assure you. I don't know anything about you that she doesn't already. Did she tell you I did?'

'It was all there could be. What else is there?' He got to his feet, cup in hand, and gulped down his coffee. 'It's been going on for months, colder and colder, and I can't get through to her. Damn it, I thought it was the job, here, getting her down. I thought when . . . when it finished she'd come round. Oh Christ, I dunno. I dunno a thing.'

'If,' I pointed out, 'it's been going on for a long while, why blame me?'

He stared at me. A struggle was engaged behind his eyes, and then he won through. He grinned at me, and the little boy showed through. 'You know me.' He ran a hand over his hair. 'I've gotta find somebody to blame.'

Then he looked round, nodded vaguely, and marched out into the yard.

'Jazz records?' said Angie. 'It's the first I've heard of them,' and I'd swear she hadn't taken in a word of Neville's outburst.

I was already slitting open the envelope. A plain sheet of paper again, and plain, uncompromising printing.

WHY DON'T YOU SEND THAT NOSY
BASTARD AWAY BEFORE HE DYES.

I heard Angie gasp from behind my shoulder, but I was too busy sorting out impressions to pay much attention to her.

If my assailant of the night before was the author of these notes – and it would be a coincidence if he wasn't – he'd have issued the threat, by posting it, before the opportunity presented itself, but in practice he'd been careful not to kill me. That was the first thought. Then I noticed we'd got the apostrophe in don't, this time. Being accurate. But not so good with DYES. Strange, that. He'd faltered on DIED in the first one, DYES in the second. There was a psychological block there, and the realisation sent little prickles running down my spine. We were probably dealing with someone to whom death had been a traumatic experience. Who else, then, but a murderer?

I didn't point this out to Angie, mainly because there were faults in the logic. She gave a short, broken laugh, and said there we were then, and perhaps I'd better make myself scarce.

'Would you care for a look round the shops?' I asked. 'I was rather thinking of Shrewsbury.' I'd need a town as large as that.

I'd slipped the letter into my inside pocket, the sun was

slanting through the kitchen window, and Angie grabbed at it like a lifeline.

'Oh yes!' she cried. 'It's going to be a lovely day, and I must start thinking about a winter coat.'

We did a cross-country run towards Welshpool, and cut across through Llandrinio and Coedway. The weather helped, and Angie, who'd been showing signs of tension before we set out, had it all in control by the time I found a parking space in Shrewsbury. She'd smoothed out into relaxed chatter, and only once or twice, when I caught a brief glimpse of her eyes, did I feel any uneasiness.

We found somewhere we could meet up, and I left her. Shrewsbury was a strange town for me, apart from that appointment café I'd used for Phil, and I had to search around a little before I found one of those car accessory and do-it-yourself places.

They had a rack of motor vehicle spray paints in cans, in every conceivable colour. They had a list hanging on the corner of the shelving, from which, knowing the make and year of your car, you can select the correct colour. I looked up Ford, then green, then Escort, and the year, which I knew to be 1972. There was only one green listed: Fern Green (Met).

I'd never done any touch-up spraying, but I'd heard you run through the first can just practising the distance and the movement of your hand. I bought a can. The lid was coated with the same colour as the contents, a not very vivid green.

I managed to meet up with Angie, but unfortunately too early, and had to trail round the shops she'd missed. But I had recourse to my thoughts to lessen the strain.

'I've bought the smartest winter coat you ever did see,' she told me, and there was some discussion on flyaway collars and things like that. I peered into the carrier bag I was holding, fingering aside the tissue paper. The coat was green, not too different from the can in my pocket. 'You'll love it,' she said, as though I'd be around to form an opinion.

'I'm sure.'

Lunch in Shrewsbury; I was beginning to wish we hadn't got to drive away and home to Viewlands – and trouble. But I kept my mind on the job by phoning Lynne from there and asking her if she'd run over around three and help me in the lab with something I had in mind. She sounded depressed and cold at first, but then seemed to perk up at the thought of something useful she could do, and said she'd be there.

I mentioned this when we got back. Angie hesitated, then said:

'I wish you wouldn't encourage her.'

I was dumping bags on the kitchen table. 'Oh? Why not?'

'She's been grabbing at any paltry excuse for coming here. Moons around in the lab, and there's absolutely nothing for her to do. She's only upsetting herself.'

'I've got a job for her. That's what makes her happy.'

She shrugged, and went off to change. It appeared there'd been no word from Evan, and I wondered whether he'd returned to his duties at the University.

But he had not. Perhaps he'd been perched high in a tree with binoculars, but certainly he made an early appearance, bouncing into the kitchen and standing with his hands on his hips, looking very uncertain of his reception.

'She'll be down in a minute,' I said.

'It's you I want to see.'

Liar, I thought. 'I'm here.'

He looked even more uneasy, not sure of me even when I was trying to be encouraging. 'I wanted to know if there've been any more threats.' Looking up under his shaggy eyebrows. 'You can be sure *she'll* never tell me.'

'It's all right. It's me who's threatened this time.'

He didn't know whether to smile or be heavily sympathetic. The smile won. 'Oh . . . I'm sorry.'

He didn't ask what I was threatened with. Perhaps he didn't want to hear the word death. Or maybe he didn't even like to write dies, spell it how you like.

I wandered out to put away the Rover. Having a garage was still a luxury that I liked to indulge in. I backed it in and got out. There was room and to spare. Then, my intention being to use the end door to get into the lab, I slammed down the up-and-over door from inside. It presented me with a plain surface, which gave me an idea. I retrieved my spray-can from the car, put on the light, and read the instructions. I shook it vigorously for two minutes, as instructed. After that, you have difficulty finding the reserve energy to press the button.

Not only had I never done any car spraying, I'd not even tried spray-can graffiti. My life was an unfulfilled void. So I tried it.

You hold the can only a foot away. In large, smug and self-satisfied bliss, I wrote my first exercise in graffiti. Graffito, I suppose, as it was singular.

To my disappointment, when it dried I could hardly see it. The inside of the garage door and the walls were painted green, and a shade not far from the one I was using. Seeking a better surface to deface, I strolled into the lab, just as one of the doors into the yard was flung open.

Angie stood there, Evan at her shoulder looking very close to scared. Angie's eyes were wild, and her gestures uncontrolled.

'There's no jazz!' she cried. 'No jazz at all.'

Evan shrugged expressively. I walked towards them.

'I've been looking through all daddy's records,' she burst out, reaching out a hand. 'There's not one. No seventy-eights at all. Oh . . . Harry!'

That she used my Christian name with such familiarity in front of Evan gave me a feeling of responsibility, and the sick realisation that her self-sufficiency was receiving a battering.

'They need not be there,' I said quietly. 'An attic, or . . .'

She clutched at Evan's arm. 'We'll search the attic.'

'But more likely he invented it,' I assured her. 'An excuse. He wanted to talk about Lynne, but for all his outspokenness he's shy.'

'I can't believe that.'

'You should. But don't get upset about it. Go and take a walk through the orchard, or something.'

She eyed me uncertainly, but Evan drew her away. He spoke to her quietly, but I noticed she kept her distance from him as they crossed the yard.

When I turned, still in search of a useful surface, Lynne was standing at the far end of the lab. She'd coasted in the Fiesta quietly, and let herself into her office. I suddenly realised what a basically quiet young woman she was, even withdrawn.

'What did Neville say to you about me?' she asked, frowning.

'Oh dear, how suspicious everybody is.' I took her arm and led her into the centre of the lab. 'He was worried about you, Lynne. Don't you know what his feelings are?'

She gently prised herself free. 'Neville's a fool, I've told him that. I don't like him discussing our affairs with strangers.'

'Am I a stranger?'

'All the same . . . he's got no right. I never promised him anything.'

'We didn't discuss promises and intentions – he demanded to know what I'd told you about him. I think he might've punched me on the nose, given a bit of encouragement.'

I grinned at her. My nose had been punched before, and shows it. My face has a generally battered appearance, and I was probably more experienced than Neville in nose-thumping. She smiled back, showing teeth I hadn't seen before.

'Oh, I'd love to see him try.' Then she was at once efficient. 'But you wanted me for something . . .'

'Ah . . . yes. Something I could never manage on my own. I'm sure you could do it in your sleep. I've got some little scraps of paint. What I'd like you to do is put 'em under one of these instruments and check the colours for me.'

'Little scraps?'

I'd noticed sheets of white card around, and now laid one out on the bench. I produced my envelope and shook out my scraps of paint. Two red, five green.

'Those.'

She stood and stared down at them. One had split up, and there were now three red.

'Where did you get these?' It was a very small voice.

'Don't worry your head about that. What I'd like is for you to classify them, all neatly like a scientific experiment, and perhaps mounted or something, as a record.'

'A record of what?'

'Call them evidence, if you like.'

She did not raise her head. I had to listen carefully to catch her words. 'You'll have to tell me what they're from.'

'Though of course, if you'd rather not do it – Evan Rees is around somewhere. I'm sure he'd know what to do.'

'I don't want him touching my instruments!'

'Of course not.' I made an unconcerned operation out of filling my pipe and moved a few feet away. 'Which instrument will you use?'

Prompted by her reaction, I was deliberately giving her the opportunity to destroy them in some way, sweep them from the desk and grind them underfoot perhaps. It was a risk, but I'd judged her accurately. When I turned she was staring at me, her face expressionless, but with no sullen look to match the voice she'd been using.

'I'll get the mounting adhesive,' she said, and she walked off into her office.

There was a little window between the lab and the office. I could see her moving beyond it, taking more time than necessary. She returned, carrying her equipment. I said nothing as she drew a stool up to the bench and slid, without realising it, into a professional intensity of concentration that must have been worth a fortune to Gledwyn. She was mounting each piece of paint, using tweezers as delicately as a brain surgeon's scalpel, on little plaques of white plastic. She glanced up at me, her mouth in a wry smile.

'How do I label them?'

'Red one, red two, red three and so on.'

'All from the same source?' There was efficiency in her voice, but she was still probing.

'Put: ESCORT underneath. In capitals.'

Her body was still, but the tweezers vibrated like a tuning fork. Her voice was very low. 'These are from Gledwyn's car?'

'That is so.' Gravely formal.

'You should have said.'

'Would it have made any difference? Does it upset you to handle tiny bits of his car?'

'No. Nothing like that. I just . . . didn't want to get involved with all this . . . he's dead, gone . . . why do you have to rake around . . .'

I waited, lighting my pipe laboriously. There always seems to come a time when you become aware that vital information is being concealed. Sometimes it's possible to wait, and allow it to emerge in its own time. Sometimes there's more urgency, and you have to put on the pressure. I'd deliberately set up the scene, knowing what the answers would be, but something very strange was restraining Lynne, and the pressure had to be stronger. I felt lousy.

'It's a matter of how his death came about,' I said.

'You know how!' Her upturned face was red. 'It was an accident.'

'Then . . . why? Shouldn't we know why he had the accident?'

She spoke stubbornly to the bench. 'I don't know what you're saying.' And she returned to her task, clearly not expecting me to continue the discussion.

Gradually her hands lured her into relaxation. She loved to use them. She got up from the bench.

'I think we'll use the Lovibond,' she said chattily. 'The Burnham-Wright's really for portable work. You take the instrument to the job.'

She plugged in the Lovibond. I caught a splash of brilliant white light, then I moved to her shoulder and got a closer introduction to this instrument. It was a square box with an eyepiece in one corner and a set of nine slider controls on the top to operate the filters. From the left side there were two flexible tubes that led to a little feeler. She told me the tubes were optic fibres, and the feeler was in fact the viewer. She adjusted the two light-intensity controls on the top. She placed the viewer on the sample on the bench, put her eye to the eyepiece, and began juggling the levers at the top.

'He was always talking about getting a spectrophotometer,' she said, 'but they're very expensive. This is more fun, though.'

Fun? 'One thing I just don't understand,' I said. 'Cast your mind back to the night Neville brought him back from Aberystwyth.'

'This one's easy,' she said, eye well down, voice muffled. 'A bright red.' She consulted a notebook from the drawer. 'I make it 2R 10/4 on the Munsell scale.'

'The night Carla died,' I reminded her.

She glanced up. 'If I'd been able to leave earlier . . .'

'Try another red.'

'Why are we talking about Carla?'

'To remind you of the night we're talking about.'

'I'm not talking about it. I don't ever want to remember that night.'

'I wanted you to remember the night Gledwyn got home from his visit to Paul. Try another red. Now . . . wait.'

I caught her by the arm before she could get too far, and levered her persuasively back onto the stool. She was protesting.

'You ask me to do something for you, then you deliberately upset me.'

'I'm sorry about that. It wasn't anything upsetting I was going to ask.'

She sat. She placed the viewing head on one of the other reds. 'Go on then, ask.'

'You told me he tore up his speech and stormed out,' I said to her bent head. 'And you set to and re-typed it for him.'

'This red's the same.' She marked it up.

'But that wasn't quite true, was it?'

'I'm sure I don't know what you're talking about.'

'You said he came back in an hour. That's a bit presumptuous of him, isn't it! That really is a bit much, assuming you'd do it again, and not even looking in and saying, "Sorry Lynne," or anything.'

'He might've done that,' she murmured, 'and I didn't hear.'

'That's possible of course. But if I'd been you, I'd have been very annoyed, and I'd have bounced out and driven away.'

'I *was* upset.'

'And bounced out?'

'Well, if you must know,' she said angrily, 'I just walked out of my side door, banged off the light, and sat in the car crying for a bit.' She was looking at me with pitiful defiance.

'I'm not surprised,' I said with sympathy. 'And then you changed your mind?'

Her face puckered. 'The damn car wouldn't start. I'd over-choked it or something. So I sat and cursed, and *then* came back in and did the typing. So . . . you see . . .' Her grimace was almost mischievous. 'If he'd shouted he was sorry, that's why I didn't hear him.'

'The other red?'

'No point, is there? I'll do a green.'

'But the snag is,' I said, 'that if he'd looked in to apologise he'd have seen your office dark through that little window, and if it wasn't during the time you were trying to start the car it would be quiet, and he'd assume you'd gone home.'

She threw one of the plaques across the lab. I retrieved it. It was one of the reds.

'You trapped me into that,' she stormed.

'Into what? Into admitting he might've thought you'd gone home?'

'It's not fair.'

It was not, I'll admit. I'd had years of practice, and I'd been aiming for circumstances I'd deduced had to be there.

'Try the green,' I suggested.

'Do it yourself.'

'Can I be trusted with your lovely Lovibond?'

'Oh . . . you make me mad.'

As she bent her eye to the eyepiece again, I said: 'But why should you be mad? All you've told me is that he could've thought you'd gone home. Is that so terrible?'

'This one's different. It's a metallic colour.'

'Though of course,' I conceded, pretending to give it thought, 'there'd have been no reason for him to come back an hour later, if he believed you'd gone home.'

But she was not to be drawn. 'Munsell didn't allow for metallic colours,' she explained. 'This was eighty years ago that he did all his work. Perhaps they didn't have metallic colours then.'

'Perhaps the car industry invented them,' I agreed. 'Like they invented bumpers.' But she'd withdrawn into a deliberately stubborn mood. 'Do your best with it, there's a good girl.'

She consulted her notebook again. 'Then I'd classify it as 7G 4/5.'

'Try another.'

She sighed dramatically, and did it. 'It's the same.'

'Then . . . the next.'

'There's no point.'

'Please.'

She placed the viewing head on the third green. This time she was longer. Frowning, she consulted her notebook. 'It's the same metallic green,' she said, 'but it's higher on the value scale. Say 7G 6/5.'

'Which means – to me?'

'It's a fraction lighter.'

'Try the other two, then.'

They came out at 7G 6/5 as well.

She sat, one leg half off the stool, her frown so intense it shadowed her eyes. 'What does it mean?' she whispered.

'A poor match, perhaps. Here, try this.'

I'd thought of a distraction. There was no harm now in demonstrating to her a theory I'd now discarded. I made a joke of it, because she was deeply shaken. She was watching me agitate my spray can again. I snapped off the cap and sprayed the wall behind her, assuming she could reach it with the viewing head. As I watched, it dried, and seemed to disappear, just as in the garage. At my obvious expression of dismay she gave a choked little laugh.

'Silly,' she cried. 'We sprayed the wall 5G 5/5. It's not much different.'

'Good Lord, is that how the scientific mind works? Most people would paint their woodwork in apple green, but you people do it in 5G 5/5. You walk into the paint shop and say: "I want a gallon of 5G 5/5, please." How amazing.'

She sighed. Suddenly she'd had enough of it, and looked exhausted. With both hands she swept back the hair that had fallen forward when she crouched over the eyepiece. 'It was one of his experiments, oh, two years ago. The effect of colour on the environment. Psychological.'

She gestured to a row of cupboards along the end of the lab, and I walked over and opened the doors. There were hundreds of screw-top jars of coloured pigments, in powder form, each one labelled with its basic Munsell rating. All began with the number five, followed by one of the ten basic codes, R, YR, Y, GY, and so on, and then a variation of the theme of the series 2/2 to 9/12.

'We could mix anything we liked from that. He bought gallons of base and thinners – there's still a lot of cans left – and he came up with some beauties. Once or twice it nearly drove us crazy. *Me* crazy, rather. It didn't worry Gledwyn, of course. This on the wall now is the last one we tried. Then he lost interest.' She sighed. 'We went on to something else.'

It seemed to me that I now had confirmation of what I'd theorised. 'I really am grateful,' I told her.

'But what does it mean?' She was off the stool now, plucking at my sleeve.

'I was checking on the Escort's colours. I'm afraid it means it was re-sprayed, Lynne.'

'But we *knew* that. It was green, and it was re-sprayed red.'

'I didn't quite mean that. It shows – what you've told me – that the one wing, the nearside front, was re-sprayed green again. Recently.'

She leaned back against the bench. All colour had drained from her face. She tried to smile, probably in contempt and dismissal, but it didn't come off. 'How can you possibly know that, from what I've said?'

'The fact that you got readings for two slightly different greens. The light green bits are from the original and the darker green from a recent re-spray, just a fraction wrong.'

I was walking towards her office, forcing her to tag along with me. I wanted her to draw the obvious conclusion. I was not sure I could handle her distress, so I hoped she'd do it later.

But she saw it straight away, plunking down on her office chair, her eyes staring and her clenched fists on her knees.

'You're telling me that the Escort was the car that killed Carla!' she said, choking on the idea.

'It does seem like it. Particularly as there're signs on the wreck that repair work's been done on that wing. Probably a headlamp shell was put in, and then the wing was repaired and re-sprayed.' I sighed. 'Green,' I added, 'but just a fraction wrong.'

She buried her face in her hands. 'Oh dear God,' she whispered.

All I could think of was tea. I'm not much use with distressed females. 'I'll put the kettle on . . .'

She was at once on her feet, all flame and fury. 'And all you can think about is bloody tea!' she shouted.

Then she slammed out of her side door, and for a few moments I thought she'd over-choked her car again, but it spluttered and caught and she revved it high, scraping into reverse and backing out as though I was chasing her. Or something else was.

Worried, I went and tossed the spray-can into my car, and found them in the long sitting room. More drama. Phil had phoned, and unfortunately Evan had answered it. There'd been a coolness, even when Angie took over from him, and though there was now silence in the room, apart from Mahler on low volume, it was the silence of inward strife. Angie was flipping through a magazine, Evan standing staring out of the window.

Still on the same theme, I said: 'Anybody ready for a spot of tea?'

Evan pounced on the idea eagerly, as though it triggered something. 'Is it that time? I really ought to be off.'

Angie raised her head. 'Should you, Evan? If you say so.'

And he left, with a weak smile for me. I wondered, later, what Phil had said to him.

It turned out to be one of those evenings. I could barely sit still, with my mind churning ideas around – dying to express them to somebody, and not daring – and trying not to allow Angie to realise. I caught her eyes on me from time to time, worry in them. She had the brooding uncertainty of a young lady poised between decisions, barely restraining herself from dashing out and across to the Rees farm, and probably, thereby, burning a few bridges.

At around eight, Paul phoned. He'd obviously been reconsidering his situation, having heard that the chair of Philosophy had gone to a Dr Wright of Oxford, and invited himself plus Rena for a visit.

'They're coming tomorrow evening,' declared Angie, in a tone of despair and desperation.

'He can't eat you.'

But it worried her for too long, and I couldn't shake her out of it. She went up to her room early, and distracted herself by trying on her new coat. Women's therapy. I was half asleep on the settee when she came tripping down. 'Trala! What d'you think?'

As though it mattered what I thought! I made admiring noises, but didn't give her the truth. However she came, that was fine with me. But perhaps I stared. It seemed to please her, anyway, and off she went to take it off.

Green. I sat, eyes out of focus. The thought gradually crystallised, and I dashed out into the hall and dialled Lynne's number.

It rang a dozen times before she picked it up. 'Yes?'

'It's Harry Kyle. I wanted to ask you something unpleasant. I'm sorry.'

Her voice was thin and toneless. 'Then ask it, and get it over.'

'On the night Carla died, Lynne, what colour coat or costume or whatever was she wearing?'

I could hear her breathing. It was irregular.

'Lynne?'

'It was . . . it was green.'

The last word faded as she removed the phone from her ear. I thought she was sobbing. 'Lynne, Lynne,' I called.

At last she came back, her voice empty. 'Is that all?'

'Are you alone?' I asked, worried for her.

'I can't say any more.'

'Are you alone?' I repeated intensely, but the phone was already buzzing in my ear.

I replaced it, got the dialling tone again, and dialled Phil's flat. Fortunately, he was home.

'I've got to see you,' I said.

'Harry . . . if you only knew . . .'

'Tomorrow. I've got to talk to you.'

'I'm up to my neck . . .'

'It's a bloody Sunday,' I snapped impatiently. 'You're entitled to a break, so give yourself one.'

But all the same he couldn't make it until the evening. We arranged to meet in the pub on the square in Llanmawr, the Mitre. I'd impressed him with the importance of it, but I was annoyed with him by the time I hung up. He wanted to get his priorities right, I thought.

I'd got it all, the full story, and I didn't like one word of it.

12

Sunday, for me, was very difficult, because I didn't want Angie to know what I was thinking. So I had to look busy, and intent on momentous discovery.

The day was fine, and over breakfast she said she'd take out the gelding for an hour. We hadn't thought of looking in the hall, there being no post delivery, but when I wandered through, wondering whether to drive down to town for a paper, there it was.

There was no stamp and no postmark, the envelope having been delivered by hand in the night, but all the same the identical name and address was printed on. It was almost as though the intention had been to post it, but urgency had dictated an earlier hand delivery.

'We've got another,' I called out cheerfully, walking back into the kitchen.

This sort of thing loses its effect from sheer repetition. If you want to make an impact with threats you have to do something about it, or at least show a potential. A rain of threats is futile.

IF You Do NOT LEAVE AT ONCE IT WILL BE THE END FOR BoTH OF You.

This time he'd avoided the use of death or die in any form. It was to be our end. It was pathetic. Angie even managed a weak little laugh. I said: 'What about this riding you mentioned?' and managed to sound quite cheerful.

I watched for a while as she cantered round the paddock, then Evan rode in from the field beyond on a big black stallion and made mock jeering sounds, which caused Angie to meet the challenge. With wild shouts they rode off into the valley. I've never been on a horse.

All the same, not displeased with the distraction for her, I drove down for my Sunday paper, read it until Angie returned to cook a rather heavy meal, then had a little doze. She didn't seem surprised that I wasn't out detecting. Maybe she assumed detectives had a Sunday break like other people, during which their brains grew numb.

Mine certainly must have been. The facts had been handed to me, and I'd missed out on the important one. Evan's arrival awoke me. Everything was normal between them, judging by the cheerfulness in his voice. It was just turning dark, and with a start I recalled that I was going to meet Phil. I'd make a secret of it. I hadn't even told Angie. Especially Angie.

But there was still time. I said I'd be going down for a drink, and nobody queried it, so I wandered out into the yard on the way to my car. I threw up the door, and realised that Evan was standing at my shoulder.

'A word?' he asked.

I refrained from looking at my watch. We walked through the garage and into the lab.

'Somebody's left the Lovibond on,' he said.

I switched it off quickly. It was smelling hot.

'What's the matter with Angie, Mr Kyle?' he asked, taking it head on.

'Hasn't she told you?'

'A domestic thing – I didn't like to pry.'

'No, of course not.' He was a stolid non-pryer. 'I think we'll soon get it sorted out,' I said, sounding confident.

'If you think it'd help . . .' He shook his head. His mouth was firm. 'If you'd advise me . . . I could easily go back to my work.' He didn't know how to get to it. 'Mr Kyle,' he tried, 'was she like this before I came here?'

It had cost him a lot, and he blushed with the effort.

'Like what?' I asked carefully.

'You know. She was always highly-strung, was Angie. Always living on the peak of some mood or other. But now – touch her and she flinches, and her temper's showing at a word. I don't understand. She laughs at things that would usually hurt her, and sometimes a smile nearly has her in tears. She's . . . unbalanced. Is it me? What am I doing wrong?'

All this he said with his head turned away. I didn't know what to say to him. 'It's something she can't handle herself.'

'Then I *can* help?' he asked, turning quickly.

'By being around, perhaps.' I couldn't just send him away, he was so earnest.

'You'll tell me what I can do – any time?'

'Of course.'

He seemed to relax a little. It had all been prepared and he was glad to have got it out.

'Who's been using the Lovibond?' he asked, touching it to test its warmth. It'd been on all night.

'That was Lynne. Something I asked her to check.'

'It's a great pity.' He smiled at me. 'Gledwyn was really a splendid scientist, but you'd have thought he'd have lashed out on a spectrophotometer. A man in his line. Colour.'

'I don't understand.'

'These two instruments are colorimeters. They depend entirely on the colour judgment of the user. I mean, Lynne could be good – most women have perfect colour vision. But for truly scientific work he should've used a second operator to check the results. A top-class spectrophotometer would have covered it. He could even have used that himself. But with these he was absolutely dependent on his assistant. A colorimeter's no earthly use to somebody who's colour blind, as he was.'

And I'd missed it. I'd watched Lynne using her excellent colour vision, and I'd still missed it. I'm afraid I was short with him. I pushed past him. 'Excuse me.'

Then I ran past the car and across the yard, and galloped through the house into the hall. I dialled Lynne's number. When I looked round, Evan was watching me from a far doorway.

She answered. I told her who it was.

'What is it now?' she asked in a dead voice.

'You let me go on believing it,' I said severely. 'You let me show you why I thought the Escort killed your friend.'

Her uneven breathing was in my ear. She was not interrupting.

'And you knew what I was getting at. Lynne, are you

listening? You knew I was assuming he could make up a match for any colour. Himself.'

She gasped: 'I don't want to hear. Why can't you leave me alone!'

'Don't hang up.'

'I don't want to discuss it.'

'I've got to talk to you.'

'Go away.'

'I'll come over.'

'No!' she almost screamed. 'I'm not going to talk to you. Not ever . . .'

I controlled my voice. Calm, I told myself. Calm and confident. 'Now you know I'm not going to shout at you. It'll take me a quarter of an hour to get there. Will you wait for me?'

'No!' she shouted.

'Please! It's so important.'

'It's no good.' It was a whimper now. 'I can't tell you –'

The line went dead. I stared at the wall. Evan said: 'What is it?'

I caught his elbow. 'You can help me. Keep quiet about this. I've got to go over and speak to Lynne, but I'm supposed to be meeting somebody – the pub at the far end of the square.'

'The Mitre?'

'That's the place. A tall, fair-haired chap. Go there, and tell him I'll be along. Don't let him get away and don't let him come up here. You'll do that?'

'Who is he?'

'His name's Phil Rollason.' His face was abruptly lifeless. 'You'll do that, Evan?'

'Yes, I'll do it.'

I ran out into the yard. Angie called to me, but I simply waved. She must have thought I'd gone mad. Well – I was. Mad at myself. But I did manage to remember something else I'd missed.

Cursing, I ran through into the lab again. I could spare two minutes. I found the cans at once, the row of eight gallons of base and thinners for paint mixing. They were lined up under the bench along the side, and with them, tossed aside negligently, there was one of those electrically operated spray-guns. Its nozzle was covered with green paint. I couldn't tell whether it was the green of the walls, which Lynne had catalogued as 5G

5/5, or the green of the Escort's wing re-spray, which she'd said was 7G 4/5.

It was just another thing I should have thought about. I should have deduced that the spray-gun had to be there – because she'd spoken of *spraying* the walls – and asked her to make a check of that, too. But the thought carried the assumption that she'd have told me the truth, which would have been pushing her a bit far.

By the time I got to the end of the drive I had reached that point of self-criticism where one begins to feel very old and insecure. I was moving too fast. I admit it. I very nearly crushed a large car, which was just turning in. There were exchanged comments. I realised I was swearing at Paul. His wife, beside him, recognised me and joined in. My wavering self-confidence received a further blow when I realised she was far beyond me in swearing ability.

I drove on, taking a right onto the back road Angie had showed me. With the turns and dips, and the tightly restricted width of the road surface in places, I could have done with a sports car. I tried to pretend the Rover was, and pushed it into the swinging curves. Only once did the tail slide. I caught it, banged down into a lower gear, and let the revs mount. Fifteen minutes, had I said? The loom of the block of flats came out of the night at twelve, and I was turning in at thirteen.

Every flat was illuminated in the windows that faced inwards, all curtains drawn back. I parked the car by the row of garages and began to run. The light in the courtyard was directionless, and I realised the balconies were lined with shadows, and the muttering whisper I'd taken for wind was voices. There was a patch of shadow near the swings. A light flickered. Red spots became the rear lights of a parked, silent ambulance. The group around it was caught in the petrified awe that always accompanies an accident. They allowed me through with no comment and no resistance.

They were just loading her onto a stretcher. I pushed my way forward. The face was at peace, I saw, before they covered it. Then they slid the stretcher into the back. I turned away.

'You knew her, sir?' asked a young constable.

'What? Yes. Her name's Lynne Fairfax.'

'We know her name. But . . . did you know her?'

'I was on my way to visit her.'

There wasn't much in my voice. I hadn't got any reserve. He had his notebook out, and I could see myself stuck there for hours. I tried to straighten my shoulders. I gave him my name. I told him I was a detective sergeant, to indicate I knew procedures. I told him where I was staying, and I mentioned that Sergeant Timmis knew me. I said I'd be pleased to answer any questions the sergeant had to ask.

'But not now, Constable. Not now.'

Sensible chap, he nodded and smiled, and moved away. Then I found myself wandering back to the car, and only professionalism halted me. I knew nothing about what had happened. Nothing. I went back and mingled. There'd be police in her flat, and I wouldn't be welcome there, so I moved around. Dozens of women, hugging their arms, were full of it. One was saying that Lynne just came tumbling down.

'Seemed to run out and straight over the rail. I've always said . . . haven't I always said? . . . they're not high enough . . .'

I wandered back to the car, fumbled around for a while looking for my keys before remembering they were in the ignition, then fell inside and did the only thing I was capable of at the time. I filled my pipe. I lit it and sucked on it. My head was aching again and the double vision had come back. I smoked, and wondered what I was supposed to be doing, remembered Phil at the Mitre, switched on the engine. Then I smoked a little more.

Finally I drove out and found the road to Llanmawr, going gently because death was in the air. Sunday evening. My tyres thrummed on the cobbles and I saw Phil's Sierra parked at the kerb. Nothing moved except a ginger cat, streaking across the road as though it might be pouring with traffic. I got out and stood beside the car. It was a ghost town. I felt like one of them.

I found them in the snug, chatting quietly over half pints. As I approached I heard Evan say:

'It's a matter of rods and cones. It's why we know cats see only mono, like an old TV set.'

They saw me. Phil got to his feet. 'Harry?' My face was now in full light.

I sat down. 'Expected you'd be later,' said Phil.

'I would've been, but I didn't get to do the talking I wanted.'

'I'll get you a drink,' Evan offered.

'Lynne's dead,' I told him flatly. 'She fell off her balcony.'

Of the two, Phil knew me better. My voice had sounded strange to me, and he probably detected it. 'No, I'll get it,' he said, and Evan and I sat silently until he returned with a double whisky. I rarely touch spirits. 'Get that down you,' he said.

'I'm sorry,' said Evan gently. He'd barely said two words to her. 'I liked her.'

I took a mouthful of scotch, searing my throat. Phil was watching me with interest. Evan finished his beer and said he'd be going. 'You'll have things to talk about,' he murmured, knowing the things would be Angie.

The spirit had shocked my brain into action. 'You're going back to Viewlands?'

He nodded. 'Thought I would.'

'Her brother's there. You know him. Don't let 'em talk about Gledwyn.'

'I'll do what I can.'

He walked out, one of your solid and dependable types who always get caught holding the sticky end.

'You found her?' asked Phil solicitously, though he hadn't known Lynne.

Lynne's death was the only one in my life for which I could be held directly responsible. I cleared my throat.

'Not exactly.' I tossed down the rest of the whisky. 'I want this finished, Phil, and quickly. I've handled it like a clumsy oaf. I want to see an end.'

'You blame yourself . . .'

'I've been blind, idiotic . . .'

'Why don't you tell me, then?' he asked, annoyed at me. 'Tell me, and let me judge.'

'I'm the judge, mate,' I told him.

'For God's sake – why have I come all this way?'

I needed a minute to collect my thoughts. I spent it getting in two pints, banged them down on the table, and sat opposite him again. I led in from the beginning, telling him everything I'd done and discovered, as well as I could remember, trying to miss out nothing, not even about Lynne's death.

'Oh hell, Harry,' he said.

'I missed it, you see,' I told him. 'I'd assumed he'd be able to mix a perfect match for any colour he came across, as near as damnit. I didn't realise he'd have to use Lynne.'

'What am I going to tell Angie?' he asked in dismay. 'I know she liked her.'

'Yes . . . well . . . that's the point. That was what I wanted to see you about. From what I've already said, you'll have gathered something of what you're up against. This isn't just a nostalgia trip for Angie, like a man going back for a day's trip to the place he was born. For her, the house is a symbol of her father, and her father's the most wonderful thing that's happened to her in this rotten world. You've heard. I've had contradictory evidence about Gledwyn. Listen to Paul and his wife, and he was a poor specimen, a failure, covering his failure with hypocrisy and self-martyrdom. But I don't think that even scratched the surface. It all came from Paul, and he's blind in any direction but his own. I think Gledwyn *was* a fine man, weak perhaps, but making something great out of even that weakness. I think his wife died knowing he loved her. I think she believed he had gained by leaving his research work at Aberystwyth. If that's so, he did a good job.'

I paused. Phil had appeared to be listening carefully. I couldn't tell how much was penetrating.

'Angie realised, I think,' I told him. '*She* was the one who lost out, because she could've stayed on and got her degree, and nobody the poorer. But she doesn't see it like that. She sees that she spent her mother's last few years in a warm and close relationship with her father, smoothing her mother's life to the best end it could possibly be. And because of that, the house where it happened has got a special place of its own in her life. She can't let it go, Phil, she can't let her father go.'

He'd let me run on, talking the distress out of me. But I'd deliberately gone into it in detail, hoping to impress on him how important it was to Angie. I was no longer thinking directly about Lynne – she was an ache in the background.

'You think I can compete with that?' he asked miserably.

'I think you were making a pretty good go of it. God knows what she ever saw in you . . .' He gave a twisted grin at that, but I was serious. 'Maybe you're like Gledwyn, though I can't see it. If so, you ought to be proud of that. But you know the place where she was brought up, so what d'you think it's done to her, moving to a town flat, and with a husband who's always missing at one of his other garages. And . . . I'm guessing this . . . I bet she got a share in what Gledwyn was doing, whereas now . . .'

'You know I can't involve her in what I'm doing now.'

'Not if it's illegal.'

'Now come off it, Harry. You know what I mean. I'm breaking through and seeing a profit. And Angie knows that.'

'Maybe she does. I think she blames herself bitterly for not being able to fall in with it all, and for leaving you like she did – and for knowing she can't go back.'

I'd got to shock him, preparing him for what was to come.

'But she can't do that,' he burst out. 'Harry, you're crazy. I'm not having that.'

'Keep your voice down. You'll need it for later. I'm going to ask you to consider the effect on her if you tell her that Gledwyn was the hit-and-run driver who killed Lynne's friend, Carla. No – worse than that – who knocked her down and didn't stop, didn't do anything about it, but left her to die.'

Only his ears retained their colour. His face was quite white. I'd given him all the facts, and he hadn't seen the obvious conclusion until I handed it to him.

'You'd better prove that,' he said, and there was threat in his voice.

'I think I can. Listen. That day he'd been to Aberystwyth to see his son, Paul. It wasn't a visit he wanted to make, and he was worried about the paper he was preparing for the Convention he was going to. It was a terrible confrontation with Paul and his wife. He heard a lot of home truths that must've shocked him to his heels, if my understanding of him is correct. Neville drove him. It was a rotten return journey for both of them, and Gledwyn was barely civil to his nephew when he got out of the Escort. Perhaps that trip, with his bit of treated windscreen, had convinced him his work was no use. Anyway, he marched into the house, leaving Neville in the car in the drive. Right? Are you with me?'

'With you,' Phil muttered. The bounce had drained out of him.

'Gledwyn was in a right bad humour. I know he marched straight through the house, because he'd still got his keys in his hand when he reached Lynne's office. He took it out on her. Imagine how he'd feel. He'd seen a year's work – and possible acclaim – sliding down the drain. He didn't even notice Lynne'd stayed late for him. He tore up his speech as a gesture and walked out. Back to the house . . . and then what?'

I waited. I'd intended it as a direct question, trying to provoke Phil's poor imagination. But he simply shook his head.

'Imagine,' I said forcefully. 'He was a weak character perhaps, but he hadn't shown himself to be thoughtless. He'd realise how he'd treated Lynne. She'd become important to him. He'd go back after a minute or two to apologise, but she told me she could have been out at the side, sitting in her car at the time. He'd see darkness, because she'd put off her light, and assume she'd gone home. So he'd go back indoors, would he? Probably. But I'd suggest that suddenly he'd realise how much he really needed her, not just because of the speech, but simply to talk to, perhaps. Somebody who'd got faith in him. So . . . what would he do, Phil? Come on. Think.'

His eyes brightened. 'He'd climb into that Escort . . .'

'Well now, you *do* see it! Yes. The Escort, when he hadn't driven for years.'

'And chase after her. Is that what you're saying?'

I nodded. 'And I reckon it didn't matter to him whether or not she'd return to the lab with him, so long as he could be with her. But he'd got his special glasses, and there weren't any traffic signals on that road, so it should have been all right. But it wasn't. There was a broken-down car and a woman standing beside it, and through those glasses the rear lights would look like white sidelights, which would confuse him, and her green coat would look a dark grey and almost invisible. He hit her – and because he was the type who can't look at other people's pain, he drove on. Maybe he even went to Lynne's flat, and found it empty. Yes, of *course* he went to Lynne's flat!'

'Why're you so sure?'

'When he got back, he went into the lab expecting to find her there, so he must have failed to find her at her place, and guessed she hadn't gone home. So that would put him in a panic to get back to Viewlands, and it'd mean a roundabout route – back through the traffic signals.'

'He seems to have managed all right there.'

'He'd be driving like an elderly nun, you can bet, half in shock, half in fear.'

'And he got back just in time to find Lynne was still there, and just finishing off the re-typing of his paper. He'd have to try to act normal, and she'd leave. Then he'd put away the car in the garage.'

I was beginning to have more respect for Phil's imagination. Maybe, after all, it would be all right.

'And then,' I said, 'the really terrible thing would start. His panic and his weakness had killed that young woman, and he'd be disgusted with himself. He wouldn't be able to bear the thought of anybody finding out what a poor specimen he'd turned out to be – especially after that session with Paul and his wife. He'd got a week in Blackpool. He had to do something about the near-side wing of the car. The only possible thing for him to do was hire a car in Blackpool and take daily trips back to Viewlands, and work on it. He wouldn't really be missed. Evan Rees said they talked for hours, but that'd still leave him huge gaps of time.'

Phil's professional interest stirred. 'And he'd need it all. A big job, that.'

'I'm sure it was. He'd have to buy a new headlamp and do a build-up job with fibreglass. It'd need to be good enough to fool Neville, next time he came. But when it came to the finishing – well, if there was one thing Gledwyn was an expert on, it was colour. Wasn't that his own subject? He'd be able to make up his own spray paint.'

'If he'd got the necessary . . .'

'He'd got everything. I've seen. Even a spray-gun. But you can see the mistake I was making. Lord, it was nothing less than criminal. I assumed he'd do the colour matching himself. You see his difficulty? His only way of matching was to code the colour and mix it up like a mathematical exercise. He picked off some scraps of paint from the damaged wing. Now . . . it'd been buckled. Parts of the red re-spray were broken off, and I'm guessing he picked off bits of the original green by mistake, and used 'em to get his match. The fact that the coding showed it as a green wouldn't alert him to anything. The registration document told him it was green. So he didn't know it, but he was spraying one wing green on a red car. But I thought any matching he'd be able to do himself, that's where I was wrong, and it wasn't until Evan told me he couldn't do it without Lynne . . . oh Lord, and I'd watched her doing it! I watched her match it by eye, through a damned eyepiece, and still I didn't realise!'

'I'll get you another drink,' said Phil uneasily.

'No.' I stared at him. 'Don't you realise it means she'd have to help him?'

'Of course I realise it.'

'Well then . . . But obviously she never saw the battered car. One glance at it and she'd have said, "But it's red!" No, he'd have to have given her one or two bits of paint, and not tell her what it was for. She'd put them in that machine and tell him it was 7G 4/5, or whatever the damned number was. She'd do *that* for him. She just couldn't have known why he wanted it.'

Phil watched me with concern. 'When?' he asked, reaching for a crack in my theory.

'When what?'

'When did he give her these scraps of paint? She drove him to Blackpool the next morning.'

'Then,' I decided. 'He'd have come back the previous evening with the Escort battered. He'd go into the lab, having a good idea she'd be there – and she'd re-typed his speech for him! Ye gods. He'd try to act normal, and send her off home – and she didn't notice the Escort, out there on the drive, so he'd put it away in the garage after she was gone. In the morning he'd decided what he had to do, and knew what part of it he couldn't do himself. Before they left for Blackpool he asked her to do a reading on one or two bits of paint. He wouldn't need to tell her why. And then, later, he could mix a paint that fitted the formula. It was a bit too dark, that was all. But with trips back to do the repair job, the spraying . . . by the Friday he was ready. He phoned for her to pick him up. She drove him home, and she says she left him at the drive entrance. Says that. Said it.'

I stared at my empty glass, mourning its emptiness.

'But I know that young woman,' I went on. 'She'd realised he was upset and under strain. D'you think she'd leave him on his own? No! Phil – have you realised that Lynne must have been in love with him! Maybe she was no more than his assistant. But it explains why she went cool with Neville. The poor young bugger didn't know whether he was coming or going. But she would not leave Gledwyn to fret alone. She'd give it a few minutes, and then follow him up to the house . . . and find what? Find Gledwyn looking at his handiwork in the garage? The Escort with one wing green and the rest red! Can't you see her standing there and realising that this wonderful man of hers had run down her friend and left her to die?'

I'd used up all my inspiration. I fumbled with my pipe. Phil seemed to be doing very little to help. At last he said:

'Then what?'

'Oh, for God's sake, how do I know!'

'You've done all right so far, with that imagination of yours.'

'Imagination? It fits the circumstances. All right. See how you like it. Say she walked up to the house – or drove up. There was Gledwyn – and he'd had a lousy time the last week. He'd be as low as you could push anybody, and standing there looking at what he'd done to escape the consequences of his bloody feebleness. Not feeble, then, if you don't like that word. His whole life had been a kind of nervous moral courage. Perhaps he saw the Escort as evidence of his complete failure. What d'you want – Freud? And when she stood there, realising . . . what if he *was* in love with her, and hadn't ever admitted it because of his age? What if he couldn't stand it any more, looking at her, knowing what he'd done? I'm trying to see it, Phil, and you're not helping. Can't you imagine him getting into that Escort – hell, he'd even have the spectacles with him, from the Convention – and driving off, anywhere away from her.'

'Anywhere? To do what?'

'What do I know about his thoughts? Suicide? Or to go to the police and confess? I'd guess either. But Lynne might see suicide in his intentions. Jump into her own car, blind after him. She'd do that. It was late, he was out of practice with cars, and her car would be faster. If she got past him – where could she brake and be sure he couldn't get past her – make him stop – talk to him – tell him . . . whatever she *could* tell him? At the single-lane stretch by the new roadway, that's where. If she'd been able to get in front of him just before then, and braked . . . hell, haven't I told you how he'd see braking lights as white! He'd ram on *his* brakes, and go off the road.'

'You make a good case, Harry.'

Good – and I hated it. My voice was dull when I went on: 'There *was* an anonymous caller. Hysterical, I was told. As she'd be, watching him go up in flames.'

He was silent. I'd run out of tobacco and went to the counter to get an ounce of flake. I hadn't really run out; I wanted to give Phil time to absorb it.

Sergeant Timmis was suddenly at my elbow. 'Join you?' He nodded over at the table, where Phil was sitting like stone.

'You interrupt now,' I told him, 'and I'll kill you.' I eyed him with anger. 'And why aren't you at Wilmington Court?'

'It's what I wanted to talk about.' But he smiled, and raised his glass, watching me return to the table.

Phil said: 'Harry, how can I tell her *that*?'

'It's difficult,' I agreed savagely. 'Her brother's with her now, with his wife. They'll be painting a sour picture of her father, you can bet. So you go to Angie and you tell her the truth – and you can't do it without all the character background – then what? Maybe she won't be able to get away fast enough. You tell me. But you might not like what you take back with you.'

'You're exaggerating.' His mouth twisted. 'It depends on how I put it across.'

Which was what I was afraid of. I searched round for any way the story could be softened for her.

'You wouldn't have to tell her why Lynne killed herself,' I said.

'I don't know, anyway.'

'Isn't it obvious, you fool? She saw me getting close to it. She didn't want to have to face the thing, and perhaps have to give evidence of what she knew. Maybe . . .' I glanced at him. He wasn't great on imagination, so perhaps I was pushing him too far. 'Maybe she'd been able to hold it all back in her subconscious, and she dreaded having to take it out and look at it.'

'You dream things up, Harry. That's your trouble. The same with that business over the cars – suggesting I was faking-up stolen vehicles.'

How he could think of side issues at a time like that . . . I was furious with him. 'So who the hell d'you think's been sending those threatening notes? She saw me getting closer and closer to the truth. Who tried to smash the evidence of the Escort's repaired wing?'

'This is a woman you're talking about.'

'Don't let Angie hear you say things like that. Angie could climb a gate and swing a sledgehammer. Ask her. And it's typical of a woman to bash me on the head with the lighter end of the thing.'

'You don't believe a word of it!'

'No? But it must've been Lynne. She's the one who's been hiding the truth.'

'In the mood you're in . . .'

'She threw herself off a balcony tonight, Phil. I'll explain all that to Angie, if she wants to know, because I caused it. The rest, you can do. She's your wife – you tell her about her father.'

'I don't like it. There ought to be other ways. Damn it, Harry, if I have to drag her home . . .'

'You asked me to find out the truth.'

'Not *this* truth, for God's sake.'

'How many d'you want? There's only one truth.'

He drank up, and we left. He followed my tail-lights back to Viewlands.

13

All the lights were on in the house, like a distress signal. I parked in the drive, Phil behind me, because I wanted to use the front door bell with the hope of interrupting anything acrimonious that might be going on.

Angie answered the door. 'Harry! Where *have* you been – and . . . it's Phil . . .'

'Has it been bad?' I asked.

She shook her head numbly. Even when Phil took her hand and tried to kiss her she did not respond, merely lifted her cheek. Then she turned away, and we might not have been there. Phil glanced at me, and then it was clear what had happened.

Evan had given the news of Lynne's death. But he hadn't been able to give any reason for it. I could hear Rena's voice biting through the woodwork.

'. . . it's not surprising – the poor young woman. How long was she working with that man? It's enough to drive anybody crazy. Correct me if I'm wrong.'

I would have loved to. The opportunity was neatly presented, but I could not correct her without exposing the truth. She'd have revelled in it. I followed Angie into the room and tried to take it all in with one glance.

They were using the sitting room at the rear, Rena and Paul on the settee, sitting well apart, both holding glasses. Evan was leaning against a corner of the mantel. They had a wood fire going. Angie headed for the wing chair she'd been using, and sat, returning at once to her previous attitude, knees together, lips compressed, eyes glazed in the concentration of deliberate withdrawal. The fire was warm and cheerful, but made little impression on the atmosphere. Evan hadn't managed to steer the subject away from Gledwyn. It had been asking too much of him.

'Ah, Mrs Griffiths,' I said. 'How splendid to see you again. And Paul. You're looking fit. I was sorry to hear that you missed out on the professorship.'

Evan was obviously keyed up. He'd spotted Phil in the doorway and tried desperately for a diversion. 'Did you go for that, Paul? Oh dear – everybody knew Wright had got it. Months ago, we knew.'

Paul smiled thinly. Rena was staring round, eyebrows raised, eyes bulging, waiting to be introduced. Angie said, from a great distance: 'This is Phil. My husband. Harry Kyle . . . you know.' Animation was returning to her voice, colour to her cheeks.

Evan edged towards the door. Phil stood, uncertain. Something he'd not expected was a social interlude. He was unable to carry off the moment; his business was too urgent for chit-chat to intervene. The atmosphere was frigid, but Rena was quite impervious to it. I found a seat and pretended to be at my ease, trying to banish the recurring image of Lynne plunging from that balcony.

'You'll be going back to the States?' I asked.

Paul waved his empty glass. 'We'll look around first.'

'Professorships are probably thin on the ground.'

'There's always room for a good man,' put in Rena.

'Of course,' I agreed.

Phil was signalling Angie with his eyes, but she ignored him. I clenched my fist over my pipe, clamped my teeth on the stem, and hung on.

'I'd like to see him as a don at Oxford,' Rena was saying, putting the emphasis on the second syllable. 'But of course . . .' A sneer crept in. '. . . they'd be very selective.'

'American degrees,' said Evan suddenly, 'are much sought after in Oxford,' probably with the intention of keeping them away from Aberystwyth.

'In Wales,' I explained, 'they're apt to burn down your house.'

'What?'

'Nationalists.'

Then Phil's patience ran out. He advanced into the centre of the room, looked round, and said:

'Well now, I guess that's it. Sorry to hurry you off, Paul. And Rena. Things I want to say to my wife.'

Somehow I didn't think that smile would have sold anybody a car. It froze Rena. She got to her feet.

Evan took it in his stride. He'd been aching for the excuse. 'Well . . . fine. I was leaving, anyway. Good night all.'

He pushed past Phil, almost breaking into a run. Rena was gathering up her belongings, which seemed to have spread themselves around. Paul made clucking noises. Phil shuffled them out to the front door.

For a minute, perhaps two, I was alone with Angie. She was watching me with wide, staring eyes.

'What is it, Harry?'

'Something Phil's got to tell you.'

'Can't you do it?'

I was wishing I hadn't brought him back here. 'It ought to come from him.'

She flapped her hands on her knees. 'Is it about poor Lynne?'

'No. That's my bit. My fault. I pushed her too hard, not realising . . .'

'Harry!'

'Listen to Phil, Angie. Try to understand.'

That frightened her. She was half to her feet when the door opened and Phil returned. I grimaced at her. She looked from his face to mine as I backed off. I wondered whether I should be in the room at all, and tried to fade, finding a chair in the far corner.

'Something that's got to be said, Angie,' he told her, and damn me if he hadn't decided to be jovial about it.

Then he swung around one of the Queen Anne chairs and placed it down in front of her, like an inquisition, and sat with his back to me. Suited me fine – I was being excluded. But I could hear every word, and I could see her face, full on, every distress and agony clear-cut. I sat. My pipe was out and I didn't dare flick my lighter, the silence was so expectant.

He started all right, all the correct words, talking like a kind old uncle, and almost as though he'd memorised what I'd told him. But the intonation in some way was a challenge, the emphasis was wrong, the pauses carried too much weight.

This he seemed to realise, and it annoyed him. Anger crept in, and uncertainty with it. He began to toss phrases at me, without turning his head.

'Isn't that right, Harry?'

And I'd grunt.

It wasn't right. No part of it was right. When telling it to Phil I hadn't been able to suppress a certain sympathy for Gledwyn, but to Phil it obviously seemed that it was Gledwyn's fault that he was now in this awkward situation, appealing to Angie when he should simply be asserting his authority. So his attitude drifted towards impatience and anger. Perhaps her stony, unresponsive expression irked him. My original words gradually became more and more distorted.

Where I'd said, referring to Gledwyn's attitude to Lynne, something like: 'Suddenly he'd see how much he really needed her, not simply because of the speech, but perhaps just to talk to', this came out as:

'But the old fraud couldn't manage without her. She'd been crawling after him for years, doing anything he wanted. So all right, he wanted a speech typing, and the stupid bitch had gone off home . . .'

'Oh Christ, Phil,' I whispered.

She could not have heard, but Angie threw me a flick of a glance, mute appeal. Help me, Harry. I felt sick, but I could do nothing. Phil was involved in a frantic effort to strike interest in her eyes.

I'd credited him with intelligence, but he was certainly bereft of imagination. Faced by her stunned lack of response, he bored in with more persistence, his voice rising. He knew he wasn't getting through. Couldn't she see what a hopeless failure her father had been?

He came to the part where Lynne must have walked up the drive and discovered Gledwyn looking at the repaired car with its green wing. Then, at last, imagination showed itself. He could not see behind Angie's glazed eyes. His was not that sort of perception. He was simply carried away by his own words, shouting it as a challenge to her lack of response, and embroidering as he hotly threw the words at her.

'You're not trying to understand,' he bellowed. 'You're just sitting there, telling yourself it's not true. Lynne followed him up the drive. Don't ya see it? Followed him, and caught the old bastard gloating over his handiwork. And she'd see straight away. A green wing on a red car! Ever heard anything so daft! Can't you just see her, pointing at him, and saying, "So it was you, you creepy devil. Killed Carla, and tried to cover up."

She'd tell him. *She'd* see, however stubborn you want to be. He'd killed her friend, and left her to die. What sort of louse does that? Tell me. Say something, Angie, damn you . . .'

But I didn't let him get any further. I was on my feet – couldn't remember doing it – and pulled him round.

'What the hell!'

'That's enough, Phil. It's enough.'

I was trying to drag him to the door, he fighting me off with the ineffectual flappings men like him make, and I had a brief glimpse of Angie, on her feet, hands pressed to her face and the rest of her all frantic eyes. She was making weird keening noises behind her fingers.

Somehow, I got him out into the hall and the door closed behind us. He was completely beyond self-control. It's quite often the case with these controlled characters, who tailor their faces to the body of necessity. The effort to maintain the pose presses them to the limit, until a time comes when it all breaks apart.

I had to slap his face to bring him back to normality – or as close to it as I could expect. I was doing him a favour, if he'd only realised it. Apparently he didn't. For one moment his face was rigid, nothing in it apart from the eyes, and from these only the most virulent hatred I've ever faced. Then it was gone. He shrugged his shoulders free. His teeth showed briefly.

'Not now, Harry,' he said quietly.

He opened the door into the long room and for a moment stood in the doorway. 'I've had enough,' he declared. 'Three days. I'll give you that to get things organised. Then I'll send a couple of the men for you. Right?'

The fact that his voice was unemotional gave his words more emphasis. A pity he hadn't used that technique before.

I watched him leave, and heard the tyres scrabble at the drive surface. Then I went back to Angie.

She sat, dry-eyed. She did not look at me. I circled her. I did not dare to say a word, and certainly dared not touch her. Physical contact would have dissolved her, and I could not have retrieved the same Angela. She had to make her way herself.

I sat in the same corner chair and lit my pipe. Knocked it out when it was finished and re-charged it. You're not supposed to do that. Let it cool, that's the rule. Two pipes later I sensed a change in her, went into the kitchen and brewed tea, and returned with the tray. She watched me moving furniture about, the low, tiled-surface table to her knees, one of the other winged chairs from the wall to face her, found her cigarette pack on the mantel and slapped it down in front of her, my lighter on top of it.

'You told him that, Harry?' she asked quietly.

'Not in exactly the same words.'

She nodded. Her eyes met mine, and I'll swear there was a smile in there somewhere. 'Then can I have it in yours.'

I obliged. She listened intently, nodding occasionally. I covered the lot, including the facts that had led to Lynne's death. She shook her head.

'You mustn't blame yourself.'

'No.'

Then there was a pause. She was looking beyond me, smoke round her head.

'What did he mean, Harry, two men?'

'To fetch you home.'

Her eyes sparked. 'He can't do that.'

I took that as a question. 'It's tricky, legally. Assault, I suppose, but it'd be domestic. The police wouldn't dare to intervene – short of physical violence, I suppose.'

'Police! I don't need protection. I can look after myself.'

'Of course you can.'

Soon after, she said she thought she'd get off to bed. I was hungry, and poached in her cupboards for the makings of cooked cheese on toast. Then I locked the side door and went out by way of the front. There'd be no more unlocked doors to that house.

In the morning I was sitting on the caravan steps, sneering at the gelding, when she came out to water him, or whatever she had to do. She paused in front of me.

'You'll be leaving?' she asked.

'It's the end of September. Nowhere to go, really.'

Her eyes softened. 'Till you make up your mind . . . you're welcome, Harry.'

I waved a hand. 'Thanks.'

A cold tap in the corner of the yard; an outside WC. What more can a man want?

This was Monday. I went for a walk in the afternoon, up the lane outside in the direction of Whitchurch, down it in the direction of the traffic signals. Nothing. Too early, I supposed. He'd said three days, after all. When I returned, she'd gone for a ride over the hills. The house seemed cold and empty. I settled into the caravan.

When she came back I asked if there was a spare side-door key. She seemed to understand, and produced it without comment. I'd need to be able to lock up from outside, yet have access to the house. But something had changed in our relationship. I was now living fully in the caravan, she in the house, with no casual comings and goings. There was a cool familiarity about it, as though neither of us dared to venture too close, like neighbours who can chat over the frail, crumbling fence, but neither dares touch it in case it collapses.

The following morning, early, I used my key because I'd run out of milk. I put my head into the hall to listen for signs of movement, and noticed the post had arrived.

There was another of the threatening letters. It had been posted in Whitchurch the previous day, Monday. I slipped it into my pocket and left the rest – trash mail – in the hall. I locked up as I went out.

From then on, I went out each morning early enough to meet the postman at the gate. They came in a steady flow, becoming more vicious, promising more dire consequences. I didn't think that Angie need know that Lynne, after all, had not been the one sending them.

We were not short of visitors. Evan was home until the end of the week, and dutifully called. He knew nothing of what had happened, and whether Angie told him I don't know. But he remembered the jazz records Neville had mentioned, and took her on a search of the loft, where they found them. Angie phoned Neville, and he came to fetch them.

Lynne's death seemed to have hit him hard. He was quiet and repressed, and though I searched my brain for memories of Duke Ellington, I couldn't find enough comment to interest him, and he soon left. The inquest was to be on the Thursday, and he said he'd see me there.

Timmis had called on the Tuesday to say I'd be needed, and did he have to subpoena me? He was Coroner's Officer, it turned out. I said no, I'd be there, but I thought I saw in his set face the condemnation I was levelling at myself.

It was on that same Thursday that the two men appeared.

There was nothing overtly threatening about them, and I'd not even have known they were there if it hadn't been for one of my patrols up the lane.

The breakdown pick-up was parked two hundred yards from the drive entrance, two men sitting inside and drinking coffee from a flask. I recognised one of them.

I paused. 'Clancy, isn't it?'

'That's right, Mr Kyle. And this is my friend, Charley Boggis.'

I nodded. So that was how it was going to be, friendly pressure. We chatted a few moments, then I walked back. An hour later, I saw them drive away past the end of the drive.

I wondered why Phil had sent his men in such a vehicle, when he'd got any number of cars available, in for repair or for sale. Then I realised there was a certain subtle logic in sending a wagon eighty miles with his name blazoned on the side: ROL-LASON GARAGES. It declaimed his presence. His. And a pick-up! There was a crane on the back. They hook steel arms under the drive end of your car, then they can drive it away. Whether you want them to or not. Like the police. The hint was there. Harry Kyle had better clear out, or they'd take his car and dump it somewhere.

I wondered whether to have a new lock put in the garage door, but that afternoon I was busy. The inquest.

I had been dreading that inquest, though I should have trusted Timmis, who had his ear very close to the ground. These senior policemen in country districts have great influence and authority. A word from Timmis to the Coroner, who just happened to be Gledwyn's solicitor, smoothed things along no end. I was asked only for the fact that I had spoken to Lynne just before she died, and said I'd be straight over, and that I'd detected the fact that she was distressed. No details were extracted. The verdict was: Suicide whilst the balance of her mind was disturbed.

Nobody asked who'd disturbed it.

When we got back from Llanmawr the breakdown pick-up was there again, but this time closer to the gateway. I said nothing about it, but for the next few days Angie's routine comments became more and more terse, with undertones of despair. Evan had returned to his lab at Aberystwyth, so that

Angie had been riding alone. She must have used that lane often, and seen the encroaching pick-up.

'You're still here then, Harry?' she'd ask.

It got to the point where I'd just nod, but then there came the morning when the pick-up was visible at the end of the drive. It seemed to have been there all night.

Her comment changed. 'You must go, Harry.' She knew they'd have to do something about me before they could reach her.

I added a grunt to the nod. That morning's threatening message had been desperate.

I went inside and phoned Neville. He was the only one I knew, apart from Timmis – whom I wanted to keep out of it – who'd know these sort of things.

'The best chap round here for putting a new lock in the garage door, Neville,' I asked him.

He said he'd do what he could.

When I hung up and turned away, Angie was standing in the kitchen doorway, watching me. Her voice was close to hysteria.

'You're stubborn, aren't you!'

'It's a new car.'

'You make me mad!' Then her voice softened. 'I don't want you here – if there's trouble.'

'There won't be any trouble.'

I sat up that night in the darkened caravan, with all the windows uncurtained, waiting for it.

14

But of course you nod off. Unable to brew coffee to keep me alert, unable even to flick my lighter and light the pipe, I dozed on the seat beneath my rear window. The Rover was tucked away in the garage, but still without a lock to the door. I was recalling the last message.

I CAN'T WAIT ANY LONGER.

IT'S GOT TO END.

Nothing ambiguous, nothing wrongly spelt.

I jerked awake, and a ruddy glow was flickering on the roof surface above my head.

I ran to the door. I could see it through the lab windows opposite, flame mounting and smoke already seeping through the roof. I burst into the yard. The fire was extensive, I saw at once, and it would be fatal to fling open the doors to get at it. I couldn't remember seeing any fire extinguishers in there, but I did remember with sudden fear the row of paint thinners and base under one of the benches.

Somebody was screaming, and then I realised it was the gelding. I ran to the corner of the house and raised my voice.

'Angie! Angie! The lab's on fire. Ring the fire brigade.'

She must have been lying awake, more successfully than me. I heard her cry out, then I turned and ran across to the stable. The top door was open. He was rearing about, nostrils flaring and eyes wild, and I didn't think I dared to go in there amongst those flying hooves and the seeping smoke. I tried, but the hooves scared me into retreat, and I couldn't reach his halter. Then she was there, in pyjamas, gasping for me to give her room. She ran in beneath him and I turned away because she'd got it in hand.

The roar of the flames was like blood pressing in my ears. I remembered the Rover. Already the flames were through the lab roof. The whole building was mainly wood, and was lost, I knew. I ran towards the garage at the end. If I was quick enough, I might get it out.

The heat reached me when I was still well clear of the up-and-over door. I flinched, but ran towards it. The impression could be deceptive. The door was solid metal, but fire could already be reaching inside there. The end doorway inside led directly into the lab, and I had the car parked tail in, so that the tank would be vulnerable. But I did run towards it, aware that flinging up the door would provide the gasp of air that the flames demanded.

Dully, from my left, I heard the explosion as the thinners went up, a rumbling thump against the roar of the main fire. In the corner of my eye I caught the flare as flame rose high, taking up with it sparks and dark shapes flying. I was ten feet from the door when the Rover's petrol tank went.

The outrush of hot air and flame hit the door. If it had been locked, the pressure would have built up until it exploded in my face. But the lock wasn't in operation. The door flew up in front of me, tore itself from its upper mounting, and the whole thing came out at me like a leaf torn from a tree by the wind. Tumbling over lazily, it spun over my head, and I heard it crash onto the cobbles behind me.

Following it there was a rush of hot air and a tongue of blue-red fire. The pressure of it had me over, but I rolled, unable to take my eyes from my lovely new car, enclosed in a ball of flame.

As I watched, a minor explosion inside the car sprayed flame from the side window. I had time to realise that that was my can of spray paint going up, then I became very busy, because my jacket was aflame – my hair also, I was told later.

It was not the first time I'd had a jacket on fire, as this is a pipe smoker's hazard. You should never put a lighted pipe into your pocket. Once I walked all the way down a high street before an old lady stopped me. 'Did you know your jacket's on fire?' I'd felt the warmth. I tore it off and stamped on it, but that was the end of a tweed jacket and a favourite pipe.

This was worse. This was actual flame, and though I struggled with it, still rolling, the damn jacket didn't seem to want to come off.

Then somebody was saying: 'Keep still, you bloody fool,' and Clancy was plunging his hands into the living flame and creeping cinders of my jacket, and with a great effort, because panic was very close, I managed to keep still. The jacket came off. My head was rolled in a wet towel, I was thumped and slapped in the most tender spots, probably by Boggis, and at that point I think I passed out.

How long I was unconscious I don't know, but the next thing I remember is sitting in the kitchen on one of the chairs, being held firmly upright while a doctor did something to my face, and somewhere Angie whimpering: 'His eyes! His eyes!' But they were all right. I could see her. The fastest moving things in your body are your eyelids, and mine had worked well. They no longer had lashes, but they'd done a good job. I turned my head. The hands on my shoulders were bandaged. Clancy bent forward.

'I've seen some stupid things in my time . . .'

'You bin lucky,' said Boggis from behind a mug of tea.

If that sort of pain was luck, then I decided I'd be glad when I ran out of it. Then I closed my eyes again, because my eyeballs felt tender, and the next thing was that I was in the bed in the long rear bedroom, with the bedside light on, and Angie sitting beside me, carefully picking the remains of my jacket to pieces.

'Oh, you're awake,' she said calmly. 'You gave us a turn, I can tell you.'

All was quiet. Some considerable time must have elapsed. There was no fire-glow, and no sound of operating fire appliances.

'What time is it?' My lips moved strangely.

'Four,' she said, 'in the morning, and you're to keep still and behave. You can have a drink. Would you like that?'

'I'd love it.' I tried to sit up, but needed her arm. 'The lab?' I asked, gulping. 'The car?'

'All gone. Stable, lab, car, garage, the lot. But they stopped it from spreading. Now . . . you must rest.'

'Anybody else hurt?' I croaked.

'Clancy's hands. But I got the horse clear. Nothing to worry about.'

Yet there had been a strange undertone to her voice. She had been sorting through the remnants of my jacket, salvaging what there was. On the bedside table I saw my wallet, my pipe, my tobacco pouch, all looking healthy, and a pile of slightly singed letters from the inside pocket.

She saw the direction of my eyes. 'You're not to worry about it now.' But clearly she was doing enough for both.

'Do I lie and worry, or do we talk about it?'

'Talking must hurt your mouth,' she observed.

'And worrying makes my head ache.'

She frowned. 'All these letters – you've been hiding them from me, Harry. That was very secretive of you.'

'Sorry. But there was no point. When Lynne died, they should have stopped. Or so I thought.'

'But . . . then . . . who?'

I shook my head. She bit her lip and got up to walk to the window. She came back.

'And this?' she asked, showing me the envelope on which Evan had drawn the genetic charts. 'Whatever are you doing with this?'

'That was Evan,' I told her. 'He was showing me that your children, if you had a son, would stand a fifty/fifty chance of being colour blind.'

'And that mattered to you?'

'If the father's normal,' I amplified.

'Phil's very normal. Knows just what colour to re-spray a car.'

I think I grinned. I tried for a grin, and got the appropriate pain. 'We'd better get Evan to test him.'

'There's nothing funny about any of it,' she said firmly. Then, not having forgotten it: 'But if Lynne didn't send those filthy threats . . who did? Do you know who, Harry?'

I was suddenly very tired and couldn't make the effort to think round it or stall. 'Who d'you think? Who's wanted to get you away from here? Who's threatened and badgered and sent his men . . .'

'He . . . wouldn't. Not Phil.'

'And set the fire,' I murmured.

'But that's ridiculous. It was Clancy and Boggis who helped you.'

'Perhaps,' I suggested, 'they weren't told about the fire.'

'Oh, you're impossible!'

But she didn't go away, just sat quietly, thinking about it. After a few moments I realised she was holding my hand. I was lying back, making the most of it, when she said:

'I suppose that's flattering. All that trouble, because he wants me . . . needs me.'

I opened one eye. Couldn't resist putting a word in. Or maybe I was half asleep and thought I'd dreamed of saying it. What came out was:

'Or needed your money, Angie. More like. Who knows how he's fixed financially? Things could be rocky. With the sale of this place and the furniture . . .'

She reached over and put a finger to my lips. 'Now who's being naughty!' She'd have allowed herself to be angry if I'd been stronger.

I moved clear of the finger. 'But if I persuaded you to go home, Angie, peacefully and voluntarily, then you'd lend him your money?'

'My husband – yes.'

'But if he had to drag you from here?'

'I'd have his eyes out!'

'So that's why he's been so patient, and why he needed an expert persuader like me.'

I closed my eyes again, my last sight of her including her lower lip being severely bitten and worry in her eyes. But I was still awake when the hand crept back into mine. I'd been forgiven for such cynical words. Still awake, too, when she suddenly remembered.

'And this?'

I opened my eyes. She'd found the knobbly lump of melted plastic that'd been a cigarette lighter.

'It was a plastic lighter.'

'But surely . . . was it as hot as that?'

'It isn't mine. I found it.' I was dozing off. 'Don't throw it away,' I whispered.

Then I drifted off to sleep, and woke to a dull dawn and a fine drizzle of rain, and the desire to get on my feet and become mobile.

They like to tell you how bad you feel and how helpless you must be. Women love nursing. But I knew how I felt – like hell. When I got as far as the bathroom I saw I looked worse. There was a great wad of cottonwool covering the left side of my face, no eyelashes or eyebrows, and a singed stubble of hair. My hands were red and painful.

I insisted on going down for lunch.

'A right intrepid character I look,' I said to Angie. By that time I was talking with more ease.

From the kitchen window I could get a good view of the damage. The stable and lab were an untidy pile of charred timber, still steaming in places. At the end, the Rover stood naked on its rims, all signs of the garage around it having disappeared. It had the general shape of a car, but that was all.

'I hope you had it comprehensive,' she said.

'Fortunately. Where's the caravan?'

'They got it out onto the front drive.'

Something saved. I nodded. I wondered where she'd stabled the gelding. Probably with Morgan Rees.

'I've been on the phone to Bryn Thomas, in town,' she said. 'The car sales.'

'Have you?'

'I've hired you a car.'

'We'll need to be mobile,' I agreed.

'It's for you. A Range Rover, with a tow-bar. For your caravan.' She looked uneasy. 'As soon as you're fit to drive, I want you to go, Harry.'

'I'll go when you do.'

'You're a fool,' she said angrily. 'What might it be next?'

I laughed. It took effort. 'I'd be safer here. Anything that comes up – hell, I'd need you to protect me. You can't send me away.'

'I've got no patience . . .'

'It's all we've got between us.'

They delivered the Range Rover that afternoon. To test my ability I climbed into it, and went a short run. It was agony, but the trip did show me that the pick-up was no longer around. A pity, that. I couldn't remember thanking them.

Then I hitched it to the caravan, which I worked back into the same position it'd been before. Without the horse to snigger at me, I did it quite neatly. I was pleased. Stuck out there in the drive, it'd been a symbol of imminent departure.

'Oh, you're so damned stubborn!' She slammed the door.

By that time, though we hadn't discussed it, I was a fixture in the house and sleeping in her father's room. But she was becoming increasingly annoyed with me, especially as I wouldn't respond to her concern for my safety.

That evening she turned on me. 'Don't you see, you stubborn idiot! Whatever they did, they wouldn't dare treat me with violence. They'd force me to go home and then . . .' Her eyes flashed. 'Then we'd see! But you, Harry, you'd try to intervene.'

'Between man and wife? Me?'

'You *would*, you damn fool.'

I raised my scarred face to her. 'But I'm not fit to drive.'

'Damn you!' she shouted.

The following morning the locksmith came to mend the lock on the buckled garage door. Somebody had leaned the door, upside down, against the house wall next to the caravan. The outside was showing, so that he could easily have got at the lock, but as I pointed out, it would be locking the garage door after the garage had gone.

When he drove away, I noticed the pick-up outside in the lane again.

That seemed to decide Angie. She mooned around the house for a while, then she came to me, where I was leaning over what was left of the paddock rail and smoking, and said:

'I've made up my mind, Harry. We're getting nowhere, and . . .' She looked beyond me over her beloved valley. '. . . and I'm scared. I've just phoned Phil to come and get me. It's the only thing.'

'Not the only one.'

'Why don't you shout at me!' she shouted at me. 'Why don't you tell me what you're thinking?'

'It's not just you any more, Angie. Don't be so selfish. I'm not going to let you go back to him.'

'You're not . . .' A glance. 'Be serious, Harry, please.'

'When's he coming?'

'Tomorrow evening. Late.'

'But you don't really want to go?'

Her eyes were on the view, her voice soft. 'But it's not the same any more, Harry. The house – it's changed. Cold and empty. I don't seem to be able . . . oh, I can't explain.'

She didn't need to. Phil had destroyed more than her father-image. I stared at my raw hands, flexed them, and when I winced she understood my intention.

'I want you gone before he arrives, Harry.'

And if he used the same delicate diplomacy as last time, I could see it all disintegrating into violence. Oh, she was quiet enough now, but one touch on the wrong nerve . . . I hadn't realised how much I hated Phil.

'I think I'll hang around.'

'Oh . . . I could strangle you!'

'A watching brief, call it.'

With one furious glare at me, she whirled away and into the house.

But she was back in half an hour. I was still in the same spot. She seemed quietly confident.

'We shan't need you, Harry. I've managed to contact Paul. He's staying at Oxford, and he's promised to come along.'

'That's nice.'

'And Evan . . . he'll drive over from Aberystwyth. Just for the evening.'

I said nothing.

'Even Neville. He said he'd find time . . .'

'A kind of going-away party.'

'Just to *be* here! So that you can leave!' She thumped the rail.

'But now I shan't need to, shall I? With all that manly protection, I'll be safe.'

She went off into the house. That door wasn't going to stand much more slamming.

It should all have worked fine, except for that fact that Phil gave himself time off and arrived early in the evening, casual in jeans and a T-shirt to indicate confidence, sporting a Jaguar XJ6 to show how much he cared. Clancy and Boggis followed him into the yard with the breakdown pick-up, rather spoiling the effect. They were uneasy, but Phil spotted me, sitting quietly on the caravan steps, and told them to stay close. I wandered after them into the house.

There was no sign of any of Angie's reinforcements.

She'd been upstairs to do some packing, and had changed into a neat two-piece in olive green— flared, tight-waisted skirt and a little jacket, with beneath it a white shirt with ruffles down the front. Like a honeymoon going-away outfit. I'd been expected to comment, but I hadn't been able to say anything.

We went into the long sitting room at the back. The sun was setting, and Angie moved round putting on lights. Phil was impatient. He'd thought it was just going to be a quick in-and-out.

Angie nodded towards Phil's two helpers. 'I've decided to come home,' she told him. 'You didn't need those two.'

'With Harry here?' He was nervous. Clancy waved a bandaged hand at me cheerfully. 'I bet he won't be able to keep his mouth shut.'

'There was just one thing,' I admitted.

'You see!'

And Angie shook her head at me.

'Somebody's been sending threatening letters,' I told him. 'We've kept 'em all. It could be your writing, or printing rather, I reckon . . .'

'That proves you're insane!'

'You might have thought it was worth driving to Whitchurch every day,' I went on stubbornly, realising it sounded thin, 'to make it look reasonably local. And then, when that didn't work, tried something a bit more scary – a fire.'

He laughed. 'I always knew you were crazy.' Then I knew I was on a wrong tack. He'd relaxed. There'd been something he was nervous about, but that wasn't it. He was standing with his palms raised, as though testing for rain, and smiling round at my stupidity.

'Did y'ever hear the like?' he asked. 'You packed, Angie?'

'All I need.' But her eyes were on me, and she was tense. 'Let it drop, Harry,' she pleaded.

'Yeah,' said Phil, pleased at what he took for her support. 'Relax, Harry. You and your threatening letters and your fires! You're out of it now. It's over. Angie's coming home.'

'And that's it, I suppose?' I demanded. 'Angie's coming home, and it's voluntary.'

'You did well, Harry,' he conceded.

'I made a botch of it,' I snapped. 'I started off all wrong, with the idea it was all for Angie, because she was upset about her father's death. But it wasn't for Angie at all – every bit of it was for you.'

· Angie was becoming restless. Clancy and Boggis were at my shoulders, looking stern. Phil could afford to take it all casually.

'Of course it was for me. I wanted her home.'

'But bringing with her the proceeds of the sale of the house – and still friendly enough with you . . .'

Angie turned away. 'Oh, for God's sake!' she said in disgust.

It was at that moment I knew I'd lost. Angie had surrendered completely to his pressure, and I could offer her nothing.

'All the same,' I said weakly, more quietly, morosely.

He slapped me on the shoulder, and spoilt it all. 'That's the ticket, Harry. Chin up. We've always been friends.'

'Friends?' I said. 'My god, d'you think I didn't see through it all, getting me to come here, well away from the investigation into bribery, and have your own say with no contradictions?'

'It wasn't like that.'

And Angie moaned impatiently.

'You don't have to be in such a hurry,' I said angrily, and she tossed her head. I returned to Phil.

'You sent a Renault 5 round to my place. Was that friendly? It was intended as a bribe, but you knew I'd have to bring it back.'

He shrugged, looking round at Angie, who was twisting a lock of hair in her fingers, worried, distracted, not liking what she was hearing.

'So you'd bring it back. Where's the bribe, Harry?'

'I didn't manage to get it back, did I?'

'Why don't you leave it alone,' said Angie. 'It does no good. I want to go home.' She lifted a hand wearily, then turned away.

But I'd seen something in his eyes. I persisted. 'That Renault was a bribe, and you can't get round it. I can't *prove* I'd have run it back.'

'It was a deal. I offered you a bargain.'

'You! A bargain. It'd kill you, losing a quid. Why, you mean bugger, you couldn't even run a car up here, for Angie to use. The blasted breakdown pick-up can do the run a dozen times, when you need it for a threat, but never towing something for Angie.'

Phil was white. I'd hit a nerve. God, how I wanted to hit something! But Angie wasn't pleased. The tip of her tongue appeared and ran along her lips. Her eyes were bleak, and they were on me. Was this all I could do for her, this pitiful attempt at denigration?

'We use the breakdown pick-up for breakdowns.' It was an empty excuse, and Phil knew it.

Clancy stirred at my elbow. We'd ventured into his territory. 'Now that ain't always true, is it Mr Rollason?' he asked, being completely fair.

'You see.' I smiled.

Phil waved a finger at me. 'Now you just listen . . .'

'Just 'cause a car's towed,' amplified Clancy, in case we hadn't got it, 'it don't mean there's gotta be something wrong with it.'

'And you shut your face!' Phil bellowed. I couldn't understand why his nerve was cracking up. Angie gasped at the outburst, but Clancy, who was probably used to it, was unmoved.

'I took the Renault 5 up to your place,' Clancy told me proudly. 'Towed it on the crane. Don't have to mean there was something wrong with it.'

These things pounce out of nowhere, catching you unprepared. I whirled on him. 'You mean you *towed* the Renault to my place? You'd got it lifted on the crane?'

Clancy beamed. 'Under the front.'

Never for one moment had I suspected this possibility. If the car had been safe to drive, it would have been driven there. I'd assumed Cynthia had simply had an accident; she hadn't driven for years. That it should have been intended . . .

Clancy might not have been bright, but his instincts were good. He clamped a hand on my arm, Boggis attaching himself to the other. It was hurting Clancy more than me.

'By God!' I shouted at Phil, 'it was never intended as bribery. You *expected* me to drive it back.'

Seeing me restrained, Phil could afford to sneer, looking round for Angie's support. But she was staring past him, her eyes on me, and in them something . . . was it appeal? I didn't have time to work it out, because I was thinking: this news to my superintendent! They'd dig in deep . . .

'Try proving one word of it,' said Phil.

'I was getting too close for comfort,' I claimed, 'and you knew it was no good offering me bribes. The accident was supposed to be mine!'

Now I was able to grin at him. They'd pin him down like a butterfly, and admire the intricacy of him. 'You make me laugh,' said Phil, but he wouldn't be laughing for long.

Angie sat down abruptly on the settee, her hand to her

mouth. Her eyes never left me, and every line in my face must have been crying out my triumph. Couldn't repress it. I was aware that it must seem I'd abandoned her problems. I needed time alone with her.

And Phil, I think, realised this, and had no intention of allowing it. With Angie, he had to keep himself in the clear. He spoke confidently. 'And don't say I had anything to do with the threats. Nor the fire. Angie's coming home, and it's what she wants.'

I stared down at the hands on my arms. I now had myself under control and shrugged myself free easily enough, Clancy sighing with relief.

'There's more to say.'

'Such as what?' he demanded. 'You and your blathering about rigged cars and hidden bribes! There's nothing – nothing at all left to prove a thing. It's an obsession . . . all you can think about.'

I heard a car draw up outside – it seemed to be in the yard. The reinforcements had arrived, but I couldn't think why we'd needed them. The castle had been surrendered, judging by the way Angie was standing, smoothing her skirt, looking prepared.

'It's all he's *ever* thought about,' she said, her voice uneven.

She'd worked it out. Phil's previous visit had left her with very little to hold on to, but there'd still been one person devoted to her interests: good old Harry Kyle. And who'd spent the last few minutes telling her it was a lie? Who'd demonstrated that his only reason for being here at all was to sort out his own problems and clear himself of bribery charges? Your good friend, Harry Kyle. That's who.

'Are you ready, Phil?' she asked. She was lifeless, withdrawn.

'There's more to say!' I appealed frantically.

'And I thought you really wanted to *know*.' It slid off into a whisper.

And who, I realised she must be thinking, had stalled frantically for the past few days, refusing to leave, just in order to bring about this confrontation with Phil? Who but . . .

'Harry,' she said, almost unable to use my name, 'I think you'd better leave.'

This was said so quietly and with such cool dignity that it cut me worse than her anger. She'd thrust her fingers into the tiny pockets of her jacket, jutting the points like fluttering wings, and suddenly I felt drained and useless.

Two months before – ask me and I'd have said my ultimate ambition was to trap Phil Rollason, and prove he'd rigged me into a corruption charge. Well . . . I'd done that. I'd done more; I had evidence that he'd killed my wife. But the triumph was tasteless. I'd gained nothing. I saw that I'd lost everything.

Angie was staring at me with cold rejection. I couldn't take her in my arms and plead; half a room intervened. Sunlight slanted onto one cheek, blood red, like a slap.

'All right,' I said, defeated, 'I'll go.' I could just detect her teeth between dry lips. I waited for them to open. One word, just one . . . but there was no protest at my decision, only contempt.

'I'll go!' I shouted.

I turned, and marched blindly out of the door, with Clancy calling after me:'It don't mean there was anything wrong with it.'

Only the brakes and the steering perhaps.

I discovered Neville in the kitchen, calling out was anybody there. He saw my face and stood aside quickly. Paul was just drawing up in the yard, with Rena staring at me through the side window. Oh, they'd all made it easy! No dignified departure for me, when there were three cars and a pick-up scattered around. I climbed into the Range Rover, backing it up wildly and causing Paul to reverse and give me clearance, and when I clambered down it was sheer luck that the cup on the caravan was reasonably close to the towing ball. With my hands crying out, I lifted the caravan into position, forgetting to wind up the little wheel at the front, forgetting the lowered braces at each corner of the caravan, and ran back to the seat of the Range Rover.

I got it into four-wheel drive, for extra traction, and with a grinding lurch moved it three yards. Then Evan drove in. I rammed on the brakes, cursing, and tried reverse. It locked on the caravan's over-run brake, but all the same the Range Rover backed it all, rasping and scraping, with smoke from all four tyres. There was a crash from behind me.

You can't see the back end of a caravan, but I knew where it'd got to. I'd bashed into the house. I fought the box into first gear again, and moved it away, stopped with the front wheels in a pile of charred timber, cut the engine, and got out to have a look.

I'd backed into the garage door. As I watched, it slowly toppled forward, and fell flat at my feet with a clang. I was staring at its rear side. The only light out there was from the kitchen window, supplemented by Evan's dipped headlights and the failing sun.

The door was by now considerably buckled, its up-and-over lever arms standing up, but bent. The heat had had a strange effect on the paintwork. The metallic paint I had used for my exercise in graffito now stood out dark and strong against the non-metallic green that Gledwyn had sprayed on the inside door surface.

'You signed it,' said Sergeant Timmis at my elbow.

'Where've you come from?'

He tapped the side of his nose. 'I hear things.'

Then we both stared at the door. The graffito was now graffiti. Underneath my signature, at a point that would have been close to the ground with the door in position, had now appeared:

'I'm surprised at you, Mr Kyle.'

'Not me, you idiot. I didn't do that.' Then I understood. 'Oh my God!'

'What's up?' he asked.

'So *that* was why we had the fire – to destroy this.'

Somewhere in the back of my scrambled mind I realised I was staring at the one clue that linked up all that had happened. A little time, a little thought – I needed time.

But I wasn't going to get any. Angie was standing in the open doorway, a dim and distraught silhouette.

'Why don't you go!' she screamed.

'I think she means it,' said Timmis.

15

He took my elbow in the proprietorial manner of policemen, and I shook him off.

'D'you know about the threatening messages we've been getting?' I asked. 'Do you?'

'How could I? Now calm down, Mr Kyle.'

'Calm down! One a day they've been coming, threatening all manner of things . . .'

'And I wasn't told?'

'. . . but all with the object of getting Angie and me away from here. Until the fire. None since then. Heavens above, I thought I'd got everything sorted out, except for those threats. And – don't you see – it looks like it's all opened up again.'

'No, I don't see. You're not wanted here.'

'The *reason* for the threats and the fire, that's what's there, on that door.'

'All I see is an unpleasant reference to a Lesbian Cow, whatever that might mean – and your signature. Let's get moving, shall we. Into the Range Rover with you . . . and away.'

'Will you listen!'

The group around us – the scattered cars, the people poised as though for flight, but caught on curiosity – was silent, listening. There was a pall of embarrassment for my predicament. I appealed to them.

'Doesn't *anybody* see? I came here, and later I started using the garage. That's when the threats started . . .'

'Nobody's interested,' Timmis said. 'You're causing a disturbance, and I'm asking you to leave.'

'Now wait!' I looked round in appeal. Blank faces. Phil walked out into the yard, pushing past Angie, who appeared to be clinging to the door frame, and joined in.

'Is he still here? Let's get some cars out of the way. The Jag along here a bit – I'll do that. Paul, if you'll just back up.'

'Phil,' I said, 'I've got to have time.'

'You've had enough time. We've heard enough from you. Just go.'

'It's good advice,' said Timmis. 'There's nothing you can do here.'

I looked to Angie for support. She, of all people, had to realise what the graffiti must mean. But she was unresponsive, and looked away.

'Now,' said Timmis.

He took my elbow again. Now I realised that Timmis usually got his way. Weight and strength carried me forward, and I stumbled, like a drunkard being escorted. Sheer pride forced me into shaking myself free. 'All right.' And into climbing with some remnant of dignity up into the Rover. Numbly, I started the engine. I could see nothing through the windscreen. The sun was so low and afire that it cast a sheen of blood in front of my eyes. Or maybe it was mine.

'Wait, you fool!' Timmis shouted.

I wound down a side window. He had run to the caravan and grabbed the jacking-tool from its clip. He'd waved to Evan to come and wind up the portable wheel, while he himself started on the corner supports. Impatient now to be away from there, I gritted my teeth and revved the engine. Behind me, somewhere, Phil was shouting as he manoeuvred vehicles this way and that to give me free passage. There was a stink of hot oil and petrol.

Timmis straightened. 'Right hand down, and you're free. Then go, Mr Kyle, and keep going.'

I crunched offside wheels through charred timber. The red sheen melted from the windscreen, and I saw my way clear, vehicles huddled and human shapes watching my progress. The caravan followed me neatly beneath the brick archway and onto the drive. There I stopped, switched off, and reached for my pipe.

It took two minutes, and then I was calm, with everything lined up in my mind, and I knew I could no longer leave. I started up the engine, took a large arc that included a few yards of lawn, and came back nose-in to the arch. I stopped, took out the ignition key, and put the headlights on full beam. I climbed back to the ground.

There had been a commiserating group in the light from the

side door, where Angie was sitting now on the top step, her face in her hands. They all turned, facing the fierce light, and I walked out from it with Timmis striding towards me looking purposeful.

'One word out of you!' he said, his fists bunched at his sides.

'I'm going to have my say, Sergeant, and nobody's going to drive out of this yard till I do.'

He walked over to his Land Rover and climbed inside, the microphone to his lips. I turned back to the side door.

They could have walked away from me into the house. Phil could have summoned Boggis and Clancy from the shadows. But the stark, dramatic light caught them, that and my own intensity I suppose.

'The threats,' I said, picking up from where I'd left off. 'They started when I arrived here and showed interest. And why? Can anybody tell me why? Because from that time there wasn't much chance of anybody getting at the inside of the garage door. There I was, a few yards away, living in a caravan and hearing every sound. Not a chance. Then in the end, when it was obvious I wasn't going away, and Angie wouldn't budge, there was only one thing to do. That was to set the lab and garage on fire, and hope it'd burn off the paint from the garage door. That might destroy those dangerous words, Lesbian Cow.'

Rena began to edge away towards her car, Paul looking after her but not following.

'And then we get a nice little twist,' I said. 'Funny, when you come to think about it. I'd been playing around with a spray-can, and written my name on the inside of the door. But it didn't show, because I was using a green paint that was very close to the green that Gledwyn Griffiths had used to spray on the inside of the door. And all the while – because it had to have been there before I did my bit – there was that other comment about a Lesbian Cow, and on the same surface. But I couldn't see that either. So the fire revealed the words that it was intended to destroy, because the graffiti were done in metallic paint in both cases, and Gledwyn had used a plain paint for his door.'

I paused, waiting for comment. Nothing. I might as well have been talking to myself.

'All right. Does anybody know what that means?'

'Damned if I do,' said Paul, but Evan was nodding, nodding.

'Evan's got it,' I said. 'But he would. It means that somebody had sprayed on Lesbian Cow, and must have thought it was visible. It wasn't. But he assumed that the fact that *he* couldn't see it didn't mean a thing. As far as he was concerned it was grey on grey, but he'd know that for anybody else it could look like green on yellow or green on red. It means, you see, that he was colour blind on red and green. All that trouble to hide something that nobody could see! Oh dear me.'

I looked round. Timmis was suddenly a massive presence at my elbow, but now he had no intention of interfering.

'Who knows somebody who's colour blind?' I demanded, walking forward, scanning their faces. I poked a finger towards Paul. 'You, Paul?'

He took a step back. 'Not me! My father . . .'

'We know about your father. But not you?'

'Come in the car, honey,' said Rena, her head out of a side window. 'Don't talk to the man.'

He glared at her, and stood his ground. 'Not me,' he repeated.

'But of course not,' I agreed. 'I can prove it, as it happens, with genetic charts. Ask Evan.' Who was nodding in agreement.

'But what *about* Gledwyn?' I asked. 'We're talking now about a bit of practice with a spray-can. Words that came to the mind: Lesbian Cow. Can anybody here really imagine Gledwyn using those words?'

Rena blew cigarette smoke out of the car window, her voice following it. 'I can imagine it. He'd do anything.'

'For God's sake!' said Paul. Everybody else ignored her. While a silence built up I stuffed my pipe, wondering how best to go on. Angie had lifted her head. Her lips were slightly parted. Phil stood beside her, reaching down with one hand to her shoulder.

'Let's try it from another angle,' I suggested. 'I'd decided that the car that killed Carla, Lynne's friend, was the Escort that Gledwyn had been using. He used it to go to Aberystwyth to see Paul, with Neville driving him. There'd been a resin-bonded repair on the wing, and I managed to get some chips of paint out of cracks, some red and some green. It'd been a re-sprayed car, you see, originally green and called Green Dragon by one of the previous owners, then sprayed red. I asked Lynne to check them for me, and the green chips showed two shades, slightly different. That meant, to me, that the wing had been re-sprayed green, but the re-spray colour wasn't exactly a match for the original. Do you see what that means? The wing of a red car had been repaired to hide the damage – and re-sprayed green. You get the point? Our colour blind friend again. And blatantly giving himself away, but not knowing it.'

'That's fine, as far as it goes,' said Evan judicially. 'But it'd have to be a pretty severe case of red-green blindness. I could give you percentage figures . . .'

'Let's assume, shall we?' asked Timmis heavily. 'I'm accepting it.' He stared blandly at me. 'So far.'

'I hadn't finished that bit,' I complained. 'The point was – and Lynne told me this, but I missed it – that the original car colour was a metallic green paint. So was the re-spray. I'd had the idea, you see, that Gledwyn had been involved with Carla's death, and that Lynne had helped him make up a matching colour by using her instruments. But Gledwyn hadn't got the facilities for mixing metallic colours, and Gledwyn wouldn't use such words as Lesbian Cow. I was pushing Lynne, though, and she knew what I was thinking. Gledwyn, that's what I was thinking. So I was pushing her . . . and she died.'

I stopped. Angie raised her head. Phil's hand fell from her shoulder as she moved it.

'I blamed myself,' I said in disgusted anger. 'I did – but I'm not now. I thought I'd driven her to suicide . . .'

'Keep to the point,' Timmis growled.

'It *is* the bloody point!' I shouted. 'Whatever I might have thought, Lynne *knew* it couldn't have been Gledwyn who'd re-sprayed the car wing. It was a metallic colour, and she'd realised what that meant. That the re-spraying hadn't been done by somebody using the lab instruments and mixing pigments – it'd been done by somebody who'd bought a can of spray paint from the do-it-yourself shop, somebody who believed the car was painted a colour called Fern Green, and they thought that because it was called Green Dragon. And because the registration document said it was green. Lynne knew who that person had to be, in fact she had that person with her when I phoned her the last time. There was no reason for suicide, but a damned good one for murder, and so easy with only five feet of walkway separating her door from the balcony rail.'

There was silence. Somebody drew in a hissing breath but did not speak. Timmis raised his head. Clancy and Boggis stared impassively at the vanishing glory of the sky. I sighed. Eyes fastened on me.

'There was the lock on the garage door, you see. Broken, by force. It was broken because the garage was the best place for the repairs to be done, in the week while Gledwyn was at Blackpool. But Gledwyn came back a day early. Gledwyn walked up his drive alone, which I know because Lynne told me she dropped him at the drive entrance. I thought perhaps she hadn't told me the truth, but now I believe she did. If she'd come up to the house, she would have seen Carla's killer working on the Escort, and she would have seen at once that one wing had been sprayed green on a red car. In that event, she wouldn't have remained alive as long as she did. But Gledwyn saw – and knew. He would notice the light on in the garage and investigate. Perhaps the last spray coat was being put on – in any event there'd be all the evidence, empty spray-cans around, the containers for the resin-bonded mixture, the mixing trays, the wet-or-dry emery paper, the smell of acetone. Maybe, even, with his special glasses on, he'd *see* the wing was sprayed a different colour from the rest. But in any case, he'd *know*.'

I stopped, not really wishing to go on. The rest should've been obvious. Paul had moved to his car, and was standing by the open door, Rena plucking at his elbow.

'Then what?' he asked harshly.

'What *would* he do?' I demanded. 'But you wouldn't know, Paul. You never really understood him. Evan – can *you* guess? No, don't go away, we might need you.' He'd been moving towards the paddock. Angie hadn't noticed, and flashed him a quick look of reproach. 'Evan?' I asked.

'Gledwyn? Given that situation . . . I reckon he'd be furious. Outraged.'

'My thoughts exactly,' I said. 'Do *you* think he'd be outraged, Neville?'

Neville was fumbling with a cigarette, and dropped it. 'Well . . . I guess . . . well, sure he would. Uncle Gledwyn . . . but I never saw him lose his temper.'

'No? Perhaps you were lucky. That night he would. And guess what he'd do about it? He'd probably heard by that time about Carla's death. It would all come together in his mind. I can see him . . . see him getting into that Escort, and though he hadn't driven for years driving it out of there . . .' I turned and pointed towards the spot where the garage had been. '. . . over empty spray-cans – the lot – on his way to the police station to show the sergeant here.' I stopped.

'You can't stop there!' cried Angie.

I glanced at Timmis. He nodded. I went on: 'But he didn't make it very far past the traffic signal. Perhaps the murderer had driven after him and forced him into taking it too fast. Or got in front, and Gledwyn confused braking lights as head-lights. I don't know. I only know . . .' I stopped again, then turned to Timmis. 'Shouldn't Angie go inside? It's getting cool.'

A pause. His eyes clouded. 'Of course.' Cleared his throat, as he got the point. 'Certainly.'

'No,' she said angrily, shaking her head, hair flying. 'Get on with it.'

'It's best . . .'

'I must *know*, Harry.'

And I saw that she had to, if she was ever going to see it through.

I said, forcing myself onwards against the ring of dark, expectant eyes: 'The car turned over. It didn't set on fire. Very few do. It lay on its back, and by this time our friend knew that he'd used the wrong colour for spraying the wing, because even Gledwyn had noticed it. So that evidence had to be destroyed. Petrol would be dripping from the tank. I found this.'

I took the melted piece of plastic from my pocket and held it up.

'The remains of a zip lighter. All you'd need to do would be flick it on and toss it in. That's what he did. Without,' I said flatly, 'even checking whether Gledwyn was still alive.'

Rena screamed. For once she'd done the right thing. I thought that it saved Angie. Rena's hysteria caught at Angie's sympathy, and it held her past that moment. But her face was a mask, wild with stark eyes, and her fingers clawed at her knees.

'He's now sporting a gold Dunhill,' I muttered.

'Is there much more?' Timmis demanded hollowly.

'We're looking for somebody who's colour blind, but who went to some trouble to persuade me otherwise.' I took out the envelope with Evan's genetic charts on it, and passed it over to

Timmis. 'I should've known all along. It was written on here.'

The Range Rover's headlights, having been on full-blast with no charge, were beginning to fade.

'Bring it over here,' I said, nodding towards the car. Timmis frowned at me. 'You too, Evan,' I added. 'We might need you.'

The three of us bent in the headlight stream. I pointed.

'The top one,' I said. 'Evan drew that for me, to show me how Gledwyn's colour blindness came from his mother. You understand the symbols, Sergeant?'

'Sure. The one with the arrow for male, the one with a cross for female.'

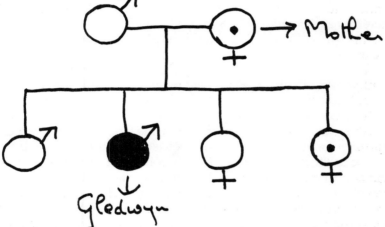

'You can see from that – Gledwyn's sister had a fifty/fifty chance of being a latent carrier of it. Here, let's do it again.' I used the top of the bonnet. 'Remember, Gledwyn had a sister.'

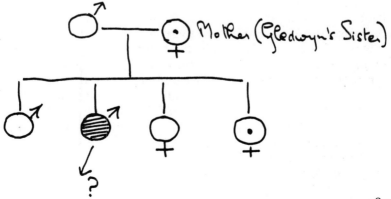

'So, who does that give you, in place of Gledwyn, now?'

'Neville!' Evan whispered at my elbow.

'That's Gledwyn's sister now, only she's become a mother. What does that make Neville? It makes him a fifty/fifty chance of being a colour blind murderer. He's colour blind, yet he chatted to me about red and yellow poles. But he knew, rather than saw, because he'd told his assistant to use red ones one place and yellow ones another.'

We had been speaking softly to each other. You could almost hear the ears creaking into cocked position. I was giving Timmis warning, but I reckoned he was ahead of me. He glanced round. A dark shape loomed beyond the caravan, another in the paddock.

'So what d'you reckon happened that Saturday night?' he asked, walking me back to the group. 'When Carla died.'

'I reckon,' I said to them all, 'that Neville drove back here from Aberystwyth, cold and fed up and hungry, his uncle left him flat, so he drove away. But not home, as he told me, and not in his Metro, as he'd have me believe. His Metro was in the garage, locked away. There was a lock on it at that time. Gledwyn marched through the house and straight through to Lynne's office, and threw the keys at the wall. The garage key was on that bunch. Neville couldn't get at his own car, so he used the Escort. He didn't even get out of it. But he didn't drive home. He'd had a rotten day, and he'd want comfort and sympathy. Lynne, he'd want. But Lynne wasn't there. She was in her office, where he wouldn't notice her, and Gledwyn was tearing up his speech, and then Lynne was out the side crying, and Gledwyn crept back – and saw her out there weeping, so crept away again for a while . . . so . . .'

'You're wandering off the point,' said Timmis severely.

I was, because I didn't want to get to it. I cleared my throat. 'So Neville drove to Lynne's flat. And on the way he came across Carla, standing by her car and waving, and ran her down. Then what would he do? Drive to Lynne's, shocked and horrified. And find her not there. Drive home to his own place. Hide the Escort for the night – he hadn't got a garage of his own – and then return here the next day, to use Gledwyn's garage, knowing he was away.'

Silence. They waited. Neville stood, frozen, glazed eyes staring at me.

'But then he made a terrible mistake,' I said. 'He got all his repair stuff together and he tried out a spray-can. Somebody who can't tell red from green isn't going to worry when it doesn't show up. Lesbian Cow. Think what that means. We know it was critical to him, because he began to worry about anybody seeing it. Here was a chap, writing the first thing that came into his head. He'd caused the death of Carla. He had to tell himself it was her fault, even that she deserved it. By that time it would've grown into a great rumbling accusation against her. The trouble she'd caused him by getting herself killed The rotten cow, he'd think. But why Lesbian Cow? Because that was what he thought of Carla. Things had been growing cool between him and Lynne. He didn't know – *he'd* never see – that she was in love with Gledwyn. What! Lynne and that old fool, he'd think, if the thought ever crossed his mind.'

'I should think so, too!' put in Rena, and Paul snarled at her.

'So he had to discover the reason for this coolness, and there was Carla and Lynne, too friendly by half, round at each other's places. His assumption had to be that Carla had persuaded Lynne into a lesbian relationship. And so: Lesbian Cow. His hatred centred on those two words. But they'd give him away, he thought. Anybody seeing them might be able to reason it through to Carla. So *he* thought.'

Neville croaked: 'No!' Nobody looked at him. I went on:

'So he drove towards Lynne's flat that night, and suddenly there was Carla, in his headlights, his hated rival standing there and waving at him, presented to him. Then,' I said wearily, 'he simply put his foot down and drove straight at her. As hard as he could go.'

I felt I was swaying on my feet. I reached back for a chair, but there wasn't one. Neville gestured, and fainted. The gold lighter clattered to the cobbles. He hadn't got round to lighting the cigarette.

'And it was his birthday,' I said.

There was a general shuffle. Everybody wished to distance themselves far from Neville. I saw Timmis make a gesture, and the two constables approached. Angie was on her feet, Phil plucking at her jacket. She looked at me for one moment, then turned away into the house.

I went back to the Range Rover and cut the lights. There was just about enough left in the battery to start the engine. I did a neat bit of backing, and like floodwaters the cars broke free. The Land Rover was last. Timmis looked across at me, not smiling, from the wheel. The Jag pulled round on the drive and stopped in front of the porch. They were going out in style, it seemed.

Slowly and wearily I wandered back across the yard, and into the kitchen. There were voices from the hall. I ambled towards them.

They were in there, Angie and Phil. She turned. 'You look tired, Harry.'

I nodded, too tired to agree.

'These your bags?' he asked. 'Got everything you need?'

Two massive suitcases stood against the wall.

'Yes,' she said meekly.

'I'll call Boggis.'

'No,' she said. 'Harry will take them.'

Would he hell! With sore hands, an aching back, and my head tearing itself to pieces . . .

He grinned. 'Come on, then, Harry. Carry the lady's cases. The Jag's out front.'

'I know where the Jag is.'

'No Phil,' she said. 'I meant back upstairs. I'm not coming home with you, Phil. Ever.' She turned to me. 'My father's room, Harry.'

I stood between the cases and raised them from the ground. I grinned into his dark, furious face.

Angie was eyeing him up and down. She owed him an explanation. 'It's a better view in that room,' she told him. Told me.

I lifted the cases and galloped up the stairs.